Fatality by
Firelight

By Lynn Cahoon

Fatality by Firelight

A Story to Kill

The Tourist Trap Mysteries:

Hospitality and Homicide

Tea Cups and Carnage

Murder on Wheels

Killer Run

Dressed to Kill

If the Shoe Kills

Mission to Murder

Guidebook to Murder

Fatality By Firelight

Lynn Cahoon

KENSINGTON BOOKS

http://www.kensingtonbooks.com

KENSINGTON BOOKS are published by

Kensington Publishing Corp.
119 West 40th Street
New York, NY 10018

Copyright © 2017 by Lynn Cahoon

All Kensington titles, imprints and distributed lines are available at special quantity discounts for bulk purchases for sales promotion, premiums, fund-raising, educational or institutional use. Special book excerpts or customized printings can also be created to fit specific needs. For details, write or phone the office of the Kensington Special Sales Manager: Kensington Publishing Corp., 119 West 40th Street, New York, NY, 10018. Attn. Special Sales Department. Phone: 1-800-221-2647.

Kensington and the K logo Reg. U.S. Pat. & TM Off.

ISBN-13: 978-1-4967-0437-5
ISBN-10: 1-4967-0437-1
First Kensington Mass Market Edition: March 2017

eISBN-13: 978-1-4967-0438-2
eISBN-10: 1-4967-0438-X
First Kensington Electronic Edition: March 2017

10 9 8 7 6 5 4 3

Printed in the United States of America

To the Cowboy:
My love, my life, my soulmate.
I love this journey we're taking together.

Acknowledgments

When I first started writing, I thought the process was all on me. Since that time, I've realized there are many hands involved with the making of a book. There's me playing with all my imaginary friends. There's my editor, Esi Sogah, who tells me when I'm running off track and when I need to tighten the leash on my fictional friends. And all the people behind the scenes at Kensington, from cover designers to copy editors to my marketing mavens, Alex, Michelle, and Lauren. Thank you all so much for your diligence at making my stories shine.

Of course, there's lots of others who help keep me sane during the writing process, including the people who bring us delivery when neither the cowboy or I feel like cooking on deadline nights. I am blessed to have someone in my life, like my husband, who believes in me and my stories.

Chapter 1

The world outside still clung to the previous night, the shadows not quite releasing their hold to the breaking light over the mountain ridge outside Aspen Hills, Colorado. With the first rays of morning, the fresh snow glistened and covered the lawn all around 700 Warm Springs.

Cat Latimer, owner of the Warm Springs Writers' Retreat, housed in the old Victorian, sat at the kitchen table drinking a mix of hot chocolate and coffee. With a dab of freshly whipped cream, Cat thought Shauna's winter concoction was just about the most perfect drink ever invented. Her friend, Shauna Mary Clodah, had taken over the role of cook, planner, and manager for the writing retreats. Shauna was a petite, pretty, Irish redhead that cooked like an angel. The small group sitting around the table was drinking the "virgin" version of her mixture. Later, the retreat guests would have the option of adding a shot of Bailey's Irish Cream or Kahlúa to their cups, an invitation to the muse.

Right now her guests were tucked in their beds, sleeping. Which was where she wanted to be instead of sitting here in the kitchen. But then she took in the smell of coffee and chocolate mixed together and she sighed in delight.

"I can't believe you're taking the group up the mountain. I thought this was supposed to be about writing. They aren't going to get many words written by spending the day skiing." Uncle Pete had become a regular at the breakfast table, both when the retreat was in session and when it was just Cat and Shauna milling around the empty house. Her uncle was Aspen Hills' police chief and Cat's closest relative.

"It's part of the Colorado experience," Cat explained, thinking about her own manuscript sitting on her computer waiting for her to make time to write. The phrase *making time to write* was a joke. She either wrote or didn't, and today her word-count chart would show a big fat zero, unless she had the mental energy when they returned from skiing. During the first retreat, she'd managed to get a few pages written— before one of her guests wound up dead in his room. This retreat she'd promised herself that she'd focus on her own work, even when they had guests. Shauna was in charge of the day-to-day activities when the retreat was in session. Cat's job was to be the resident writer *and* set a good example as a professional writer. A job that sometimes was harder than other days, especially if she got drawn into a Facebook rotating loop of cute kittens or the occasional photos of hot guys—or worse, one simple question that grew into a research project on the entire history of the Salem Witch trials.

Today was about building relationships and having experiences. Writers needed both.

"Who do you have visiting this month? Anyone I need to put some eyes on?" As the town police chief, Uncle Pete could be a little overprotective when it came to Cat. At least that was her experience. Cat had moved back to Aspen Hills when her ex-husband died and left her the huge Victorian. She and Michael had bought it when their marriage was young, before he started cheating.

Now the house was hers. Not hers and the bank's, just hers: The mortgage insurance had paid off the loan when Michael died. Karma was sweet.

"We have five guests, including the student from the college. They're writing sweet romance, historical fiction, speculative fiction, non-fiction, and poetry. They all seem pretty harmless." Cat had a list of the guests in front of her. They'd all arrived yesterday and for once, Seth had only had to do one trip to the Denver airport as the planes had arrived within an hour. Last night had been casual with the group hanging out over soup and homemade bread in the living room. It had been nice to get to know the group before the retreat got started. Cat pointed to one of the names on the list. "We have one guest who is not joining in the ski trip. Bella Neighbors told me last night she has no interest in skiing or going outside in this weather."

The door blew open, and on the wind a few

snowflakes entered around the tall man covered in skiwear. "Who ever said that is a smart cookie. It's c-c-c-cold out there."

Cat watched as Seth Howard stomped his feet, then shrugged out of his heavy coat and sat on the bench to take off his shoes. He shook his head, letting the snowflakes fall from his brown hair onto the wood floor. Seth had been her high school sweetheart, and apparently, was now her after-divorce boyfriend. She forced herself to focus on Shauna instead. "Are you going to be okay here? Bella's the historical fiction author, so I'm sure she'd be interested in the history of the town. I know I have several books in the house library about the area."

Shauna nodded. "We'll be good. I'll send her over that way when I see her. Miss Bella can write or go wandering through town, and I'll have a fine dinner of shepherd's pie waiting for you when you get back."

"Sounds great." Seth made his way over to the table, taking the cup Shauna held out for him. He kissed Cat on her neck, sinking into a chair next to her. "Hey, Pete. How are things in Aspen Hills?"

"If we didn't have the book thief over at the college, my days would be filled with counted cross-stitch. Why someone would want to steal an old book is beyond me." The big man drained his cup and stood. "I'm heading back to the station. You guys be careful on the road to the ski resort. I'm getting reports of slide-offs every day."

"I put the chains on the tires just now. We should be fine." Seth sipped his coffee. "I hear that guy stole some rare books from the library. You got any suspects?"

Uncle Pete pulled his belt upward and put on his coat. "I can't comment on an open investigation, but since I have squat for evidence, I guess I still can't comment on nothing."

"See you tomorrow?" Cat called after him as he made his way to the kitchen door.

Uncle Pete didn't turn around as he waved. "Yep."

Cat watched through the window as he made his way to his police car. The black Charger looked more like a white hill, so much snow had fallen in the hour her uncle had been in the kitchen visiting and having breakfast. She turned back to the others at the table. "Does he look tired to you?"

"You worry too much. Your uncle looks fine." Seth took the plate of fried potatoes and ham Shauna handed him. "Thanks."

"I don't know. He didn't eat as much as usual." Shauna returned to the counter where she was finishing the buffet items for the guests. "I think the college is putting pressure on him about that break-in."

"That could be it." Cat wasn't convinced, and tomorrow she'd ask him about the last time he had a physical. Uncle Pete was a widower, and with her mother in Florida, Cat was the only relative around to make sure he kept his routines. She took her plate to the sink and poured herself another cup of coffee. Glancing around the kitchen, she paused. "Do you need help with anything?"

"No. I've got it handled." Shauna waved her away from the stove. "I don't need you messing in my kitchen."

Cat put up her hands. "Fine, I was just asking." She focused on Seth. "When are we leaving?"

"No later than ten. So yeah, you have time to sneak up to your office and write. I'll come get you when we're ready to go." Seth didn't look up from his plate of food. "Just be ready to lose when we race down Mountain Top."

"Who said we were racing?" Cat smiled at the memory of winters growing up skiing at the local resort. Back then, they'd gotten their season passes as early Christmas gifts as soon as the snow arrived.

This time he did look up and the look he gave her seared her with desire. "We always race."

She ignored his comment and left the kitchen with a filled carafe of coffee Shauna handed her wordlessly. Her office was in the third floor turret, the same floor where she and Shauna had bedroom suites. The guest rooms were all on the second floor with the first floor open for guest use including scheduled and unscheduled group activities and of course, breakfast.

Except for Michael's study. After one quick look around for anything vital, she had locked that room. It held too many memories that right now Cat didn't need to be dealing with. Especially with a house full of writers to herd. She looked forward to this new group. An introvert, Cat was drained by running a retreat. What surprised her was last time, when the retreat was over, how much she needed that writer-to-writer interaction.

She entered her office, turned on her computer, and promptly got lost in the world of her teenage witch trying to navigate the horrors of high school.

True to his word, Seth knocked on her door exactly at ten. The writing was done for today. She saved her document, then turned off her computer. "Just a minute."

When she opened the door, Seth eased his body up next to hers and walked her back to the office wall. He leaned in for the first kiss. Even in high school, he had known just how to kiss her to make her toes catch fire. She relaxed into his arms, feeling the desire she'd only just brushed against a few hours ago flow through her. After a few minutes, she turned her head and whispered in his ear, "I thought we had to leave."

He groaned and stepped away from her. He waved her through the open door. "We do."

Everyone had already loaded into the van by the time they got downstairs and Cat slipped into her ski jacket. Shauna handed her a bag. When she peeked inside, she saw a thermos of cocoa and what looked like a Tupperware container of sandwiches. "In case we get snowed in?"

Shauna shrugged. "I know they just ate, but sometimes people need a little something to tide them over."

Shauna was right. The sandwiches were gone before they arrived at the Little Ski Hill's parking lot. As they unloaded their passengers, Cat gave everyone a card with her cell and the house numbers listed. "Call if you need something. We'll be meeting in the great room in the main lodge at three to return to the house."

As the guests made their way to the rental shack, Seth took his and Cat's equipment down from the rack on top of the SUV. "Do you have a season pass?" He jiggled his laminated pass that hung on a chain around his neck in her face. "I guess you'll have to stand in line with the newbies then. I'll see you after my first run, if you're set up by then." He started to turn away but Cat put a hand on his jacket, stopping his movement.

"You mean this?" She took out the season pass from her pocket. She'd bought it last month when the ski hill had been advertising a buy one, -get one half-off sale for Aspen Hills residents. She and Shauna had already been on the slopes a few times.

He grinned and grabbed her skis. "Bring along the poles and we'll get going. The line for the chair lift gets long on Saturday's."

They skied together for hours, taking the same runs they'd taken back in high school. The snow was powdery, and Cat felt like she was running on feathers except for the spray of cold that sometimes snuck around her goggles and scarf. Rays of sunshine on the hillside turned the white into bright. Ending a run, Cat waved Seth over as they slid into the area around the lodge. "Let's go in and warm up."

They took off their skis and left them and the poles standing in a rack near the door. Stamping the snow off her boots, she entered the warm lodge. The lodge, the ski runs, being with Seth—it all left Cat feeling like she'd stepped into a time machine. The leather couches surrounding the stone fireplace in the middle of the great room looked just like she remembered. A hum of excited chatter filled the area, echoing off the cathedral ceilings and wall-to-ceiling windows highlighting the mountains they'd just left.

Taking off her gloves, she checked her phone to make sure she hadn't missed any calls. She hadn't, but she was shocked at the time: 2 p.m. already. They only had another hour before they would be meeting up with the guests. Laughter echoed out of the bar area, and they followed it inside.

They squeezed into the last two seats on the edge of the bar. "What can I get you?" A man in his early twenties stood in front of Cat, clearing the empty glasses and wiping the bar in front of them. His blond hair was too long and messy, just the style girls loved. And he had the most arresting green eyes. His Little Ski Hill shirt had *Martin* embroidered over the front pocket. Cat figured the bartender did all right in the tips department.

"Hey Martin, I'll have a coffee, black." Seth looked at Cat. "Merlot for you?"

Cat pulled the knitted hat off her head. "I don't know. I guess I'll take a beer. You got a dark on draft?"

"For being so far away from civilization, this

place has a quality draft list. Let me get you a sample." Martin walked toward the taps.

"You see any of the guests?" she asked Seth as she looked around the crowded bar. But before she could recognize anyone, the bartender was back.

"Tell me if you like it." He pushed a small glass filled with a dark amber liquid toward Cat, then set a coffee cup in front of Seth. "You sure you don't want me to Jack that coffee up a bit?"

"Black is fine. I'm the designated driver." He took a sip of the brew.

"Too bad, man. I make a mean mixed drink. You two are going to have to check out our condo rentals. They're cheapest during the week when we don't have out-of-town visitors. Of course, I'm only here on weekends. Getting my degree in both accounting and mixology; at least I'll be employable after four years." He turned toward Cat who had finished the mini-beer. "Do you like it?"

"Most definitely." She turned to Seth as the young man went to get her a normal pint of the draft. "I think he's got a great idea about the condos. Maybe next week when the retreat's over, we should look into staying a few days."

"Ski by day and snuggle by night?" Seth raised his eyebrows. "I could be talked into playing hooky for a few days."

"You're only working for me," Cat reminded him. The promise of two days of skiing and relaxing were almost enough for Cat to get through the retreat without a major breakdown. She knew she'd come up with the idea, but sometimes having so many people around was challenging, if not downright crazy. She'd book the mini-vacation online as soon as they returned to the house.

A loud cheer sounded from a table across the room. A very drunk woman stood on the table and downed what looked to Cat from this distance to be a boilermaker. As she raised her hands in victory, a man swept her off the table and into his arms on the couch. The couple started kissing. The kiss continued so long, Cat felt uncomfortable watching them and turned back to Seth.

"Kids." She shrugged and sipped her beer.

"That's one of your writers." He pointed to the girl. "Don't know her name, but there's another one, Nelson something."

Cat choked on her beer. "What did they do, just ignore the slopes and come right to the bar? That girl is hammered."

"Furthermore, she's kissing the wrong guy. Tommy Neil is engaged." Seth pointed to a third person sitting farther down at the bar watching the scene unfold on the couch. "There's another one, the poet?"

"Jeffrey Blank," Cat answered absently. "How do you know the guy kissing Christina is engaged?"

"I've met him before. He's kind of a jerk, but he's Brittany's fiancé. You remember Brit, the bartender down at Bernie's?" He saw the confusion in her eyes as she tried to place the names. "Don't you read the local papers? I'm pretty sure

I've brought in the *Aspen Hills Post* from your doorstep."

"Shauna reads the local. I'm too busy." She sipped her beer and glanced at the clock. "So we're only missing one. Maybe we should start moving everyone to the van. I can call Jennifer and have her meet us there."

"No need. She's at the same table with our party girl." Seth pointed to the last retreat guest sipping a glass of wine. He focused back on Cat and shook his head. "Brit's not going to like this one bit. And Bernie has connections."

"That's just a rumor." Cat finished her beer and dug in her purse for cash. Seth stilled her hand and took out his wallet, throwing some bills on the bar.

"Not a rumor I would want to test out." He looked at her. "I don't think Tommy's going to like it if his future father-in-law finds out about his extra-curricular activities. The guy might end up skiing down a mountain side with some specialty concrete boots."

Chapter 2

Luckily, Shauna had made enough of the shepherd's pie for the entire group, as Cat didn't trust any of the guests to be able to make it into town for dinner walking on the slick sidewalks. The dining room was filled with an evening buffet of not only the individual pots of the creamy main dish, but breads, a green salad, and a pot of Shauna's homemade clam chowder on the sideboard.

After the guests were settled, Cat followed Shauna into the kitchen. "Thanks for setting up a dinner for the group. I know you didn't expect to have to serve tonight."

"Actually, I did. Nate at the lodge called when the group showed up and started drinking. He wanted to make sure they had a ride off the mountain and a place to stay." Shauna pointed to the table. "Are you eating in here or with your guests?"

Seth was already halfway through his dinner and looked up as she considered her options.

He patted the chair next to him, a lazy grin on his face. "You can sit by me."

"I'm tempted," Cat admitted, keeping her eyes on Shauna so she could ignore Seth's invitation. "I'm not great with drunk people. I can't believe you bartended for so long. Didn't you just want to pour them into a cab and get them out of the bar?"

"They were funny. And the trouble makers we got out of the bar quickly." Shauna shrugged. "I enjoyed seeing them playful."

"Well, I'll enjoy seeing them nursing hangovers in the morning. We might have to have a mini-workshop on why not all authors are alcoholics. Maybe I'll call it 'Taking Care of Your Body and Mind.'" Cat sighed and opened the door. "I'm the hostess; I'll go watch the children."

"Let me know if you need anything." Shauna filled a bowl with salad and set it on the table next to Seth.

As Cat left the kitchen, she squared her shoulders. The tradeoff for her writing full time and keeping the Victorian house was making the writers' retreats successful. And the trick for that was to be a gracious hostess. Even when all she wanted to do was have a nice meal with her friends and then go hide in her room with a fire and the book she was currently devouring.

When she opened the dining room door, she was surprised to see several guests had already finished and retired to their rooms. She sat next to Christina Powers, who played with the mashed potatoes on her meal, one hand holding up her head. "Hey, Christina, did you have fun skiing?"

A small smile crossed the girl's face and Cat remembered thinking how young she'd looked when she'd first arrived. Christina wasn't over twenty five. "I loved it. I really enjoyed meeting Tommy. He's such a dreamboat. I might just have to move here after the week's over."

"I'm not sure that would be a great idea." Cat's words were out before she could stop them.

Christina narrowed her eyes and looked at Cat for the first time since she'd sat down. "Why, are you after him? He told me that he has girls falling all over him all the time. It's really hard for him to be true, but he thinks I might be the one to change all that."

"I'm not interested in Tommy Neil." Cat shook her head. The guy had gotten into Christina's head in what, three hours? She would have to watch her closely during the retreat. Of course, it really wasn't Cat's place to keep her guests from getting their heart broken. "I hear he's engaged to a local girl."

The shock on Christina's face slowly hardened, and she pushed the food away, getting up on her unsteady feet. "I didn't think you were one of the mean ones. Tommy told me there were ugly rumors going around town about him, but I thought you were nice."

She stumbled out of the room as Cat watched. Should she follow her to her room? Before she could move, Jeffrey Blank, the poet, stood, pausing at her chair. "Eat. I'll make sure she gets to her room." When Cat hesitated, he held up his hand in a Boy Scout salute. "It will be my good deed for the day."

Bella Neighbors, the historical author that had stayed behind from the skiing adventure, called after him. "You just make sure you keep your hands in your pockets, mister."

Cat laughed and Bella smiled at her.

Bella broke off a piece of bread. "Poets, they always see the good in everyone. All the world's a playground for their words." She looked around the table. "Looks like I'm the only one who will be in shape to work after dinner. Which means I'll probably be alone in the living room researching."

"I'm sorry. I could come join you." Cat took a bite of the shepherd's pie and almost groaned. The comfort food filled her mouth and, with the creamy mashed potatoes, warmed her down to her toes. Perfect after-skiing dinner. Shauna was a genius.

"Sorry, you thought I was complaining?" Bella's face lit up. "I worried that I'd have too many people around all the time to get anything done, but today's been perfect. This is the best retreat ever."

"I'm glad you're enjoying your stay." Cat buttered a roll. "We'll head over to the library tomorrow after breakfast, and you'll get your temporary cards for the week. I'm sure you'll love the collection."

"I've been dying to get into that library for years. This week is going to make my book shine as long as I can find the documents to prove my historical theory. Your town is just full of surprises." Bella pushed away her plate and stood. "I'm going back to work. I'll probably be up until after midnight; is it okay for me to stay downstairs?"

"The first floor is totally available 24–7." Cat thought about Michael's locked office, and quickly added, "Unless a room is locked. I don't let people use my late husband's study. But other than that, you're free to wander. Shauna will have beverages set up in here along with some treats if you get hungry."

"Perfect." Bella paused at the dining room doorway. "This really is the best retreat. I swear I might come back every year."

By the time Cat was finished eating, she was alone in the room and thinking about her work in progress. Staying on top of a teenage witch who not only had to deal with the testing for her magical lessons, but also navigating the hells of attending high school kept her on her toes. But at least she always enjoyed returning to her fictional world to write.

"Do you know how to clear a room or what?" Shauna started picking up plates and putting them on a large serving tray.

Cat started at the question. "You caught me. Daydreaming and plotting. But I didn't run everyone out. They just kind of left. At least Bella's happy with the retreat so far. She says she's getting a lot of work done."

"I think the others are happy too. Not everyone takes a vacation just to write." Shauna pointed to Cat's plate. "Was it good?"

Cat scrapped the last bit of mashed potatoes out of the bowl with a small piece of bread. She handed the empty dish to her friend. "Not good, great. You are an amazing cook."

"I'm trying. I'm working on some recipes my mom sent me last week from the family cook-book. Of course, they need a little modernizing, but they're turning out yummy." She frowned as Cat stood and started cleaning up the table. "What are you doing?"

Cat froze, an empty glass in her hand. She looked at it, wondering if Shauna had a clearing up system. She cocked her head. "I'm helping?"

"Well, stop it. Most of the time I sit around playing with recipes in the kitchen. One week out of the month, I get to feel useful. So stop doing my job." Shauna waved her toward the kitchen. "Go and see if that man of yours has left yet. He needs to be reminded to come and clean off the sidewalks first thing in the morning so you can take your tour of the library."

Cat set the glass down on the tray. "Yes, Mother, I'll go remind him."

"No need to be sassy." Shauna cleared off an-other part of the table. "Just get out of my way; you're slowing me down."

Seth *was* still in the kitchen, a cup of what smelled like hot cocoa in his hands. He looked up from his phone when she entered. "Hey, beautiful. I didn't know if I'd see you again to-night."

Cat went to the stove and poured her own cup of the steaming cocoa before she sat down. "Shauna won't let me help clean up, so she sent me in here to give you your marching orders." Cat repeated the instructions Shauna had given.

He held up his phone. "Already set a reminder." He looked at her. "I'd stay and talk about how fun skiing with you was today, but you look beat. Your eyes look like they're about to close."

Cat rolled her shoulders, aware of the tension. "I've only been out to the hill three times now. It's going to take a while to get back up to speed. I've missed it though."

"Me too." He drained his cup, stood, and kissed her gently on the lips. None of the passion from this morning's kiss lingered, even though Cat could still taste his desire on her lips. "Sweet dreams. I'll see you in the morning."

As Cat left the kitchen she heard Bella moving books around in the living room. Shauna had returned to the kitchen and was cleaning up the supper dishes, humming to herself as she worked. Cat looked left, down the darkened hallway that led to the back door and Michael's office. She hadn't even been in the room since Uncle Pete had told her that he didn't believe Michael's death had been from natural causes. She wouldn't even think about opening that can of worms during a retreat. Next week. She'd deal with that stuff next week. But once her mind had opened the subject, she wondered if there was a clue in Michael's work notebooks or the journal she hadn't had the guts to completely read yet. Okay, maybe she hadn't had the guts to go back to reading. She rolled her shoulders, willing the confusion to go away. She didn't need the distraction, not during a retreat.

And with one decision made, she went up the stairs to her bedroom, started the gas fireplace,

and curled up with her hand on the memoir
she had planned on reading. Instead, she closed
her eyes.

The next morning, by the time she got the
last straggler ready to leave, they had to walk
quickly to make their ten o'clock meeting with
Miss Applebome, the college librarian. As they
made their way down the recently plowed or
scraped sidewalks, Cat kept up a monologue
about the different houses and their history in
the town. She pointed out the routes to Main
Street, where they'd find diners, bars, and some
small shops. Bella walked next to her and kept
asking questions about the town.

"Where is Professors' Row? I know it's around
here somewhere as your house used to be part
of the college's administration housing, right?"
Bella grinned at her. "I found an article about it
last night from an archive of the local paper."

"It's a couple streets over." Cat pointed toward
the left. "When I started remodeling for the
writers' retreat, a reporter came and did an
interview about my turning the house into a literary mecca." She laughed as they waited for the
one streetlight on their route to change from
STOP to WALK. Stamping her feet to loosen any
ice or snow, she kept her gaze forward, not
looking at the woman next to her. "I think they
overestimated my contribution to Aspen Hills'
educational history."

"I don't. You are letting people enjoy the past
as well as putting the house to its best use. You

should be proud of what you've accomplished only in a short time. The retreat is getting great buzz in the writing world." The light changed and they began to cross the almost empty road.

"I think that's more morbid curiosity about Tom Cook's death than the actual retreat process. Although, I hope we take off and the retreat becomes successful." Cat turned to make sure the rest of the group was still with them as the walk sign was now flashing orange. "Hurry up, guys, we're missing the light."

They turned the corner and were on the campus grounds. Bella uttered a cry of what appeared to be joy, and she pulled her cell out, snapping pictures of every building they passed. At least someone was enjoying the trip. The rest of the gang behind Cat seemed to be working on autopilot. Maybe next time she'd schedule the extra ski day at the end of the trip; then all the guests would have to deal with was a travel day home.

Cat made a mental note to mention this to Shauna and have her add it to the *Improvement Suggestions* file they planned on reviewing at the end of each retreat. The first thing they'd added last time was *No Dead Bodies*. That should be simple enough to follow. Smiling, she walked into the library and paused. At the glass entrance to the room that held the Hemingway papers, a row of yellow crime tape still blocked all the way to the display. And instead of being at the desk to welcome them, Miss Applebome's office door was closed. Cat made her way to the desk and rousted a work-study student who seemed to be writing a paper on the library's computer.

"Hey, we have an appointment with Miss Applebome"—Cat looked at the clock, which showed ten exactly—"now."

The kid didn't even look up from his work. "She said she'd meet you in the conference room as soon as the fuzz left."

"She said 'the fuzz'?" Cat waited for him to pause and look up at her. "Really?"

He shrugged, obviously embarrassed to be called out. "Okay, maybe she said she was with the police chief. Anyway, you're supposed to wait in the conference room."

"Did she leave anything for us?"

The kid looked around and found a large manila envelope. "This. She said to give you this."

She took the envelope. "Anything else?"

He sighed and rolled his eyes. "No. That was all."

"Thank you, you've been so helpful." She hoped the sarcasm wasn't lost on the guy who'd called her uncle *the fuzz*. She might not always agree with his methods, but he worked hard to keep Aspen Hills safe for little twerps like this.

She turned toward the group. "This way."

As they settled into the conference room, she took an envelope from the backpack she'd been carrying and opened it. She matched a shiny new library card and a dark blue journal with WARM SPRINGS WRITERS' RETREAT embossed on the front, then handed out the gifts.

"I didn't know if you'd all have paper, so here

you go. A gift to remember us by." She held up the library card. "This will get you full access to the stacks and to check out books. Don't worry about returning them; we'll have a book return box at the house where you can drop them off if you're not coming back to the library."

"I don't think you'll see much of me now that I have this." Bella held up her card. "I am so looking forward to digging into the stacks."

"And that's where I come in." Miss Applebome breezed to the front of the room. "I'm sure it's been a few years since you've been in a library. Well, except for Miss Simon. Nice to see you again, my dear."

Jennifer smiled. "I spent all last summer holed up in a graduate student room on the fourth floor. I left the library to eat and sleep, but other than that I lived here."

"Which is why we always leave one of the retreat spots open for Covington graduate students." Cat stood behind Jennifer. "She's your guide if you can't find me or Miss Applebome."

Bella turned in her seat and stared at Jennifer so long the girl glanced at Cat, adding a nonverbal *what did I do?* to the look.

"Anyway, I'm turning you over to Miss Applebome," said Cat. "If you want an escort back, I'll be here at three to walk the group back, or there's a map in your notebook if you feel adventuresome."

As Cat left the room, she ran into Uncle Pete standing outside the door waiting for her. She gave him a hug, then nodded to the taped-off room. "Still no leads on the missing book?"

"Nothing. We were going over video recording for the last week, but someone turned off the system last Sunday after the library closed. Now I have to go through the rest of the tapes and see if someone was casing the place in the week prior. This doesn't make any sense. Why would someone steal a book?" He sighed and ran a hand through his thinning hair.

"How valuable was it?"

Uncle Pete shrugged. "According to Miss Applebome, they had it insured for a couple thousand, but even she couldn't put a firm value on it. A signed Hemingway is not as common as you might think."

"Have you asked in the rare-book community?" Cat considered the people she'd bought out-of-print books from; someone had to have an idea of the book's value. "I should have some contacts I could give you."

"That would be nice, honey. Miss Applebome was going to ask her librarian friends, but if you have some names, that might be faster. That woman doesn't like me messing with her library, she's made that clear as day."

Cat bit back a smile. As head librarian, Miss Applebome ruled with an iron fist. She only agreed to the retreat library cards if the participants took her Library 101 session, which is why they were here today. "She likes things her way."

"That's an understatement," Uncle Pete complained. As they walked out of the building, he paused as he turned left toward the parking lot. "You want a ride back?"

"Nope, I'm good. I need to stretch my legs; I'm sore from skiing yesterday." She stretched her arms. "All over."

Chuckling, he nodded. "And that's why you don't see me throwing myself downhill on two pieces of wood. I'd kill myself for sure." He paused. "Anything going on up there I should know about?"

Cat shrugged. "The bartender is really good at his job. He's a natural at suggesting the perfect drink and loves to chat up the customers. But I got the impression that they handle their customers responsibly. He offered to set Seth and I up with a room before we started drinking."

"That's because the two of you ooze couple-ness. It's probably because you dated each other for so long. You act like you've been married for years." Uncle Pete turned toward the parking lot.

As Cat made her way back home, walking through campus and the side streets, she thought about what he'd said. Sunday had felt like old times. She smiled at the memories of skiing with the gang during high school. Even though they couldn't get into the bar, they would hang around the fireplace, drinking soda and talking about the day's runs. And the ones from the weekend before. Most of the other kids weren't dating, but it didn't seem to matter. They were a tight-knit group, and everyone saw Seth and her as being perfect together. Now she had to wonder: Were she and Seth already a couple again? They'd fallen into the same routine, the same level of comfort with each other without much fanfare. She was happy they were dating, but maybe it was too soon. And the bigger question was, Was that what she wanted?

Chapter 3

The house empty now that the guests were out, Cat stopped in the kitchen to grab some coffee. The room was unoccupied too. Even Shauna had disappeared for the morning. "So what," Cat mumbled to herself. "Perfect time to head upstairs and write."

She poured her coffee and then put a couple of cookies on a napkin. She was stalling. Sometimes her writing office called to her like a new love, and sometimes, like today, she felt like she was being sent to detention even though it was her choice to write.

She made a note on Shauna's kitchen whiteboard to let Shauna know she was in the house. With guests in the house, they kept the front door unlocked most of the time, a practice that made her uncle cringe. Typically, someone was in the house at all times, either her or Seth or Shauna, but this morning the house was empty when she arrived back from the library. Maybe they needed to talk a bit about scheduling, especially on retreat weeks.

Grabbing a couple more cookies, she headed out of the kitchen and to the stairs. Pausing at the foot of the staircase, she looked down the hall to Michael's office. Then she went back into the kitchen, grabbed the key to the office from the sideboard, and marched down the hall to unlock it. Cat blamed Uncle Pete for her lack of focus. When her deadline was gone, she could spend time thinking about a future with Seth. But when she thought about being a couple, her mind twisted back to Michael. Without finding out what really happened to their marriage and her ex-husband, she couldn't move on, no matter how much anyone pressed.

The room smelled like wood polish as she pushed open the door. She'd ignored the room and her husband's journal for weeks, focusing instead on her writing. Now, the memories were too strong for her. With no one in the house, there were no distractions. No one to tell her this was a bad idea.

Shauna had cleaned since Cat had last been here. The room looked neat as a pin. She sat down in what used to be her reading chair and put her coffee on the side table. It felt strange to her that Michael hadn't changed the office once they'd divorced. Why keep the one piece of furniture she'd insisted he buy and make room for in an office that was supposed to be all his? Opening the journal she'd left next to the lamp, she bit into one of the cookies as she started reading.

She knows something's wrong. I can see my lie turning around in her eyes as I'm saying it. "Yes, I have to work late, again. Don't hold dinner or wait up for me. In fact, why don't you go out with your friends? You haven't seen them in months." I hate having her think the worst. She should know I took my vows forever, but if she thinks I'm just a jerk, it will keep her safe. I've started receiving hang-up calls at the office. Are they warning me to keep my mouth shut?

If she was to believe Michael's journal, not only had he been in trouble, but he'd lied to her to force the divorce. The idea made her head spin. She looked at the leather-bound journal. She wouldn't put it past him to make up a story about how he was the noble one. Especially since he'd looked like quite the jerk in the divorce proceedings . . . which, from reading this entry, was his plan all along. "Oh, Michael, what did you get yourself into?"

A door slammed and she jumped, her hand knocking a cookie to the floor.

"Cat? Are you here?" Seth's voice echoed through the house, and she knew he was standing at the foot of the stairs, looking upward. She closed the book, being careful to replace the bookmark between the pages and picked up the last cookie and her coffee. She shut the door and locked it before she answered.

"I'm here."

Seth turned toward her voice, and his face darkened a bit when he saw the key in her hand. As quickly as that emotion had registered, it disappeared and Cat was left wondering if she'd been imagining things. "Hey, I told Shauna I'd stay until you got here, but I got called to an emergency water issue on a job in town."

"No worries. I wondered why the house was empty." She put the key away in the kitchen and then returned to the hallway where Seth waited. "Are you leaving again?"

"Yeah, I just had to pick up a drill I left upstairs." He brushed a stray hair away from her face. "You okay?"

Cat knew he wasn't just talking about her being alone in the house. Trying to figure out the real Michael had twisted her insides up more than once. And Seth knew it. "I'm fine." She looked upward toward her office. "I'm heading upstairs to write while the house is quiet."

"I should have this leak fixed in a couple hours. I'll be back around five to check in and see if you need anything." He pulled her close and kissed her. "You're pretty amazing, you know that?"

"I'm just a normal girl with a crazy big Victorian to renovate."

He laughed, and then bounded up the stairs to the room he'd been remodeling. Seth fit in the work on the Victorian when he wasn't busy with the rest of the odd jobs he got as the only repair person in town.

As she turned to follow him upstairs, the door opened again. There was no way they could be back by now. She glanced at the grandfather clock before turning around. Miss Applebome's class should have gone longer than forty minutes. Plastering on a smile she didn't feel, she turned to see

which one of her guests had already returned
and cancelled out her writing slot.

Instead of a retreat guest, Professor Turner
stood in the foyer, looking around, confused,
until he spotted her at the stairs. "Miss Latimer.
I'm so sorry I missed you at the library. I wanted
to talk to you about tomorrow's session."

And with those words her writing time disappeared. She'd have to get up early tomorrow to
make up her word count she missed today. She
moved toward the professor. "Of course, would
you like something hot to drink?"

"A cup of tea would be nice." He stomped his
feet on the rug, trying to get off the snow that
had accumulated during his walk here. She wondered if the professor even had a car.

"Take your coat off and meet me in the living
room. We can talk there since you'll be speaking
there later; that way, you can get reacquainted
with the set up." She went to the kitchen to make
his tea. She added a few of Shauna's fresh baked
cookies to a plate, refilled her own coffee cup,
and put everything on a tray. Before she left the
kitchen, Seth came up from the basement, tools
in one hand, and grabbed a couple cookies with
the other.

"I'll see you later." He kissed her and looked
at the tray. "Who's here?"

"Professor Turner." She forced a smile. "And
I'm the hostess with the mostest."

He left through the kitchen door, calling back
to her, "You're just too nice. Always have been."

When she entered the living room, Professor
Turner was already practicing his lecture. He

flushed as she walked in. "Sorry, I've been working on my speaking presence since, as dean, I'm called into many meetings, and sometimes I even have to make an impromptu presentation."

"You sounded great. Last session, the group adored you." She set the tray down on a coffee table. "What did you want to talk to me about?"

He took a sip of the tea and then added a couple of teaspoons of sugar. Trying another sip, he nodded, then set the cup down. "I suspect you know I've been wanting to make this dean appointment permanent, not acting. It requires a lot of my time for the administration processes, so I'm afraid tomorrow will be the last time I'm able to talk at your retreat."

Cat smiled, wondering how long it had taken the guy to get up the courage to talk to her. Professor Turner—well, soon to be Dean Turner if he had his way—didn't like saying no. "I suspected as much. I appreciate you letting me know. Will you be asking for volunteers, or can I choose who I'd like to replace you?"

"Now, that's just the thing. Professors are a busy lot. I did the task out of my love for all things Hemingway, but we will no longer be able to subsidize your retreat in this manner. If you want a professor to speak, you will have to pay them their speaker rate." He ate the cookie, not looking up at Cat. "I'm sure you can get some of the newer professors at a reasonable cost."

"The college offered the guest lecturer as part of our agreement with the library. In exchange, I give you a slot for one graduate student for free, minus the room charge." She leaned forward. "It's all in the contract."

Professor Turner frowned. "I didn't see a contract in Dean Vargas's papers. Do you have a copy?"

"I'm sure I do." Cat thought about the mess on her desk upstairs. Would it be there or would the final copy be in Shauna's files? "I'll bring over a copy as soon as I find it. Wouldn't the college's legal department have a copy?"

He shook his head. "I tried there. I didn't want to bring up all this money stuff, but honestly, Dean Vargas was very free with his spending. I suspect several of his deals weren't approved by the board."

"Since you're here, you must mean specifically the one between the college and my writers' retreat." Cat blew out a breath. She had spent hours hammering out a fair agreement between the college and her retreat. Their logo was on her marketing materials. If they were no longer a partner, what all would she have to change? And at what cost?

"I don't mean to be snippy, but yes, unfortunately I don't believe you have a valid contract with the college. Until you can come up with your copy, I'm afraid I will have to ask you to pay the required speaker fee." He stood and took two cookies off the plate. "I look forward to meeting your group tomorrow. I hear you have a determined historical fiction author in your group."

Cat was nothing if not determined. "I'm sure

they will enjoy hearing you speak." She stood
and followed him to the foyer.

He slipped on his coat, held his hat in one
hand, and the doorknob with the other. "I'm
sorry to bring bad news to you on such a lovely
day."

Cat stood by the doorway, watching the professor make his way to the road. The snow plows
had been doing their job, and the streets were
white but had clear driving lanes. Unless a new
batch of snow fell, they might just clear off with
the heat from the bright sunshine today. The
clock chimed noon and Cat made her way to
the kitchen, hoping that there was a leftover
shepherd's pie in the fridge she could microwave
for lunch. Or, barring that, a big bag of potato
chips and salsa. She deserved a treat after the
morning she'd had.

And after lunch, she'd go upstairs and write.

Under her earlier note on the whiteboard,
she wrote *Where's the contract?* Between her and
Shauna, one of them should remember where
they filed it a few months ago.

Otherwise, she was going to be footing a huge
cost to remove Covington College as one of her
sponsors, along with paying a visiting professor
for each of the retreats where they already had
guests confirmed. Either that, or she needed
to take the item off as one of the perks of the
retreat.

She shook her head. No use thinking about it
now. Now was time for food. She spied several of
the individual portions in the fridge, so she took
two out and popped them in the oven to heat. If

Shauna didn't arrive home in time for lunch, Cat would eat both of them. Not that she was starving; instead, the warm food eased her anxiety. Food made her feel safe and in control, not the best way to deal with the unknown, but it would work for today. Between spending time with Michael's journal and then the less-than-satisfactory meeting with Professor Turner, she deserved some food love.

While she waited for lunch to be ready, she satisfied herself with a cookie and leafed through a fashion magazine Shauna had left on the table.

She was just taking lunch out of the oven when the back door opened and Shauna arrived to save Cat from herself.

"You read my mind." Shauna plopped bags onto the counter. "I would have called to tell you to put a couple pies in, but I got talking at the market. Apparently, the stolen book was the college's signed copy of *A Moveable Feast*. It was one of a few his widow signed when it was published after his death. I loved that book when I read it at university."

"I wouldn't think grocery shopping would be a good source for gossip. I just go in and get stuff and leave." Cat started unloading the first bag.

Shauna laughed and paused at the door before returning to the car. "Then you're doing it all wrong. The grocery store is the best place to catch up on local news. I'm also hearing Brit's pretty steamed about Tommy Neil's antics. The wedding seems to be still on, but she postponed her wedding-gown appointment."

Cat waited for Shauna to return with the final

load of bags before responding. She didn't know the local bartender well, but she knew how it felt for someone you loved to betray you. Or at least believe that he'd betrayed her. Her divorce from Michael had been complicated when it happened. Now, with the knowledge Uncle Pete had shared that he believed Michael hadn't died of natural causes, and the journal, she wasn't sure *what* to think anymore. But she knew how she'd felt back when they'd divorced. She dug through one of the bags, grabbing the stuff that needed to be stored in the fridge. "Maybe cancelling is the best thing. I don't think you can fix a cheater. Although who am I to judge?"

"Now, we don't know that Tommy has actually cheated." Shauna held her hand up to stop Cat's response. "Yes, he kissed a girl in a drunken moment. Maybe he was dealing with cold feet. Or just sowing his last wild oats?"

"Even if it's just that, Brit's better off without him. She'll always be looking over her shoulder for the next shoe to drop. I say cut him now and find someone who really loves her." Cat took the steaming dishes over to the table. "You want a salad or something with this?"

"I think you're putting some of your own history on Brit's situation. Anyway, the meat pie will be fine. I do have a bowl of cut fruit from breakfast in the fridge. Get that out and it can be our dessert." Shauna moved to put away the rest of the groceries.

"Hold on a second. I need to tell you something." Cat told Shauna about the journal entry and waiting. When she didn't respond, Cat asked her the one question that had been echoing in her brain for the last few hours. "Do you think it's real?"

"The entry or Michael's fear?" Shauna placed the perishables into the fridge. "I didn't know the man, so I can't give you advice on the whole thing. Maybe you should show the journal to your uncle?"

"Maybe." Cat took a bag and unpacked the canned goods for the pantry. "He's busy with this book investigation. I guess I could wait for a few days."

"I think you need some perspective from someone who knew both of you." Shauna folded the last, now empty, bag then paused at the whiteboard to erase her status and Cat's short-lived declaration that she was going upstairs to write. She pointed at the next line. "What contract?"

Cat filled her in on the impromptu visit from Professor Turner. "Do you have the contract from Dean Vargas I can give Turner? I think we'll have to look at the budget if Professor—I mean, Dean—Turner is right."

"I know we got a final copy from the legal department." Shauna tapped her spoon on the edge of her plate as she thought. "Give me a bit and I'll find it."

"We have until the next session, but if we need to change things on the website, I'd rather do it sooner than later." Cat took a spoonful of the fruit and put it next to the half-eaten pie. They finished lunch, chatting about the new retreat attendees.

"I can't say I've gotten to know any of our new guests yet. They are so different from the last group." Shauna brightened. "Speaking of the last group, you got flowers today."

"From who?" Cat put her empty plate in the sink and ate the last few pineapple chunks in the now almost-empty fruit bowl. She offered the melon pieces to Shauna, but she shook her head.

"I have to cut fresh tomorrow anyway and there's not enough for a serving there." She headed to the door leading to the foyer. "Hold on a minute; I'll be right back."

Cat finished clearing the table and ran a rag under the hot water. She'd just finished wiping down the table when Shauna returned, a card in her hand.

"*Hope your second retreat goes smoother than the first. Thinking warmly of you all, Linda Cook.*" Shauna handed Cat the card. "I can't believe you didn't see the two-dozen red roses on the registration desk. Although red roses are kind of an odd choice."

Cat knew exactly why Linda had sent the roses: An inside joke between the two women mirroring the flowers Linda had received from a killer when she'd been a retreat guest. "She's a strong woman. I hear she's working on a book and already has signed a top-notch agent."

"She's got a lot to write about, that's for sure." Shauna looked at the clock. "Let me clean up the lunch mess, then I'll get the baking done for tomorrow's brunch. You have a craving for any specific sweet?"

"Brownies. But don't forget to look for the contract." Cat paused at the door. "I'm going upstairs to write. I'll go get the retreat guys from the library at 3:00, and Seth said he'd stop in around 5:00 in case there's something you need him to do."

"That's nice." Shauna smiled. "He's good to have around."

Cat shook her head. "I'm sure he's coming by then so he's on time for dinner."

"That's not fair. He comes by when his meal isn't included in the deal." Shauna smiled. "To see you."

"Food's a stronger driver, I believe." Cat smiled when she saw her friend start to argue. "Let it be. Right now, I'm happy with getting to know Seth again. I don't know where it's going, but it's good today."

She left the kitchen before Shauna could see the question in her face and ask her what was wrong. She didn't want her friend to worry about Cat reading the journal again. Shauna was instinctual about things like that and, honestly, Cat wasn't good at hiding her feelings.

She climbed the stairs slowly. With each step, she wondered if she'd be stopped or if she'd actually make it the entire way to her office. When she finally reached the third floor and opened her office door, she let out the breath she'd been holding. Now all she had to do was get her computer started, and she could at least write down a number on her word-count tracking sheet. When she wanted to write, things got in the way. When she didn't want to write, no one was around to bother her.

A knock on the door caused her to look up from her document, surprised at the time on the clock. She'd been writing for over two hours straight, lost in Kori's latest drama. She hit *save* and stood to stretch. "I know, I'm late to get the guests."

"Not too late." Shauna leaned on the open doorway. "It shouldn't take you more than ten minutes to get over there. Unless you want me to go?"

Cat turned off the computer. "Nope. I want to have some one-on-one time with our Miss Christina. Maybe she's more rational today about Tommy Neil and his situation."

By the time she got to the library, most of the group was hanging out in the foyer, their backpacks heavy with checked-out books. The scene made Cat smile, wondering how anyone visited a library without leaving with a to-be-read list longer than the one they walked in with. "Hey guys, sorry I'm late. Ready to wander back to the house? Shauna has afternoon snacks set out and hot apple cider to warm us up."

"No worries, we just finished up." Nelson Wider picked up a pile of books from the counter. The books were all about the Old West and Colorado. Cat wondered if he was writing about the local area or something else. Maybe he and Bella could share their research, helping each with their different viewpoints. "I went a little crazy in the history section. Looks like I'm reading and taking notes for most of the week with this gold mine."

"That's why I write fiction." Bella smiled at the man, straightening his neck scarf. "Yes, you have to have your facts straight, but mostly it's about the story, not the history."

He blushed and Cat wondered if the guy had a bit of a crush on the older woman. Bella didn't seem like a cougar but, honestly, what happened between guests wasn't her business. She glanced around. Four guests. Who was missing? She looked out the glass entry doors and saw Christina Powers climbing into a truck that had just pulled up in front of the book drop. Four-wheeled drive, jacked up, and painted with a glimmering red—there was only one person who the vehicle could belong to: the player, Tommy Neil. Cat sighed.

Jeffrey Blank, turned at the sound, shaking his head in disgust. "Some girls are just attracted to that bad-boy anti-hero type. Apparently, they can't see through the fluff to the real person. That's what's wrong with relationships these days. The kid's sweet, but she can't see the jerk wants one thing from her."

Cat nodded. "It's not my business, but I agree with your analysis." She looked back at the other three, who were watching their interaction. Writers were like magpies: They picked up everything, including unexpected tension in the everyday. "You all ready to head out?"

The group made their way through the foyer area and started following Cat back to the house.

Jennifer Simon caught up with her. "That was something."

"The library tour? I would have thought you would be bored." Cat smiled at the woman. Jennifer had long, dark hair covered with a fuzzy beanie and her puffy ski coat was high quality. She was used to the Colorado winters and wore heavy gloves. Cat had bundled the other guests with additional winter items from the retreat closet, including hats and gloves.

"Miss Applebome let me write during her presentation. I did an internship with her a few years ago, when I was thinking about majoring in library science." She tilted her head and grinned up at Cat. "I was talking about the chick running off with Tommy Neil. That guy's a loser, I don't know what Brit ever saw in him."

"You know Tommy and Brit?"

Jennifer shrugged. "Bernie's is a popular spot. A group of us in the graduate program go down on Friday's for karaoke. I'm totally into Adele. But, anyway, when Brit started wearing that rock, I told her Tommy was a jerk, but she just laughed. You won't believe what she said."

Cat didn't stop walking or respond, but the younger woman continued as if she had.

"Brit said even bad boys needed a chance at redemption." Jennifer adjusted her backpack. "I think sometimes Brit should have been the writer; she's really good at making up stories about her own life to fit her delusions."

* * *

When they returned to the house, Shauna greeted them at the door, helping to hang up coats and set aside snow boots. "Check out the brownies. They just came out of the oven."

The guests disappeared into the dining room, and Shauna put her hand on Cat's sleeve. "I see we're missing Miss Powers?"

"She's going to leave here with a broken heart, that's all I have to say." Cat ran her hand through her short hair, feeling the static cling from the hat.

"She might wind up with more than her heart broken." Shauna lowered her voice. "Brit stopped by all hot and bothered, looking for Tommy. She's tired of hearing about him hanging out with Christina."

"Brit can't be mad at her. He's the one who is breaking a promise." Cat slipped on a pair of house slippers she kept by the door.

"I don't know. Women tend to blame the competition rather than the guy who's stepping out." Shauna put away the last coat. "Anyway, I told her they weren't here and that she needed to calm down. I can't believe she drove as angry as she seemed."

"Well, I didn't get a chance to talk to Christina. I'll try again tonight when she comes back from their date." Cat followed Shauna into the kitchen. "Who would have thought that baby-sitting would be part of my duties running the retreat?"

Chapter 4

A knock on Cat's door woke her. She peered at the clock display: 3:00 a.m. Who would be waking her up at this time? She sank back into her comforter. Maybe she'd imagined the sound. The old house had a way of creaking and squeaking making her think she heard voices and noises. She closed her eyes.

"Cat, are you awake?" Seth's voice came through the door.

Now she did sit up. She grabbed her robe and slipped her feet into her slippers sitting next to the bed. The wooden floors could be ice cold during the night. "Just a minute," she called out, still not convinced Seth was really waiting in the hallway.

When she opened the door, he held out a cup of coffee. "Here, drink this, get dressed, and come downstairs. Your Uncle Pete is here, and he needs to talk to you." He looked at the flannel pajamas that peaked out from underneath the robe. "Cute Snoopy pj's. I thought you gave those away."

"You're assuming these are the ones your mother gave me in high school." She took the cup and drank deeply. "What are you doing here? Do you know it's three in the morning?"

"Drink your coffee, get dressed, and come down to the kitchen," he repeated. He kissed Cat on the top of her head. "And don't make me come back up here. Your uncle wanted me to dump a glass of ice water on you."

"He did it once when I was in high school. I'll be down in a few." Cat shut the door and turned on the room light. What in the world was so important that she had to be woken up in the middle of the night? A vision of Christina climbing into the truck ran through her mind. "Crap. I hope she's okay."

By the time she'd arrived in the kitchen, she'd gone through a list of what could have happened to the missing Christina, none of them pleasant to think about. She took a deep breath, then pushed the door open and walked into the warm kitchen, filled with smells of biscuits and a sausage gravy. Uncle Pete, Seth, and Shauna sat at the table, coffee cups in hand. They all turned and looked at her as she walked in.

"Okay, what happened?" She poured her own coffee before sitting down in the empty chair next to Seth. He put his arm around her, but didn't speak.

"When was the last time you saw Christina Powers?" Uncle Pete picked up a pen and poised it over his notebook.

"Yesterday about three. She was climbing into Tommy Neil's truck at the library. Why, did they get into an accident?" She rubbed her forehead. "I can't believe that kid thought driving that truck in the snow was a good idea."

"They weren't in an accident as far as I can tell." Uncle Pete sat his pen down. "Miss Powers is not in her room."

Cat's gaze turned to Shauna. "She didn't come back last night?"

She shook her head as she stood to grab the coffee pot and refill everyone's cup. "I checked her room and the security logs. She left with you at ten but hasn't been back since."

Shrugging, Cat sipped her coffee. "I guess she's not the first to spend the night with an inappropriate man. Why is this a big deal? This kind of shack-up has to happen often in a college town. Just check Tommy's house."

"Tommy lives with Brit." Uncle Pete leaned back in his chair. "But he wasn't there either. Tommy rented a ski condo for the week."

"Well, then look there." Cat frowned. There was something they weren't telling her; she could see it in their faces. "What? No one wants to bother Tommy the cheater during his player time? What are you all not telling me?"

Seth turned her face toward him. "Tommy Neil was found dead in the condo a few hours ago. From the look of the living room, he and someone, probably Christina, had a romantic dinner in front of the fire. A few hours ago, a guest called the front desk to report an open condo-room door. When the front desk sent someone up to check, the girl found Tommy dead. He was naked in the in-room hot tub, a knife in his gut."

"Tommy's dead?" Cat whispered. She hadn't really known the guy or liked him, but that didn't matter now. Not now that he was dead. "Did the killers kidnap Christina? Did we check the phone for ransom demands?"

"I don't believe she was kidnapped, but we'll explore that avenue too." Uncle Pete ran a hand through his thinning hair. "Look, Cat, I don't know how else to ask this, but do you think this woman could have killed Tommy Neil?"

"No." Cat shook her head violently. "The girl wrote sweet romances. If she wouldn't even imagine sex for her books, why do you think she would have the confidence to kill someone?"

"I'm not saying she did; we just need to question her."

Shauna stood and crossed to the stove. "Let's eat something before our blood sugar gets low and people get cranky."

Cat sat thinking about Tommy and Christina. The girl had been drunk on happiness the last time she'd seen her. Over the moon, Cat's mom would have called her. "I just don't see how she could have done something like this."

Shauna set down plates in front of everyone, but they all just picked at the food.

Then, the kitchen door blew open, and Christina stumbled into the room. She collapsed on the bench, shivering as Shauna ran to help her out of her wet coat and boots.

"I'm freezing," the girl choked out. "I must

have walked a mile or more. I thought the house was closer to the library, where I had the guys drop me off."

"Where have you been?" Cat knelt in front of her and pulled off the gloves. Seth reappeared to her left with a couple of large blankets. "Why didn't you come right to the house?"

"I didn't trust them. They were ski bums. I didn't want them to know where I was staying. They kept asking if I wanted to go party with them." Christina's teeth started chattering as they wrapped her in blankets and led her to the table. Shauna handed her a cup of coffee and went back to the stove to get her a plate of food.

"You're lucky. A lot of people die from being out in the weather too long. Why didn't Tommy bring you back?" Cat looked at Uncle Pete as she waited for the girl's answer.

"That jerk. All he wanted was one thing. When I told him I didn't believe in premarital sex, he laughed at me and threw me out of the room. Said I'd been a waste of perfectly good room service." She sipped more of her coffee. "When I got down to the lobby, these guys offered me a ride back to town."

"Did you tell them what happened?" Cat watched as the girl devoured the food in front of her. Cat pulled the blanket off her left hand. The shirtsleeve was covered in blood spatter.

"No. I felt stupid. I made up some story about missing my bus. They didn't really care; all they wanted was the same thing as Tommy." Christina brushed tears away from her eyes with her forearm. "That's it. I'm done with drinking and going to bars and meeting guys. If God has a plan for me to be married, he'll send my Mr. Right to my young-adult group at church."

"Christina, what happened to your arm? Is it cut?" Cat pointed to the dried blood.

The girl barely glanced her way. "No, it's Tommy's blood. He cut his hand when he was trying to open the champagne. You know, like you see on the television? He had some kind of machete and lopped the top off, but then he cut his hand on the bottle. I told him he probably had glass shards in the wine so I refused to drink it. Of course, that made him mad too."

"More coffee?" Shauna interrupted the quiet that had come over the room.

"I'd love a hot chocolate. And after that, I'm going to my room and sleeping the day away. I'm sorry I'm going to miss the Hemingway lecture." Christina shook her head. "I've been an idiot on this trip, but I swear I'll be in full retreat mode as soon as I wake up."

"You'll have to take your hot cocoa to go." Uncle Pete finished off the last bite of food on his plate. "I'm afraid you'll have to come with me and make a formal statement at the police station."

Christina stared at him. "A formal statement about what? I wasn't gone long enough to be considered missing, was I?" She turned to Cat. "Did you file a missing-person report?"

"No, honey, I didn't." Cat put her hand over the young woman's hand. "Listen, I have some bad news."

"Stop, Cat. I'll tell her." Uncle Pete stood and

turned toward Christina, blocking her exit in case she showed any plan on running. "Tommy Neil was murdered last night, and you were the last person to see him alive. I need to ask you some questions."

Uncle Pete waited as Shauna escorted Christina up to her room to change into warm clothes. As they walked out of the kitchen, he handed her a bag, "No showers, please. And I'll need her clothes as evidence."

"I didn't do anything." Christina looked at Shauna, her eyes wide. "Really, you have to believe me."

"Honey, let's just get this over with okay?" Shauna murmured. "When you come back, I'll have a nice breakfast waiting, and then you can sleep as long as you want."

When they were out of the room, Cat looked at her uncle. "Her story could explain why she had his blood on her. There's just no way she killed Tommy Neil."

He shrugged. "You're probably right. Unfortunately, she is the last person I know who saw him alive. I need to protect any evidence that might be there."

After Uncle Pete and Christina left, Cat took her coffee cup upstairs to her office. There was no way she could sit in that kitchen and worry. What was going on with her world? It had to be a coincidence that Tommy Neil was killed on the same day one of her guests was seen leaving with him.

She opened her computer and read the last few lines of what she'd written the day before. No matter what kind of turmoil Cat was experiencing in her real life, typically writing made her forget everything and concentrate on the story. As she stared at the last few lines written a few days ago, all she could see was the look on Christina's face after Uncle Pete told her the news. The girl had been crushed. Sighing, Cat tried to put the incident away in a box she could deal with later. Right now, she wanted, no needed, to write. She checked her notes, then added a sentence to the document. Then another.

Looking down at the clock on her computer, Cat realized she'd been lost in Kori-land for over three hours. She stretched, realizing she was still in the jeans and T-shirt she'd pulled on when Uncle Pete had arrived. Time for a shower, more coffee, and maybe a snack. Shauna's biscuits and gravy had been filling last night, but she felt like she'd gone for days without food. Cat glanced out the window at the snowy scene below. She couldn't tell if Uncle Pete had returned Christina last night or if they were still talking. Cat knew one thing: She had to find Tommy Neil's killer before the kid was convicted of being stupid. She turned off the computer and went to her room.

Showered and dressed, Cat slipped downstairs and into the kitchen without running into anyone. The rest of the retreat attendees had to still be asleep, unaware of the drama from late last night. Shauna started as Cat opened the door. "Sorry, didn't mean to scare you."

Shauna put her hand to her chest. "I swear, these retreats are getting more and more crazy. Can you believe someone like Christina could kill?"

"No, and neither can you." Cat poured herself a cup of coffee. "The question this morning is if not Christina, who else wanted Tommy Neil dead?"

"Besides Brit and her dad?" Shauna set a plate in front of Cat. "I made quiche and a fruit bowl for breakfast. I couldn't go back to sleep after your uncle left."

"Me neither. I spent some time in on the manuscript. I feel bad for Christina. And Brit," Cat added before taking a bite of the pie. Shauna used potatoes and bacon, making the quiche filling and amazingly yummy. Cat pointed to the egg dish. "I really like this. You need to keep this in the retreat rotation."

Shauna sat across from her, with her cup of coffee. "I'm making up a list of recipes for a Warm Springs Writers' Retreat cookbook. Something people could take home with them to relive some of the food they got while they were here. Do you think that's a good idea?"

Cat nodded. "It's a great idea. I don't know much about making a cookbook, but we could sell them on the website." She focused on eating for a few minutes. "As long as we don't have to shut the retreat down. Did you find the contract?"

"Not yet, but I plan on looking for it today." Shauna stood as the oven timer went off. "Muffins are ready. Do you want one? Peanut butter crunch."

"Please." Cat put her plate in the sink and refilled her coffee cup. She'd realized as they'd been talking about cheating Tommy that she hadn't even cleaned out Michael's desk. Maybe there was a clue there that could explain what she'd read in his journals. "I'm going into Michael's office to use his computer. I want to check into Tommy Neil and see if we can point Uncle Pete in the right direction."

"Remember, Professor Turner will be here at ten. You need to introduce him to the group before he talks." Shauna grinned. "He sent over an updated bio for you to read. I'm not sure he remembers it's just five people."

"He told me yesterday he's practicing for the bigger events." Cat shook her head. Had it just been Monday when she had the talk with Professor Turner? The week was just beginning, and she already felt like she'd been dealing with retreat business forever. "I hate to say this, but I'll be glad when this retreat is over. Too many things happening already."

"We'll have a nice, boring retreat soon." Shauna handed her the muffin on a napkin. "I promise. Maybe next time we'll have a group of literary authors who just want to be left alone in their rooms, no fuss, just writing."

"And you're saying we won't find one of them dead by suspicious means in the middle of the retreat?" Cat shrugged. "That would be heaven. You know where to find me if you need something."

* * *

Cat opened Michael's office for the second time that week. The smell of wood cleaner hit her as soon as the door opened, reminding her of when her husband had been alive. Back when she'd thought he'd hung the moon for her personal benefit. How had she been so naïve back then?

She crossed the office and sat in his large leather chair. Opening the laptop, she keyed in his password by memory and then waited for the Internet browser to open. When it did, she typed *Tommy Neil, Aspen Hills Colorado* into the search bar. A list of hits filled the screen along with images of Tommy in ski attire and on the slopes and one where he was teaching a very beautiful young lady how to ski. She could have just typed *Tommy Neil, Player* and gotten the same results. What had Brit seen in the guy?

Cat searched through the desk drawers until she found a notebook. The first half was taken up with Michael's tight handwriting, but Cat found some empty pages near the back. She ripped them out of the notebook and went to put it back into the bottom drawer. Hesitating, she looked at a few of the pages in the front. Economics notes from his classes, a list of possible stocks and their rankings on the exchange, and a list of expenses. Nothing to explain Michael's weird journal entries. She put the notebook away. One mystery at a time.

She started writing down everything she could about Tommy Neil, and by the time she'd finished, she knew where she would go next. Well, at least when she felt comfortable talking to the family. It had been less than twelve hours since they had received the news. She should take over food. People always brought food for the grieving family. Tommy's mother only lived a few blocks away, past Warm Springs. Maybe talking to the mom would give Cat more than his ski school website had revealed. If the family was even telling Tommy stories yet. Food, she'd just take food and see where that got her.

A knock sounded at the door. Shauna poked her head into the room. "Hey Cat, everyone's gathered in the living room, except for Professor Turner. Do you want me to call the office and see if he's on his way?"

Cat closed the computer and folded the pages with Tommy Neil's life highlights on the Internet. "Would you?" She met Shauna at the door. "I'll go in and entertain the group until he arrives."

In the living room, she found four of the guests. "Sorry, we're running a little late today. How's the writing going?"

Jeffrey stood in the back of the room. "As good as could be expected with all these distractions. Anyone know where Christina is?"

The rest of the guests looked around at each other and shrugged. Cat motioned for him to come and sit with the group. How much to tell them? Finally, when no one answered his question, he shook his head and sank into a chair, his arms crossed. Cat sat too and addressed the group. "Miss Powers had an appointment today and should be joining us later."

"An appointment with that cute ski instructor I heard about? I swear, I should never turn down an outing just to write. Now all of you have fun memories." Bella beamed at the group, but Jennifer shrugged.

"I like the skiing part. When everyone went back to the lodge, it got kind of boring. I probably would have liked to stay here with you. Besides, the guy wasn't that cute." She flipped her long, brown hair back. "Heaven knows, I've got a ton of research to get done on my thesis project."

"Cute enough that the girl took off with him yesterday." Nelson Wider shook his head. "Seriously, we paid good money for this retreat, and she's treating it like a spring break on the beach. I'll never understand romance writers."

"You guys don't know anything," Jeffrey burst out. He glared at the other three. "Christina isn't interested in that jerk. She's way too smart for that."

"Ooohhh, do I hear a bit of jealousy?" Bella grinned at Cat. "You might just have the makings of a love triangle here. Wouldn't that be lovely to write about? In a fictional manner, that is."

"I'm not jealous. I'm out of here. Who cares about some old Hemingway professor anyway? I'm going to write." Jeffrey strode out of the room.

The others went quiet as they watched him leave.

"I didn't mean to upset him. I was kidding, but I think the way he's acting, he might just be a little taken with Miss Powers." Bella leaned back in her chair, watching the doorway Jeffrey had just passed through. "Poets, they're too emotional for their own good."

Nelson tapped his notebook with his pen. "If you ask me, there's several groups of writers who should just go get a day job and forget about creating. It never turns out well." He thought for a moment. "Look at Hemingway. He took his own life, leaving the mess for his last wife to clean up. Creative types tend to believe their feelings over real-life facts. Like if you put a gun to your head, you're going to die and make a mess."

"*Ewwh*, gross." Jennifer doodled on her paper. "So when is this professor coming?"

"Should be anytime." Cat glanced back at the doorway. "So while we wait, my how-I-became-a-YA-author talk is scheduled for tomorrow. Do you want me to do that, and then we'll just cancel tomorrow morning's get-together?"

The group listened and asked questions while they waited for Professor Turner. When he finally came in, breathless and out of sorts, Cat stopped the question-and-answer time, promising to be available during breakfast tomorrow. She introduced the winded professor and then left the room.

Shauna was in the kitchen working on the laptop.

"Well, today's and tomorrow's seminar sessions will be over by noon," Cat said. "We might have to start scheduling a third speaker to make sure they have enough options when they arrive."

"It is a *writing* retreat." Shauna didn't look up, even after Cat got a soda from the fridge and sat down. "Did you find anything on the dead guy?"

"Only that his mother lives a few blocks away. Do you think it would be tacky for me to stop in and see what she knows?" Cat was rethinking her plan. Besides, she was sure Uncle Pete would have already thought of questioning Neil's mother.

"Not if you bring a basket of muffins and your condolences." Shauna pointed to the cellophane wrapped basket on the counter. "I put a card in there from us at the retreat expressing our sympathy at her loss."

"You're two steps ahead of me." Cat sighed and sipped her soda.

Shauna looked up from the laptop screen. "But?"

"You're sure it's not tacky?"

Shauna laughed. "Every person who stops by with food wants the real story about how the guy died. What, you think they all just feel so bad he's gone? Funerals are a gossip hot spot."

"Maybe you could come with me?" Cat brightened at the thought. Shauna was good at getting the real story out of people.

Her friend shook her head. "Sorry, I'm in the middle of retreat business. This accounting program you bought is giving me fits. It doesn't want to match up with our bank accounts. The bank manager is calling me in a few minutes to make sure I have the right passwords."

"So maybe I should go now?" Cat looked outside the window, hoping the weather would keep her from leaving. The bright sun was shining and the sidewalks clear.

"Go, find out more information." Shauna looked at her with intensity. "We both know that kid didn't kill Tommy. Now we just have to make sure someone proves it."

"In other words, I'm supporting truth, justice, and the American way." Cat stood and took her winter coat off the kitchen coatrack.

"You could say that." Shauna put a white napkin over the top of the basket. "Or you're just being neighborly in a mother's time of need."

"I just hope she doesn't throw me out of the house when I try to get more information." Cat paused. "Any suggestions?"

"Be subtle. And don't mention his dalliance with Christina. I hear the mother was a big fan of the engagement to Brit."

Cat grabbed the basket and left the house, hoping that she could pull this off.

Chapter 5

The driveway at the Neil house was empty, but the snow had been removed and the warm day had made the remaining snow on the yard, shine. The Cape Cod–style house looked like a typical middle-income family lived there. Which, in Aspen Hills, meant at least one of the owners was a professional, doctor, lawyer, or trust-fund society volunteer. Or both. Home prices were crazy high ever since the quiet town had been discovered by Denver's upper class. The town was perfect for someone looking to live out of the city yet close enough to commute.

Cat rang the doorbell, shifting the basket of muffins to one side. No response. She rang again, glancing around the large porch. She could leave the basket near the door and come back later to talk to Tommy's mother. She set it down on a nearby porch swing and was digging through her purse for a pen to add a short note to the card when the door flew open.

"What do you want?"

Cat turned toward the door and held back a squeak. The woman was in a dirty housecoat, her gray hair loose and disheveled, and she had a cigarette hanging out of her mouth. Not the image of a grieving mother Cat had expected. She picked up the basket and held it out in front of her. "Mrs. Neil? I'm Cat Latimer. I'm so sorry for your loss."

The woman squinted at the basket and then up at Cat. "You weren't one of his floozies, were you?"

"Tommy's? No. I had only met your son once." She lifted the basket a few inches. "Can I set this down somewhere?"

The woman's eyes narrowed, but she stepped back and allowed Cat to enter. A living room to the side of the door overflowed with flowers and food baskets. "Just put it over there. My husband is dealing with all the packages, but he's disappeared somewhere."

Cat dropped the basket off and stood near the couch. "So, wow, this was unexpected."

The woman dropped into a large recliner and stamped out her half-smoked cigarette. "He was murdered. You typically don't expect that to happen." She shrugged. "Well, maybe some people do."

"Was Tommy in some kind of trouble, Mrs. Neil?"

"I'm Marilyn Colfax now. Neil was my first husband." She waved at the couch. "You might as well sit down if you want to hear the gossip."

"I didn't, I mean," Cat stammered.

"Don't worry about it," Marilyn interrupted.

"At least you came by with food instead of calling me for juicy bits for the rumor chain."

"I don't want to take up much of your time." Cat sat on the edge of the sofa. Upscale furniture filled the room. The only thing out of place besides the large floral arrangements was Mrs. Colfax herself.

"Listen, I'll tell you what happened, then you can go tell all your ghoulish friends and leave me alone." Mrs. Colfax shook out another cigarette and lit it. "He was killed by the government."

Cat narrowed her eyes. "Our government? You think they killed your son?"

"It's logical. The boy was headed for good things. He would have been president, I know it." She waved her cigarette around. "He was an Eagle Scout, did you know that? And oh-so popular in high school. Everyone came over to the house for his parties."

"But why would the government kill him?" Cat tried to keep the incredulity out of her tone. "He was a ski instructor."

Mrs. Colfax's eyes narrowed and Cat saw anger. "He was in between real jobs. That was just a hobby. You have to understand: Tommy was bound for greatness." Her voice trembled as she waved her hand around the room filled with flowers. "See? Everyone loved him."

Cat stood. She wouldn't get anything from talking to the grieving mother. Unless Cat wanted to know the woman's fantasy life for her son. "I can see that." She scooted around the glass-and-metal coffee table and paused at the doorway.

"Thank you for talking to me. I'm sorry for your loss."

As she walked out onto the porch, a man came up the stairs. He carried a bag from the local drug store in his hand. "I'm Ted Colfax. Can I help you?"

"I just dropped off a muffin basket for you and Mrs. Colfax." She looked back at the closed door. "We were shocked to hear about Tommy's death."

"Good riddance to bad rubbish, that's what I think." He put his hand on the doorknob. "Who did you say you were again?"

"I'm Cat Latimer. I run the writers' retreat over on Warm Springs." Cat paused halfway down the stairs. "I take it you didn't like your stepson?"

He shook his head. "All the boy did was cause his mother grief. When he got engaged to that barmaid, I thought she'd see the real side of him, but no, all she talked about was that girl's connections. Like she was Colorado royalty or something."

"Brit seems to be a nice girl."

"Probably, but nice girls who work in a bar aren't the type of women a future political candidate dates, let alone marries. All of Marilyn's dreams for the kid went up in smoke with that one announcement." The man shrugged as he looked at the door, like he had X-ray vision and could see his grieving wife sitting in the living room. "As if the drug problems weren't enough of a clue for her that the golden boy was never going to be elected dog catcher, let alone to a real position."

* * *

As Cat made her way back to the house, she wondered about the different perspectives Tommy's parents had on his potential. She hadn't seen a budding politician in the boy. He seemed more of a honkytonk player. If she ever had kids, there was no way she would ever put them up on a pedestal like Marilyn Colfax had Tommy. That must have been hard to live with, knowing you were disappointing your mother with every decision you made.

Or maybe that had been the point.

When she reached Main Street, instead of turning left toward Warm Springs, Cat found herself wandering past the shops, her thoughts meandering as well around the murder of Tommy Neil. His stepfather and mother were a study in contrasts, with one thinking he walked on water and the other believing the guy was maybe one step up from pond scum. A door opened on her left, and a man in a long black trench coat pushed past her, spinning her around.

Grasping for something, anything, so she didn't fall, she nevertheless found herself on her way down to the icy sidewalk. As she'd begun to fall, another man's hand grabbed hers and kept her upright. When she caught her breath, she was cradled in a stranger's arms. She looked up into the deepest eyes she'd ever seen on a man. His lips curved into a smile as he saw what must have been shock on Cat's face.

"You're shaking. Come let me buy you something to warm you and calm those nerves." He put his arm around her waist and helped her inside the coffee shop. Sitting her in a booth, he pulled out his wallet. "How do you want your coffee?"

"I don't. I mean, you don't have to buy me coffee. You just saved me from a nasty spill out there." She blew out a shaky breath. "I should be thanking you."

"It's in my contract as a Prince Charming. I'm bound to save beautiful women in distress whenever possible." The man studied the coffee board menu. "I'm guessing you're a large mocha with whipped cream kind of woman. Am I right?"

Cat ran her hands over her face. "I don't know . . ."

"Please, let me buy you a hot drink. I don't feel comfortable letting you back on those icy sidewalks until you stop shaking." He laughed and the crinkles around his eyes deepened. The man was crazy handsome. "Caffeine may not be the best thing for you, but I don't see you as a green-tea type."

"A mocha will be fine." She paused, looking around at the empty shop. "Thank you." She watched as he walked up to the barista who had seen their interaction. When he came back, he set a large cup in front of her and sat across from her, a smaller version in his hands.

She took a long sip from the drink, letting the heat and sugar calm her nerves. She sat the cup down and held out her hand. "I'm Cat Latimer. Thank you for saving me from a nasty spill."

"And thank you for not making me turn in my man card. Dante Cornelio, at your service." He took a sip of his coffee. "This is good. Sometimes these places forget that a majority of people just like good, fresh, strong coffee."

She looked him over as she took another sip. The wool coat he wore looked expensive, as did the casually tied tartan scarf around his neck. He wore his blond hair cut short, his sea-green eyes sparkled, and if Cat had to guess, she would have labeled him either an attorney or a doctor. His hands looked soft and his fingernails short and clean. "I don't believe we've met. Are you with the college?"

Taking a long drink before he answered, he finally set the cup down. "No, I'm just checking in on some business investments I have in the area."

"Dante. That's an interesting name." She tilted her head. "Not a local then."

"Not like you, Catherine." He nodded. "Yes, I know about your wonderful little writers' retreat. That house of yours is a local treasure."

"You've seen my house?" Now alarm bells were ringing in Cat's head. She guessed the move from *Cat* to *Catherine* hadn't been a huge leap.

"I keep an eye on all the new businesses in town. A rising tide lifts all boats." A buzzing sound came from his pocket, and he pulled out his phone. Looking at the display he took a final sip of his coffee and stood. "I'm afraid our time is over. It was so very nice to finally meet you, Catherine. My driver is here. Can I give you a lift somewhere?"

Serial-killer movie scenes filled her mind.

"No, thank you. I have a couple of errands to do before I return home." She held up her cup. "Thank you again for the coffee."

"You are most welcome. We will continue this conversation soon." He strode out the door slipping his leather gloves on as he left.

The barista came to her booth and picked up the empty coffee cup. "That guy reminds me of the heroes in those books. I have a bit of a romance novel habit, but I never thought I'd see a billionaire type in this place." She glanced out the window. "He even got picked up in a limo. You two aren't dating, are you?"

Cat finished off her mocha and stood. "Nope. This is the first time we've ever met."

"Then I have hope." The barista smiled and took the empty cups back to the counter.

As Cat left the coffee shop, she shook off the feeling that the chance encounter was more than chance. Dante Cornelio was a mystery, that was for certain.

Seth's truck sat in the driveway when she got back to the house. Finding him and Shauna in the kitchen at the table, Cat put the kettle on for a cup of tea, then sat to wait. "What are you two up to?"

Shauna and Seth exchanged a look, then Shauna spoke. "You look like crap. What happened? I was about to send Seth over to get you out of the house."

"The house?" Cat grabbed a cookie from

the plate in the middle of the table before she realized Shauna thought she'd been with Mrs. Colfax all this time. "Oh, the Colfax place. Well, Tommy's mother is freaking crazy. I don't think it's just the grief, though. I got the impression she's been like this a while. His stepfather thinks, or thought, Tommy was a loser."

"You should have just left after you dropped off the muffins. I don't know what you were thinking, anyway. Your uncle is the investigator, not you." Seth stood when the kettle started screaming. "Regular tea or that herbal stuff."

"Regular." Cat leaned back in her chair. "I wasn't at the house all this time. I walked through town to think and some jerk almost knocked me down on the sidewalk."

"Oh, no." Shauna leaned closer. "Are you okay? Did you hit your head?"

"I didn't hit anything. Another man caught me on the way down."

Seth set the tea in front of her. "You were pushed by one guy and another one caught you? Who are these jokers?"

"I have no clue on the first guy. He didn't stick around to introduce himself. The other's not a local." Was that jealousy she heard in Seth's voice or just concern? "Dante Cornelio. He said he has business interests in Aspen Hills? Have you ever heard of him?"

"The Cornelio family is big in the New York Mafia."

They all turned their heads to the kitchen

door where Bella Neighbors stood. She rushed to the table.

"Seriously? You met Dante? He's here, in town? He's like the heir apparent for the family." Bella pointed to Cat's tea. "Can I have some of that? I'm about coffee'd out and the hot-water carafe out in the dining room is empty."

"Sure." Shauna stood and went to the stove. She poured a large cup of water and added two tea bags.

"So, why would a Mafia family member be here in Aspen Hills?" Seth studied Bella as the older woman wrapped five cookies in a napkin and put them in her jacket pocket.

Finished stashing her treats, Bella frowned at him. "Don't tell me you don't know about the connection between Covington College and the mob families? This is where they send all their kids for the undergraduate degree. It's considered a safe zone, and they all signed an agreement decades ago to honor the contract."

Cat spit out the sip of tea she'd just taken. Grabbing a napkin, she wiped up the table in front of her as she asked, "Mob kids attend Covington?"

Bella looked around the table at the three other people. "You all had to know this, right? Didn't you grow up here?"

"I'm glad we decided to move up date night this week." Seth rubbed the top of her hand as they sipped wine at the small bistro she hadn't even known existed just a few miles out of town.

"It's a nice place." Cat looked around the Aspen-chic room. Wood paneling covered the top of the walls with exposed rock foundation running the bottom. A fire burned in the river-stone fireplace in the middle of the room, and their table was set so close, her toes felt warm and toasty under the table. "And I'm glad you didn't let me get away with an 'I'm too busy' excuse. The way this retreat is going, I may need a few more impromptu outings just to stay sane."

The waitress put a platter of chicken and avocado nachos between them, setting small plates on the side. When she left, Seth leaned closer. "So what about Bella's pronouncement? I take it you didn't know about Covington's history?"

After meeting Dante that morning, Cat wasn't sure Bella's theory wasn't spot on. "I can't say I've ever heard anything about the college harboring mob kids. It's exclusive, sure, but the way Bella talked about it, the entire administration would have to be part of the cover up."

"I never understood where the college got the money to buy the Hemingway papers. You know the family wanted them to go to Boise State, but Covington came out on top in that discussion." Seth took a loaded chip off the platter. Cat paused as she moved to set one of the little plates in front of him. He grinned at the shocked look on her face. "What? You think I don't watch the news? The acquisition had been a really big deal here in town."

"Having the papers allowed the college to fund another English professor just to curate the collection as well as increased fund raising from local literary buffs." Cat swirled a chip in the guacamole, watching it cut through and divide the small pile on her plate. "Uncle Pete must have heard the rumors. If the mob was here visiting kids on Meet the Parents Day, you'd think he'd be aware of their presence."

"That's a good point." He rubbed a spot off her cheek. "So how are you doing? Do I have to worry about you and the rich guy running off to Jamaica?"

"An island vacation would be nice, but all he offered me was a coffee and a ride home." She leaned back in her chair and ran both hands through her hair. "What is going on with my writing retreats that we can't get through a week without someone dying or a guest being detained for questioning? Christina's too sweet to do anything like that to anyone."

"Rumor around town is that Tommy was found in the hot tub with his wrists cut." Seth kept eating.

"We both know that's not true. Uncle Pete said he was stabbed. Besides, that sounds more like suicide than murder. I wonder if Uncle Pete looked at the possibility that Tommy did himself in for cause of death?" She played with her fork, spinning it on the table.

"The coroner actually determines cause of death, not your uncle." He waited for the waitress to deliver their entrées before answering her.

"What? I watch cop shows. Besides, it's kind of hard to slash your wrists, then stab yourself in the gut, and then get back into the hot tub before passing out."

"The whole thing does seem like a bit of overkill. The killer must have been seriously ticked off at the guy." She stared at her plate, wanting to be hungry, but feeling sick to her stomach. No one should have to die like that. And Christina didn't have it in her to slit someone's wrists, at least not from what Cat knew of the girl. "Of course, being angry doesn't eliminate our Christina from the suspect pool. That's not good at all."

He put his hand on hers. "Look, forget I even brought the subject of Tommy's death up. Tonight's supposed to relax you, not send you screaming into the night and not trusting anyone."

"I trust a few people." She gazed into his eyes and for a moment, time seemed to stand still.

He tipped his wine glass to her. "A toast—to trust and a time for us."

As she clinked her glass to his, Cat just hoped Seth and she were actually going to have a time. She'd always laughed about the star-crossed love she'd had with her high school sweetheart, but now, being back, she seemed to have too much on her plate to totally surrender to this reenergized love. Besides, she still had questions about Michael's death and, now, about the handsome man in town who knew way too much about her and her business.

She pushed her doubts away and smiled at Seth. "To us."

Seth dropped her off, leaving her with a way-too-sexy kiss on the doorstep before climbing back into his truck. Cat wandered into Michael's study as soon as she heard the truck leave. Her hands shook as she picked up his journal. Why was she doing this to herself? Michael hadn't even been her husband at the time of his death. Just an ex. But she knew, even as mad as she was at him because of what he'd done, Michael would never just be the ex. He'd been the first man who'd listened to her as she talked about her dreams of someday being an author. He'd supported those dreams and bought her books for her library. He'd believed in her. He just hadn't believed in the marriage. Or so it had seemed when he threw it all away.

Chapter 6

Cat wandered into the kitchen. Sleep had come in bits and pieces last night, so when she'd woken the last time, she'd given up and kicked the covers off her legs. Four a.m., but at least she'd get some writing done today before she had to play retreat hostess. Now, showered and dressed, she needed coffee and something sweet before she locked herself into her office.

"I wondered if you'd stayed over at Seth's last night. I didn't hear you come in." Shauna held out a steaming cup of coffee. "Take this. I heard you in the hallway before you even opened the door. One good skill I learned as a bartender, always listen for trouble."

"No trouble, we're just still taking it slow." Of course, Seth's kiss last night was anything but safe. A smile creeped onto her lips, and Shauna held up her hands.

"No worries, I was just wondering if you were going to be honest with me today. I see you're back to covering up what you don't want me to see." She returned to the stove. "I'm making banana bread today, and we'll do banana bread waffles with Bananas Foster syrup for breakfast tomorrow. I found the recipe online, and it's been killing me not to try it out."

"I'm not covering up anything . . ."

The door to the kitchen swung open and Jeffrey Blank walked in. He looked like he had slept in yesterday's clothes, his blond hair sticking up at odd angles. He took in the scene in the kitchen and then asked, "Where's Christina? She isn't at the police station still, is she?"

Shauna poured him a cup of coffee and walked it to where he stood at the kitchen's edge. "Heavens, no. Here, take this. I haven't set up the dining room for early birds yet. Can I get you a snack to tide you over until breakfast?"

He took the cup, but held it in his hands, not drinking. "Thank you. So where is she?"

"Christina? I guess in her room." Shauna turned toward Cat and raised her eyebrows in a can-you-believe-this-guy motion. "She came in last night when I was closing down the kitchen, and I made her some soup since she didn't want to go into town for dinner."

Cat watched Jeffrey's shoulders drop as he took in Shauna's words. He sipped his coffee, and she thought she could see the wheels turning in his head as he formulated the next question. Ten to one he was going to ask if Christina had been charged with the murder. He seemed excessively interested in someone he'd just met.

Instead, Jeffrey held up the cup and smiled. "Thanks for this. I've been working on a stanza all night, and it's just not working." He turned around and disappeared back out of the kitchen.

Shauna waited a long minute, then peeked out the kitchen door. She breathed out a sigh as she came over to the table and sat next to Cat. "He's intense."

"Weirdly so, don't you think?" Cat sipped her coffee, thinking about the times she'd spoken with Jeffrey. Most of the conversations had been about Christina. Not his work, not why he was at the retreat, but about a girl he'd just met. "I think the poet has a crush on Christina."

Shauna shook her head. "I don't know. It feels more serious than just a crush. He's always watching her, but he never goes up and talks to her. I thought I was imagining the intensity, but after that scene? I think we should watch our resident poet very carefully this week."

"Why do the crazies always arrive on my doorstep?" Cat stood and refilled her coffee cup. "So tell me about Christina. Did Uncle Pete come in with her?"

"No. He had a deputy drop her off here. According to her, she's just a person of interest. They think she might have seen something and not realized it." Shauna paused, waiting for Cat to sit. "There *is* scuttlebutt around town about a mystery man who just appeared a few days ago. My source at the grocery store says the guy has to be a contract killer. He only bought cigarettes and a bottle of Jack this morning when he went through her line."

"That's very noir of him. He sounds like someone out of a movie script," Cat said.

"So do you think that's the business your white knight had in town? Could he be the same person?"

Cat thought about Dante's polished nails and high-end clothes. He'd appeared more like an executive than a stone-cold killer. Maybe the other guy was his driver? She shook her head. Dante's driver would have to be ready at his boss's whim, 24-7. A drinker couldn't fulfill that job responsibility. "I don't think so. Did your source give you a description?"

"All she said was the man had mean eyes." Shauna shook her head. "I know exactly what she means. *Mean drunks* is what we called them when I was bartending. Even if they were sweet as pie when they first walked in, you could tell that they were going to be a problem later."

"You should have been a counselor, not a bartender. You're good at reading people."

"So are you. I know you want Christina to get out from under this cloud of suspicion. She's a nice kid." Shauna held up the newspaper. "Of course, that doesn't stop the local reporters from waxing poetic about the love triangle."

Cat took the paper. "Poor Brit. She doesn't deserve this kind of crap. What did she ever see in the loser to begin with?"

"I hear he could be quite the charmer." Shauna went back to mixing in eggs into the bowl on the counter. "Christina told me all about how they met. Of course, he never mentioned the upcoming nuptials. For a girl who writes happy-ever-after endings, her week has turned into a horror novel."

"I'll check in with her a little later and see how she's doing. Since we already did my 'How to be an author' talk yesterday when she was absent, I can use that to get some alone time with her." Cat took a travel mug out of the cupboard and filled it. "And I want to talk to Uncle Pete. He needs to know about our overly attentive poet."

"Are we going to talk about your date last night with Seth?" Shauna didn't look at her as she poured the banana-bread batter into loaf pans. "Or the coffee date with your mystery man?"

"Coffee wasn't a date. And he's not a mystery. We know who he is, just not why he's here." Cat leaned against the counter watching Shauna put the pans into the oven. "Unless we believe Bella's version."

Shauna took the empty bowl to the sink and ran water into it. "I'm not from here, like you and Seth. Do you think there's any truth to the story?"

One more thing to ask Uncle Pete about. Instead of answering Shauna, she held up her coffee. "I'm heading up to the office to write. Let me know when Christina's done with breakfast. I'll make time to talk to her before she gets involved in her own work."

As she made her way up to the third floor, the grandfather clock on the first floor chimed five times. At least she was making her insomnia work for her by spending the time upstairs. One more helpful hint to share with her retreat guests: When your life turns upside down and crazy, take refuge in the story.

She needed to start writing these gems down.

Maybe she could put out a ten helpful hints for writing under any circumstances, including murder, mayhem, and madness.

Entering her office, the comfort of her fictional world surrounded her and before she knew it, she was lost in Kori's high school drama.

A timid knock sounded on her door a few hours later.

"Come in," Cat called, reading back the last line she wrote and inking a sentence in the notebook she kept open on her desk while writing.

"Sorry to bother you, but Shauna said you wanted to talk to me?" Christina inched her way into the room, glancing around, her eyes widening as she took in the office. "This is wonderful. I write at my kitchen table. All I have is a small studio back home in Seattle. It's all I can afford with the prices being so high. I'd move, but it's in a great location and I have a really good day job."

"You're not bothering me." Cat turned off her screen and waved her toward the couch by the bay windows. "You missed my lecture yesterday on being a full-time author, and I wanted to make sure you got the full retreat experience. Believe me, this wasn't where I thought I'd wind up writing either." She sat on the other edge of the couch. Of course, that wasn't quite true, as she'd started writing Kori's world in this very office when she and Michael had been married. The beginning of the marriage had been hearts and roses. She and Michael were a team, both teaching, both loving to talk about their day, both loving each other. If she had to write a perfect marriage, she would have modeled it after the first two years of her own. To be back here now, in the house she'd loved, well, that was an unexpected blessing even with the craziness the retreats had become. When she and Michael divorced, she never thought she'd step foot in this office again. The pain of giving up the home she'd loved had made the divorce even more devastating. She'd been so angry at him back then—an anger she didn't know if she still felt. She focused back on Christina. "So what's your day job?"

"I'm a paralegal at a law firm. I love working with some of the partners. They get the most interesting cases, but I'm not assigned to any criminal lawyers. I don't think I could deal with all that death on a daily basis." Christina's gaze dropped and a shutter ran through her body.

"And yet, that's what you get on your writing retreat." Cat shook her head. "That's so not fair."

Christina took a deep breath. "It was my fault."

"What?" Cat leaned forward. "Are you saying you had something to do with Tommy's death?"

The girl's eyes widened. "Oh my God, no. I mean I didn't kill him or whatever. I just meant that maybe, with me coming into his life, he was conflicted about his engagement. Maybe I caused him to kill himself. That's what everyone's saying. Tommy killed himself." Tears fell from her eyes, and she grabbed a handful of tissues out of her pocket.

"It wasn't you." Cat watched as Christina quietly sobbed into the quickly wilting tissues. She grabbed her box off her desk and handed it to her.

Christina sniffed and blew her nose. "You don't think so?"

She didn't. Besides, she knew from her discussion with Uncle Pete and Seth that Tommy hadn't killed himself. "I don't. Look, I know this is hard, but you barely knew him. And the last conversation you had was a fight."

Christina laughed, the sound harsh in the small office. "That's what my mother said. She told me to buck up, two dates does not a relationship make." She wiped a stray tear away. "Besides, I wouldn't have seen him again. He told me all he wanted out of me was of a carnal nature. Of course, he used other terms."

Cat tried to keep a smile from breaking through as she watched Christina blush, just thinking about Tommy's intentions. "Well, then, that's settled. What do you need from me to make the rest of the retreat as productive as possible for you?"

"I really want to know how you got started writing. When did you know it was real? How do I get published? Do I have to have an agent?" Christina peppered her with questions, and Cat started her normal story about her beginnings.

The conversation finally ended an hour later when Shauna came upstairs with a tray. "Hate to interrupt, but I know you haven't eaten yet. I brought you some breakfast."

Christina jumped up from her spot on the couch. "I'm so sorry. I kept you way too long."

"You didn't keep me. I enjoyed chatting with you," Cat called after her as the girl disappeared out the office door. She looked at Shauna. "That girl is scared of her own shadow. No wonder Tommy thought she'd be easy prey."

Shauna set the tray on the coffee table. "She needs to grow a backbone. How can she write strong female leads if she doesn't know how one acts?"

"You've been listening in on my lectures." Cat laughed as she took the lid off the plate. A mushroom and cheese omelet with country hash browns steamed, causing her mouth to water. "I take it Seth came over for breakfast?"

"He did." Shauna grabbed the empty coffee cup and leaned in the doorway. "And can I say he's about as cryptic on the state of last night's date as you are."

"He has never been one to kiss and tell." She tilted her head as she studied Shauna's face. "What's got you all smiles now?"

"At least I know now there was a kiss involved." As she left the room, she called back, "I'll grab the tray when I come back. Go on and write some more."

Cat picked up her fork and dug into the waiting omelet. Words could wait; she was starving.

At noon, Cat pushed away from her desk and stopped for the day on the writing front. She knew she had several emails from her publisher to respond to, but right now she wanted to talk to Uncle Pete. A few things were bothering her about Aspen Hills and the current murder that were affecting her writers' retreat. Again. Maybe one day she'd have a session where the biggest problem was a clogged drain or an argument over the rise of genre over literary fiction.

Someday. She could hope.

When she entered the kitchen, it was empty. She made a note on the whiteboard to let Shauna know where she'd gone and put on her coat and snow boots. Time to visit her uncle.

Mrs. Rice, Cat's closest neighbor and local busybody waved her down as she strolled by the house. "Catherine? Hold on a moment."

Cat wondered if she could get away with pretending she hadn't heard the older woman, but by the time she'd decided to try, Mrs. Rice was at the front gate. She held a garden trowel. "It's kind of cold to be out here working."

"Oh, I'm not working. I made the finishing touches on the decorations last week." She waved her hand like she was presenting a theatre production of the first Thanksgiving. She had a large picnic table sitting in the middle of the snow-covered yard. Three Indian and four Pilgrim mannequins sat waiting for the standing couple holding out a turkey larger than Cat had ever seen. "I've got the Christmas set up all ready and just waiting for Black Friday. Some people may shop; I'm preparing for the next holiday."

"So why the trowel?" Cat pointed to her hand.

"Don't tell me you are already working on flower beds."

The older woman frowned then followed Cat's gaze to the gardening tool. "The stray cats like to use my front planter bed as their personal cat box. I have to clean it daily or the place starts to smell like Aggie Malone's place."

Cat tried to place the name but couldn't.

"You know, that lady who raises Persians over by the high school? She must have twenty cats just running around her house. It's a shame. Someone should turn her into the humane society; that kind of life can't be good for the poor things." Mrs. Rice looked at her. "But here I am chatting away while you're clearly on your way somewhere. I just wanted to ask you if it was true about your poor houseguest finding Tommy Neil's body. I heard she screamed uncontrollably for hours and had to be sedated."

"Wow, that's some story. No, she didn't find his body. I don't know who did." Cat slipped on her gloves that she'd found in her coat pockets. "I think your gossip source must be off this time."

"Well, it happens. Especially when you don't get the information firsthand." Mrs. Rice didn't seem the least disturbed that she didn't have the right information. She leaned forward. "So what *did* she see? Was she really sleeping with Brittany O'Malley's fiancé?"

"I'm sure that's just a rumor. The girl just hit town Saturday evening." Cat looked at her watch, hoping the woman would get the point.

"Oh, dear, you know young people attach fast

these days. Couples used to court for months before they even ventured a kiss. You know relationships are much more about the time you spend with someone outside of the bedroom, not in it." Mrs. Rice peered at her. "So how are things between you and Seth Howard?"

"Oh, my, I really need to go. I told my uncle I'd stop by the station." Cat turned to walk away.

"Come by for a spot of tea next week when your guests leave. We don't spend enough time together," Mrs. Rice called after her.

"And that's how I like it," Cat said under her breath. She turned and waived as she continued to walk away. Louder, she called back, "I'll check my schedule."

Katie Bowman staffed the reception desk and greeted Cat with a hearty good afternoon. The station looked empty. "What can I do for you?"

"Is Uncle Pete available? I wanted to chat with him for a bit."

"Sorry, darling, I think he just left to go to the lodge. There was another incident." Katie lowered her voice. "I swear, he was hot when he left the building. I haven't seen him that angry for a while."

"Angry?" That didn't sound like her uncle at all. "What's going on at the lodge? Don't tell me they found another body?"

"Oh, no, nothing like that. He was interviewing one of the kids who works in the restaurant, and I guess he told him something that your uncle didn't like." Katie looked around the empty station. "All I know is I heard him yell at Paul Quinn—he's a detective now; I don't know if you knew he got promoted last year. He was in your class at the high school, wasn't he?"

Cat had to think. Paul Quinn? He'd been a year or two ahead of them, and the kid had been a total dork. If there was a someone who wore an imaginary KICK ME sign, it had been Paul. "He graduated before I did."

"Oh, really? He always talks about you so fondly, I assumed you were in his class." Katie shrugged. "Anyway, they had a few words, then both of them took off and here we are. I can tell your uncle you stopped by or I can call him on the radio if it's an emergency."

"No emergency. Just let him know I stopped by and ask him to come over to the house when he has a minute." Cat pulled a piece of paper out of her pocket. She'd written down the guests' names along with full addresses on the paper before leaving the house. Katie's husband did background checks for the retreat guests. She should have done this sooner. "Can you give that to your husband? I need background checks run on these. I know I should have done this before they showed up this week, but I've been busy."

"No problem. Harry was just talking about you yesterday. He'll be glad to process these. Besides, I bet you're really busy this week with your new guests. I've thought about writing a book; maybe I should come to one of your retreats." The phone on her desk rang. "I better get that. I'm handling all the 911 dispatch now too. I'll give your uncle the message and take this home to Harry when I leave for lunch."

Harry Bowman was sort of Aspen Hills' version of a private detective. Mostly, he ran background checks for local businesses considering hiring out of towners for positions. And he worked for the college too. He had a little office set up in the garage of their house. Cat paused at the door to slip on her gloves. In the background, she heard Katie's side of the conversation.

"Aspen Hills police, how can I help you?" After a pause, Katie continued. "Hey Mrs. Rice, what's going on?"

Cat left wondering if Katie was Mrs. Rice's fount of rumors or if she was just one of many people the woman called to get her gossip. But the question that kept rotating in her head was why Uncle Pete had taken off so quickly for the lodge. Had he figured out who had killed Tommy Neil?

She made her way back to the house in the quickly darkening afternoon. All she wanted was one of Shauna's loaded hot chocolates and a long, hot bath. Today had been strange on all counts. If Uncle Pete had solved Tommy's murder, at least one of her worries would be lifted off her shoulders.

Now all she had to do was get through the week without another problem. Three more days—she could make it. Feeling like a long-distance runner, she pushed through her tiredness and, grabbing her second wind, she headed home.

Chapter 7

The kitchen was warm and bright when Cat finally reached home. She felt like she'd walked for hours, even though she knew it had been less than twenty minutes. She sat on the bench and took off her boots, putting back on the slippers Seth teased her about for wearing around the house.

"You look like hell. Do you want a drink?" Shauna sat at the table, the laptop open in front of her.

Cat pulled on an oversized sweater she kept downstairs. "You read my mind. Can I have a loaded hot chocolate?"

"Of course." Shauna went to the stove where a pot gently steamed. "I just made up a batch for the group. They've all gone for pizza together, but I'm sure they'll need something warm when they get back."

Cat sank into a chair and stretched her neck.

"How can it only be Wednesday and I'm already looking forward to the retreat being over?"

"Speaking of, you have an informal get-together in the living room scheduled at seven. You going to be up for it?" Shauna set the cup in front of her. "Do you want a sandwich to go with that? I wasn't going to cook dinner since Seth's gone for the day and you weren't here to ask."

"A sandwich will be fine. Don't go to any trouble." Cat sipped her drink, letting the warmth fill her. "Where did Seth go?"

"He said he had some things to do back at his house." Shauna sliced bread and put together two chicken salad sandwiches while Cat watched. "You two didn't have a fight, did you?"

"No, we didn't have a fight. Besides, if we had, you and nosy Mrs. Rice would already know about it." She took the plate from Shauna. "She called the station when I was there. I guess she was trying to get information out of Katie too."

"I wouldn't doubt it. Our neighbor loves her gossip. She has lived here for years. Which means, she knows everyone and everything." Shauna paused. "I have to be honest, I sent Bella Neighbors over to see if she knew anything about the college's mob connection. I guess they're meeting tomorrow afternoon. I hope you don't mind."

"Why would I mind? Bella's here to research, and sometimes oral history is all you have on a subject. I'm sure there's several people Mrs. Rice will tell her to interview." Cat brushed a napkin over her lips. "Maybe that's a seminar possibility if the college thing falls through. We can find a local historian to come talk about the founding of Aspen Hills."

"That's a great idea, even if the college seminar is still in our price range. By Thursday, people need a break from their own work. It would be amazing for them to hear about the town's history. Hell, I'd even go to that lecture." Shauna picked her sandwich up, then set it down. "Hey, if I haven't told you this lately, thanks for bringing me along for the ride here. I adore living in Aspen Hills. Everyone is so friendly."

Of course everyone was nice to her. She was a life-size walking fantasy fairy. "You know I couldn't do this without you." Cat studied her friend. "So what's going on with you and Kevin lately? I haven't seen him around. You haven't been disappearing to visit him. He doesn't come by here much, does he?" Kevin was the owner of Little Ski Hill and the biggest ranch in the area. They'd been dating for the last couple of months. For Shauna, the relationship had been exclusive. I didn't know Kevin well enough to gage his commitment.

"He's always working. Sometimes I feel more like a bootie call than a girlfriend. Anyway, I told him I was too busy to see him this week. I've got a life too, even if it is here at the house." She flipped back her hair. "Being too available doesn't help him realize what he's missing when I'm not there."

Finished with her sandwich, Cat stood and stretched. "I'm heading upstairs for a shower and change of clothes. I'll be in the living room at 6:45 ready to play hostess."

"I baked coconut macaroons for snacks." Shauna returned her attention to the laptop.

Even though she arrived almost on time, the five retreat guests were in the living room with cups of hot chocolate in their hands. The tray of macaroons was already almost empty. Nelson Wider made a beeline toward Cat as soon as he saw her enter the room.

"I'm so glad I came. I've gotten so much done these few days, it's not funny." Nelson took a bite of a purple cookie and kept talking. "You should see my word count. If you want someone to quote on how effective this retreat is, you just come my way. I'm absolutely giddy."

Cat handed him a napkin for the cookie crumbs left on his chin and patted his arm. "I'm so glad. In fact, that's a great discussion starter for tonight's get together." She stepped into the middle of the room. "Let's get started. Can everyone pull up a chair in a circle? We'll gather around the coffee table so we can use the sofa too."

The group followed her instructions and, within a few minutes, everyone was seated. "Nelson was telling me how much work he's accomplished during the week. How is the pace for the rest of you?" She looked at Jennifer Simon, the grad student, sitting next to her. "Do you want to start?"

Jennifer nodded. "I thought it would be slow.

I mean, I work, go to school, write, and do homework. How could I just write for a week? Instead, I'm finding it liberating not to have to rush to go do something else. I'm focusing on the work, and it's heaven."

"I know, right?" Bella Neighbors chimed in. "I've been working on this book for months, and today I edited two chapters. Not just one, two. Even with all the distractions happening this week."

Everyone looked at Christina.

"It must be something in the water. I'm ahead of where I thought I'd be." She either ignored Bella's veiled reference about Tommy's death or didn't hear it. "Especially since I spent most of the last few days not writing. Today has more than made up for the original delay this week."

As Cat listened to the writers chat about their process and how a break from the everyday world had jump-started their muse, she wondered if she should step away from the office to write at least a few days a month. Maybe she needed her own writer's retreat.

Returning her attention to the discussion, she realized one thing: Jeffrey Blank hadn't said anything. Worse, he was staring at Christina like she was a painting on display in a museum. The only good thing was the girl was oblivious to his attention.

"And that's why I love romance. I'm all about the happy-ever-after ending." Christina leaned forward, engaging her listeners.

"It's a fallacy. There is no happy forever. All there is—is now." Jeffrey spoke, but his words weren't warm and supportive. Instead, he was showing an edge Cat didn't like at all.

"Is that one of your poems?" As Cat asked the question, the group was already watching Jeffrey. Writers were a curious lot, especially about other writer's processes.

He frowned and shook his head. He didn't seem comfortable with the attention, as his face had turned a scarlet red. "No, just my philosophy on life."

"I'm sure that's not true. People fall in love and have long, fulfilling lives together, all the time. Statistically, some of those couples have to be happy." Cat decided to change the subject since not all of the group had a romantic outlook, at least in their writings. "New question: What did you think about the library?"

"So crazy how much space it has, even when it's full of people. It's as if it just keeps growing and expanding. Maybe it's a magic library?" Nelson looked around the room, listening to the laughter. When it had died out, he shrugged. "No one else felt it?"

"Dude, I thought you wrote nonfiction?" Jennifer Simon curled her legs up underneath her and sipped her drink. "I've been almost living in that library for the last four years. Except for a pretty hot make-out session with an economics major junior year, nothing magical has ever happened to me there."

Laughter filled the room.

"Just because I write about historical events doesn't mean I don't enjoy reading a bit of fantasy. Tolkien, Robert Jordan, George RR Martin.

Even Stephen King has a few books that deal
with alternative universes." Nelson shrugged.
"The library just feels like a place that a portal
could exist. What can I tell you?"

"I've never considered the possibility." Cat
looked at Jeffrey who seemed to be doodling in
his journal. "What about you, Jeff? Do you find
the library time useful? You're the first poet
we've had join the retreat. I'd like to make sure
we're meeting your needs as well.

"Jeffrey." His gaze didn't move from his notebook but the pen had stilled.

"Excuse me, Jeffrey." Cat waited, but when he
didn't respond, she prodded a little more. "So
do you find your library time useful?"

Now he looked up from his doodles and snuck
a glance at Christina. "A poet finds inspiration in
the most ordinary things. So scheduled library
time"—he paused, moving his gaze back to Cat
before he continued—"or group activities like
this don't make a difference in the creative
process for a true artist."

The others were quiet for a minute. Then
Bella chimed in. "I don't think that's true, at
least not for my writing process." She went on to
share the interviews she had set up for the rest
of the week. "And if I hadn't done my homework, digging out facts and curiosities from all
the information stored at the library, these interviews could just be a waste of time."

Christina stood and stretched. "I know it's
early, but this has been a crazy week, especially
with Tommy's . . ." She paused, a pained look
crossing her face. Cat could actually see the mask

Christina slipped on to hide the pain before she started talking again. "Anyway, it's been a crazy week. I'm planning on writing straight through tomorrow. We don't have any activities planned, do we?"

Cat shook her head. "Breakfast will be available from six to nine as usual, and you're welcome at the library any time, but there's no lectures or seminars planned." She looked around the room. "We'll have a group dinner Saturday at a local restaurant to close out the week, but until then, you're on your own. I'm available any time for one-on-one discussions about process or just questions."

"Well, I'll see you around then." Christina said her goodnights to the group and disappeared out of the room.

"I've got work to do," Jeffrey stated flatly, following Christina to the lobby.

Cat glanced around the rest of the group. "We're scheduled for another hour, but obviously it's flexible if you want to leave."

"I'd like to talk about how the industry is changing. I'm getting ready to start looking for agents this summer and wanted to get your advice on the whole traditional versus self-published thing going on now." Jennifer looked at the other two left. "And your advice as well. Bella, you're published right?"

With the conversation back on retreat topics, Cat felt more grounded. The group didn't disband for a couple more hours as they talked about the state of publishing. Shauna helped her clean up after the meeting. "How did it go?

I heard people on the stairs a few hours ago, but when I peeked in, you all were talking up a storm."

"Yeah, Christina and Jeffrey bailed early." Cat took a bite out of the last cookie. "She's still hurting about Tommy."

"Jeffrey's starting to be a bit creepy. Creepy or love sick, I can't really decide." Shauna put the last glass on the tray and wiped down the coffee table. "Seems like there's always one in the group who just doesn't fit in."

Cat followed her into the kitchen. "Maybe it's because he's a poet. Maybe I should limit our groups to fiction writers."

"But then you wouldn't get people like Nelson. That man is a hoot. We were talking about his collection of first editions yesterday. I didn't know all of the names he was batting about, but it seems like he's got quite a library." Shauna rinsed the dishes in the sink as she talked. "I think it's just luck of the draw. Some people fit in, some people don't. I bet Jeffrey doesn't fit in at home either."

"I didn't realize Nelson was a collector." Cat's mind went to the library theft. She'd have to ask Uncle Pete when it actually happened. She really didn't think Nelson could have stolen the book, but hopefully the theft had occurred before Saturday when the retreat guests had started arriving in Colorado.

Thursday morning, Cat dressed and wandered to the kitchen where Uncle Pete sat eating a plate

of sunny-side up eggs, bacon, and Bananas
Foster waffles. She kissed him on the head as she
went to the counter to grab coffee. "I didn't
expect to see you today. From what I've heard,
you're swamped."

"Katie told me you stopped by the station yesterday, so I thought I'd get Shauna to feed me
this morning—and visit with you, of course." He
held up a fork full of the waffle. "I've never had
anything like this before."

"I hope that means you like it." Shauna set a
plate of the waffles and bacon in front of Cat.
"You might as well eat now too. I know you're
dying to lock yourself up in your office as soon
as your uncle leaves."

Uncle Pete grinned at Cat. "She's got your
number already." He ate the last bite of the waffles, sighed, and pushed away the plate. He said
to Shauna, "You keep cooking like that and I'll
have to marry you."

"I'm not sure you're her type. Besides, I can't
see calling her Aunt Shauna." Cat sipped her
coffee.

"You might just have to get used to it." Uncle
Pete chuckled. "What about it, Shauna? You interested in a pudgy, old police chief with a bad
back?"

Shauna smiled at him as she refilled his coffee
and took his empty waffle plate. "Sorry, I'm already dating someone."

"Someone with the biggest ranch in these
parts and deep pockets from what I hear." Uncle
Pete shrugged and cut up his eggs. "Too little,
too late, I guess."

"If you two are done with your impromptu edition of *The Bachelor*, can I ask you some questions?" Cat picked up a piece of bacon and waved it at her uncle.

"As long as it's not about an open investigation, sure." His blue eyes twinkled.

Cat pursed her lips. Okay, that took out the Tommy Neil questions. "So, one of our guests is doing research on Covington College. She says the mob sends their kids here for their undergrad because it's considered a safe zone. Is this true?"

"Of course it's true." Uncle Pete frowned at her. "I'm sure your mom told you to avoid accepting dates from the college boys, right?"

"I just thought it was *because* they were college guys. Are you telling me that you're okay with having mob kids here?" She couldn't believe what she was hearing.

"The kids haven't done anything wrong. As for the parents, there's a meeting between them, me, and the president of the college about ground rules before they are even accepted at the school." He grinned. "You wouldn't believe the people I've sat across a table from, talking about their children. I've only had to ask the school to kick one kid out, but he was shoplifting from the local stores. And he wasn't very good at it. We got him on security tape at five different shops. If you ask me, he wanted to be sent home."

"But I taught at the school. I never was told anything about this." She thought about her classes. No one had seemed out of place or even the tiny bit threatening.

"The faculty isn't told unless they move into a high-level administration position. Hell, even the feds know about the arrangement, and they haven't had a problem with it. I get a few more alerts from them when someone is wanted for questioning, but mostly they leave it to me to handle things."

Shauna had joined them at the table sometime during the discussion, and now she set her cup down. "What crime families are represented here? Any that have been on television or have names like Vinny the Knife? Or Manny the Moocher?"

"I am not at liberty to say." Uncle Pete finished his breakfast and wiped his mouth. "Thank you again for breakfast. If you ever do want to take me up on that marriage proposal, it still stands."

"Wait, I have a couple more questions." Cat pushed the mob craziness out of her head. "Do you know Dante Cornelio?"

He narrowed his eyes. "Yes, unfortunately, I do. Why are you asking?"

"He saved me from a nasty fall yesterday. When we were having coffee . . ."

Uncle Pete interrupted her. "Stay away from that guy; he's bad news. That's all I can tell you without breaking some confidences I don't want to break. So no more coffee dates."

"It wasn't a date." Cat blew out a frustrated breath. She wasn't getting anywhere with her uncle. "Anyway, one more question. And yes, it's on an open investigation: Did Tommy Neil kill himself?"

"So you've heard the rumors around town."

He finished the last of his coffee. "All I'll say on the subject is I don't see how that would have been possible. I'm convinced that your retreat guest didn't kill him herself, but that doesn't mean that someone didn't take care of her problem for her."

"That's impossible too. Or at least improbable. Christina just got here on Saturday. Who would know her well enough to commit murder to defend her honor?"

He stood and put on his coat. "I don't know. From what she told me about her past, she might have someone on standby for that."

"I don't understand." Cat started to stand, but her uncle waved her down.

"I've said more than I planned. Look, let me do the investigating; you two just keep your guests entertained and safe." He put his hat on and smiled at Shauna. "Thanks for the meal."

After he left Shauna leaned back in her chair. "Okay, now I'm a little freaked out about how normal this little town looks. So your mom knew about the college?"

"Apparently." Cat wondered if she should give her mother a call. Her parents had moved to Florida after Cat and Michael divorced. They were tired of the snow, but now all her mom did was complain about the heat. "Although I'm more interested in who Uncle Pete thinks might be Christina's white knight."

"The obvious person would be Jeffrey Blank but, like Christina, he just got here." Shauna held up her coffee cup. "Here's to our second retreat. Let's hope number three brings us less-complicated guests and no dead bodies to worry about."

"I have a feeling our problems are just the tip of the iceberg here in Aspen Hills." She shivered and pulled her cardigan closer. Had Michael found something at the college? Or someone? She still didn't know who he'd been working for in those last months before the divorce. Was that why he'd been killed? She considered the thought as she took her dishes to the sink. Where would she start researching the best kept secret everyone already knew? Filling up her cup, she put on a smile for Shauna's benefit. She'd brought her friend here; she needed to protect her if there was a problem. "It's time to leave reality and get back into a fictional world where I can control everything."

"I thought you said your characters controlled that world." Shauna laughed. "I'll come get you for lunch. I'll make lasagna and garlic bread. Seth should be here to eat with us."

"Remind him about getting the Denver guy in here for the quote for the attic heating and cooling unit. I'd like to get that finalized before the end of the year." Cat walked out of the kitchen and up the stairs to her office. She would make the retreat business profitable, no matter what surprises Aspen Hills threw at her.

Although this last retreat had been a doozy.

Chapter 8

Cat had her fictional high-school students
taking career tests. Kori had two that day: accounting and potions. As she wrote about Kori's
inability to follow a complex potion after blowing away the accounting test, Cat felt like her
heroine. The dull stuff she could do. The stuff
of magic, now that was harder.

A knock sounded at her door, and Seth
stepped into her office. "I know, I'm breaking the
no-contact-in-your-office rule, but I've missed
you." He pulled Cat to her feet and planted a
long kiss on her. When they broke apart, she
stretched her arms over her head, reaching up
and down to ease the kinks.

"I needed a break. What have you been doing?"
She walked over to the couch and patted the
cushion next to her.

He plopped down and wound his fingers
around hers. "Missing you, mostly. The college
called me early yesterday and asked if I could
step in and clean up some damage. I guess the

frat party got a little wild. Your uncle arrived to talk to the boys when I was estimating out the job."

"He was here for breakfast." She thought about the college's secret that apparently wasn't that big of secret around town. "He confirmed the mob sends their progeny here to attend college."

"Although from what I heard today from the fraternity mom, the original mob families are pretty much dying out now, and the up-and-comers are taking over the Ivy League campuses. I think Covington's exclusive market is drying up."

She took her hand out of his. "How did you know this and I didn't?"

He leaned back and stretched his arms across the back of the couch. "I guess it's just not talked about. I mean, my mom told me when I started hanging out in town. She warned me not to get in fights with the guys or get too close to the chicks. Didn't your mother tell you?"

"Apparently she thought a less specific warning was all I needed. Maybe because I was dating you at the time." Cat looked out the window in the direction of the college. "I feel like I've just found out I was living in Hogwarts all this time, and I thought it was just an unusual part of London."

"Seriously, you didn't know about any of this? Wow. I thought you were just being cryptic with Bella." He started laughing. "You are so naïve."

She pushed her hands against his chest. "Stop laughing. Anyway, is there anything else I should know? Like we have aliens on the city council?"

He grabbed both of her hands and brought them up to his lips. "Don't feel bad. I'm sure there might be one other person who didn't know."

"Who."

"Paul Quinn. His mom didn't want him to know anything about the college. So she just kept him home after school. The kid never even got to play with the neighbor kids. She thought everyone was a mobster. I hear she went to the state hospital a few years after he graduated. Kind of makes me feel bad for the guy." He released her hands and stood. "Enough of this depressing talk. Shauna told me to come get you for lunch. It smells like an Italian restaurant down there."

She let him pull her to her feet, and as they walked downstairs together, she thought about Paul. All the teasing he'd gotten over the years for his too-short pants and Coke-bottle glasses combined with his mother's smothering, he never had a chance at normal.

After lunch, Christina pulled Cat aside. "Can I talk to you?"

Cat excused herself from the table and walked Christina to the living room. It was empty, as the other retreat participants were either at the library or upstairs in the partially remodeled attic. It worked fine as a writing nook on warmer days like this, but once the sun started to fall, the room turned chilly. "No one's here. Will this work?"

Christina sank into the couch. "I shouldn't have come."

"What do you mean? Are you not getting your writing done?" Cat sat in the chair next to her, watching the girl's face closely.

"No, I've gotten more written this week already than I did in a month at home. It's a great retreat." She smiled warmly up at Cat.

"I don't understand. What's the problem then?" Cat matched her body frame to Christina's posture. She'd read somewhere that the body language showed that you were interested in what another person had to say and helped open up communication. She'd taken the body language course during her college years to try to limit the effect her natural shyness would have on her teaching skills. Michael had laughed at her when she bought a book on the subject during one of their bookstore trips. But it had helped.

"I've been having some problems at home. Someone's been following me. Leaving me gifts. My car was broken into."

"Oh my God. What did the police say? You did report it to the police, right?" Cat leaned forward, wanting to reach out and comfort her.

"Not at first, but yeah, eventually. The problem is nothing really bad has happened. The guy left roses in the car. At least I think it's a guy. Anyway, he writes me love notes. He even brought me a basket of cold medicine and left it on my porch when I had the flu last winter." She shivered. "I never did find out how he knew I was sick. I called in to work, but that's all. No one else knew."

"That's serious stalking. Are the police concerned? Have you ever seen him?" Cat wondered if this was what her uncle had alluded to during their conversation.

"Not really. The dispatcher laughs when I call them, but they always send someone out and they take a report. I've never seen him, but it could be anyone. He could be my neighbor and I wouldn't know." She stared at Cat. "Your uncle thinks I might have brought him to Aspen Hills. That the stalker guy killed Tommy because I liked him."

She burst into tears, burying her face in her hands.

Cat reached out and hesitantly patted the girl on the back. "I'm sure that's not what happened. You've told my uncle about the stalker, that's the first step. Now, we'll just be more careful around the house. And maybe by the time you get back home, he'll have forgotten all about you."

Sniffing, she lifted her head and smiled at Cat. "Seriously? You really think so?"

Cat didn't and thought she'd have a talk with Uncle Pete about calling the police in Christina's hometown to make sure they understood the situation, but she couldn't tell the girl that. Her nerves seemed already wound so tight they might break just by Cat expressing her opinion. "Of course. But really, you're here to write. How's your book doing?"

With the subject changed, Christina seemed to

come out of her shell and blossom as she talked about the book. Her characters felt so real. Cat was impressed. The girl might just have some writing chops. The chimes on the clock ran three and Christina stood. "I'm letting the day slip away from me. Sorry to be such a bother."

Cat stood with her and walked back into the lobby area. "You are not a bother." She watched as Christina sprinted up the stairs to the second floor.

"Apparently, the rumor is we have a celebrity in town." Shauna stood in the kitchen doorway.

"Dante? The guy with the limo?" Cat followed Shauna into the kitchen. She needed something to drink and to think about Christina's problem.

"I don't think so. This guy is built and has dark hair. Didn't you say Dante had blond hair? Anyway, he's been seen at the grocery store as well as Bernie's." Shauna opened her laptop. "I've been searching the entertainment channels, but no one has leaked that they're spending some time in Colorado. He's probably here skiing, don't you think?"

"So why would he be in town?" Cat grabbed a soda out of the fridge. "You know, sometimes people just stop in Aspen Hills on their way somewhere else. I don't know why you get so worked up about possible celebrity sightings. It's not like we're close to Vail or even Breckenridge. Little Ski Hill mostly caters to the younger, broker, Denver crowd."

"I don't know. I guess a girl could dream." Shauna smiled a bit and shrugged. "It's like finding a nugget of gold in the stream. It's not going to happen, but it could."

"Did you ever even see anyone famous in California? Those people live a different life than we do. I doubt they even do their own shopping." She leaned in to look at the computer screen. "How are bookings for next quarter? Are we full for the next session?"

She sat down next to Shauna and they reviewed the next few months. They had made a decision to book early in December. Next year, December would be their vacation month. Shauna already had airline tickets to fly home for Christmas, and Cat's folks were coming in from Florida. January's retreat slots had filled up quickly, even with adding on the room in the new wing Seth had finished renovating. By spring, they could host up to ten people, but Cat wasn't sure how large she wanted her groups. Ten seemed high.

She left the kitchen and wandered upstairs to her office. She probably wouldn't write, but she needed to check her email and social media accounts. After the first book was released, Cat had realized that she could spend hours on promotion via the Internet. Now, she focused on release week with a few hours during the weeks afterward. Managing the balance was tricky, because checking her social media accounts felt like work. Even though the activities didn't increase her page count, which was the most important task during a day.

Celebrities, stalkers, mob bosses. Aspen Hills had its share of strangers lately. Typically, except for the parents of the college kids coming to visit, the number of visitors was pretty low. Which is why strangers stuck out and rumors circulated. She wondered if her uncle had considered the possibility that the guy Shauna's friend had seen in the grocery store could be Christina's stalker. When she'd told Christina the guy probably would just give up, she'd been lying. But telling the girl the truth wasn't going to make her feel better. Most of the time, women had to disappear off the grid and leave town before the guy gave up. And sometimes, even that didn't help. She was glad she'd taken the time to do the background checks now. She needed to know for certain that Jeffrey hadn't followed Christina from Seattle.

She dialed her uncle's cell number and when she got his voice mail, she left a brief message. "Hey, can we talk about Christina? I'm concerned about what she shared with me."

Cat hung up and turned on her computer. Time to worry about what was happening with her book sales and figure out if she should do some marketing, or not, to raise sales. At least with writing, when you closed the file, you either had more pages or had edited the document. Marketing was a whole other fish to fry. And Cat didn't know if she was doing enough or too much.

It was six before she emerged from the office. Hearing voices in the foyer, she hurried downstairs. Maybe she should warn the group to be careful as they were exploring the town. Who knew what might happen out there? When she reached the main level, the retreat group had their coats on and were preparing to leave. "Where are you guys off to?"

"Dinner. We decided to get some pizza and a few beers. Do you want to come?" Bella seemed to be the leader of the outing.

Cat glanced at the group of five. They were all bundled in heavy coats and scarfs. Cat's phone rang and checking the caller ID she saw it was her uncle. She'd get more information before she decided to scare the guests. "Sorry, I have to take this call. Have fun."

"You don't know what you're missing. Nelson's going to tell us all about the haunted house he lived in for over a year." Bella leaned close. "I think the guy is a little crazy myself, but he's entertaining."

Cat answered the call as she walked into the kitchen. Shauna and Seth were talking at the table. "Hey, Uncle Pete, what's going on?"

She listened to him grumble about his day, but he didn't tell her why he'd gone up to the ski resort. She covered the microphone and asked Shauna, "Did you make enough dinner for one more?"

"Of course. Tell him I've got a chicken roasting along with mashed potatoes and gravy. That should get him over." She looked at Seth. "It convinced this one to stay."

Seth's face turned a bright shade of red. "I am entitled to a meal."

Cat broke into her uncle's litany of tasks he

still had to do before stopping for the day. "Leave that all for tomorrow. Shauna's got dinner ready. How fast can you get here?"

She laughed and ended the call.

"He's coming?" Shauna paused at the counter before pulling out plates.

Cat slipped into the seat next to Seth. "Four for dinner. I really want to talk to him about some of the weirdness around town lately."

"Like your mob boyfriend?" Seth put his arm around her shoulders. "Rumors get around fast in Aspen Hills."

"He's not my boyfriend." She kissed him. "I think I'm going to let you claim that title."

By the time Uncle Pete arrived and they'd consumed the tender roast chicken along with a green salad and to-die-for mashed potatoes, Cat had almost forgotten what she wanted to ask him. After cleaning the table and serving coffee and a NY style cheesecake, Shauna sat next to her. "Go ahead, ask him about the celebrity."

"You already know about the mob connections in Aspen Hills." He sipped his coffee and looked at her. "Was this entire dinner invitation a rouse to get more information out of me?"

"Mostly, yeah." Cat smiled at him. "But also, this way, I know you have at least one good meal in you for the day."

He took a bite of cheesecake and waved his fork at her. "Go ahead and ask. I'll tell you what I can."

Cat leaned forward. "So the celebrity that everyone is talking about?"

Uncle Pete frowned. "Slow down and tell me what you're talking about."

Shauna took over the story, telling him the rumors she'd heard around town. After she was done, he pushed away the now empty dessert plate.

"And it's not this Dante guy? I hear he's quite handsome." Uncle Pete sipped on his coffee.

"No, the descriptions don't match up, but he does sound like the guy who ran out of the coffee shop and almost knocked me on my butt that day I met Dante." Cat bit her bottom lip as she tried to remember what the guy had looked like. It all happened so fast and then Dante was there, catching her. "Wait, I wonder if he was meeting with Dante? I never got a good look at where he came from that day. But his driver knew just where to pick him up."

"Why didn't you mention this before?" Uncle Pete pulled out his notebook. "What day did you see him with this unknown? And what time?"

Cat shook her head. "Yesterday, after I took the basket of muffins over to Mrs. Colfax. What, about two? By the way, that woman's insane. Are you sure she didn't kill Tommy? I can't say he was with Dante, the whole thing happened so fast."

"You may not be able to, but the coffee shop has video surveillance of the entire dining room. I need to get over there and get yesterday's tapes." He stood and stepped over to the rack where he'd left his coat. "Dinner was top notch. Remember my marriage proposal, Shauna. Any time, you just say the word. My little house is cozy and almost paid off. Besides, I'm good at doing laundry."

"You are too sweet." Shauna put his plate and cup into the sink and started cleaning up the dishes.

"Wait, I wanted to ask you about Christina's stalker. Do you think this guy who ran me down could be him?" Cat hurried over and stood in front of the door, blocking his exit.

"So she told you about that. Anyway, I don't see how it could have been the same guy. According to the police chief from the Seattle neighborhood where she lives, she's never seen him. Just the gifts that he leaves on her doorstep."

"That's creepy enough." Cat shuddered, thinking about the flower she'd found by her door a few weeks ago. She'd been working in her office, alone that day. Then when she'd emerged, a single white carnation lay at her door. No one, except Michael had given her carnations. Maybe it had been a fluke, one of the retreat guests way of thanking her, but it had freaked her out. Had she told her uncle about finding it?

"Well, I'm not convinced this stalker could have followed her here. Unless she's the type to broadcast her schedule on Facebook which I'm going back to the station to check on right now." Uncle Pete kissed the top of Cat's head. "You need to focus on your book instead of my case.

You're doing too much plotting. You're seeing suspects everywhere."

"That's what a writer does." She opened the door for him and he waved at the others before disappearing into the darkness. Seth closed the door after him and reached for his coat. "I was heading home to watch Monday night's football game. I recorded it and I've been staying off all the sports stations to keep from hearing the results. But I can stay around if you need me."

"You mean if I'm freaked out about this stalker thing?" She kissed his lips and then gently pushed him away. "Go watch the game. I'm going to wait up for the writers and see if anyone wants to talk shop for a while. I'd love to find out more about what they're writing."

"And you say football is boring." He grinned and slipped on his coat. "See you tomorrow, Shauna."

"Don't forget to call that guy about the attic heating unit." Shauna didn't even look back from her place near the sink. "We'll need that space for January's group, it may be too cold to do anything but shuttle them to the library and back."

He saluted her back. "Yes, ma'am." Then he tapped Cat on the nose. "Although I'm pretty sure the reminder originally came from you."

She watched as he disappeared down the driveway to where he had his truck parked. The back tires spun as he hit a patch of ice on the road, but then he caught traction and disappeared down the street toward his house.

"He's a goofball." Shauna was looking at Cat

now, and for a minute, Cat wondered if she'd kept her back turned to give them privacy. Not that it existed in the house, especially during retreat week. Last month, retreat guests, Rose and Daisy had demanded a blow-by-blow recounting of every interaction she had with Seth. They'd claimed they were using her reunion romance as an exercise in writing relationships realistically. Cat thought it was more a gut need for gossip with the two.

She returned to the table and stacked the rest of the dessert plates to take to the sink. "Yeah, but he's my goofball."

Chapter 9

Cat sat curled up on the couch, reading. She heard the front door open and then retreat guests piled into the room. "How was dinner?"

"You won't believe what happened." Jennifer sat next to her. "We were all eating pizza and talking."

Nelson stood in front of her and took over the story. "Then I felt something digging·into my leg. I thought someone had left a textbook in the booth."

"And when he pulled it out, it was that book by Hemingway." Bella sat in the chair next to the couch, rubbing her hands together to warm them.

Cat put her book down. "The one that was stolen? That book?"

"Exactly that book. We even saw the signature in the front. Can you believe that?" Christina pulled a wooden chair from the desk to the side. "We actually touched a book that Hemingway not only wrote, his wife signed. Totally cool."

"So what did you do with it?" Cat looked around, hoping the rare edition wasn't stuffed inside someone's backpack or purse. On the other hand, it would be cool to see it in person.

"The owner of the place came by and took it. They called the police, and your uncle was supposed to be there before the place closed. Apparently, he was on another call." Bella looked around the room. "For a small town, your uncle keeps busy. Maybe I don't want to live somewhere like Aspen Hills when I retire."

"Every place had troublemakers." Nelson's gaze followed Bella's around the room. "What are you looking at?"

"Not at, for." Bella stood. "Cat, do you think there's still treats and drinks set up in the dining room? I'd love to grab a cup of tea to warm up before I go upstairs to write. It feels even colder outside after the sun sets. We should have got a taxi."

"The walk did us good." Nelson rubbed his hands together. "But I could use a mug of cocoa."

"The buffet is set 24/7 with a few items, including tea and cocoa." Cat watched as Bella, Nelson, and Jeffrey disappeared out of the living room. She looked at the other two. "Not thirsty?"

"No. I'd rather talk to you a bit about agents. I know you can't tell me exactly how I should go about getting one, but do I even need one?" Jennifer had pulled out a notebook from her backpack and sat with a pen to the page, waiting for Cat's words of wisdom.

"I can't tell you the magic formula, but I can tell you how to get started looking for one. The first question they are going to ask, if you get to talk to a real person, is this: Is your book finished?" Cat looked at both women, who nodded solemnly.

Christina laughed. "I have my required three books under the bed as well as the book I'll be finishing in a few weeks. I'm going to pitch that last one next year, when I attend a local writer's convention. I should have it polished and shining by then."

"The way you attract men, all you have to do is flip your hair back and you should get a few of those male agents to bite." Jennifer put her hand up, blocking her mouth. "On your manuscript, that is."

"Stop teasing me." Christina looked at Cat. "Some guy came up to our table tonight and tried to get my phone number. College kids, they're the worst. Too cocky for their own good."

"I don't think the guy was in college. He seemed way too old." Jennifer tapped her pen on the paper. "He definitely looked like he works out. Man, he had muscles."

"What color hair did he have?" Cat didn't want to hear the answer, but she figured she needed to know.

Both Jennifer and Christina answered at the same time: "Black."

Cat looked at Jennifer. "Come see me tomorrow about the agent question. Right now, I need to tell all of you to be careful."

"Why? Do you think he was dangerous?" Christina swallowed hard.

Cat reached out and patted her leg. "We don't know. I'd rather you be overly cautious than get into a bad spot later on. So don't go off alone and don't talk to strangers." She smiled at both women. "Just like what your mother would say, right?"

Jennifer shrugged. "My mother would probably say go for it, especially if the guy was buying the drinks."

Cat didn't know how to respond to that, so instead she stood. "I better go talk to the others."

As she left the room, she heard Jennifer exclaim to Christina, "Just think, you might have been kidnapped tonight."

The other three were in the foyer, heading for the stairs. She hurried toward them. "Hold off a second. The others told me about the guy who was hitting on Christina tonight."

"The guy was a tool, you could tell." Jeffrey's face turned bright red. "I don't know why she attracts the crazies."

Cat paused and looked at him before continuing. "Anyway, it's not just Christina I'm concerned about. Please be careful when you're out and about in town. Aspen Hills is very safe, but there's just some weird stuff going on right now. Make sure you buddy up when you leave and, like I told the girls, don't talk to strangers."

Bella laughed. "Most of my research is talking to strangers." She held up a hand before Cat could respond. "Don't get your panties in an uproar. I'll clear everyone through you or Shauna and let you know when I leave the house."

Cat nodded. "Sorry to be so limiting. I just don't want anything to happen to any of you."

"Let them bring it. I know how to defend myself." Nelson put his hands up in a defensive gesture. "I took boxing lessons last fall. Punch and jab, he won't know what happened."

"And no fighting." Cat stepped back. "Have a nice evening."

She watched as they made their way up the stairway to their rooms.

"At least they're not freaking out about the situation." Shauna stood in the hallway. "I'm locking up. Is everyone accounted for?"

"Yep." She followed Shauna to the door and explained to her what had happened, both with the book and the guy talking to Christina.

"You think he's the guy who knocked you over." It wasn't a question. Shauna turned off most of the lobby lights and they went to the stairs. "At least your uncle will have one thing off his plate. I bet some college kid snuck the book out on a prank and then left it at the pizza place knowing it would be found."

As she went upstairs to her suite, Cat hoped her friend was right. Now, all Uncle Pete would need to figure out was who killed Tommy Neil.

Sitting in the kitchen with Shauna Thursday morning, Cat vocalized the thought that had been running through her head actually, since she had drug herself out of bed. "Only four more days."

Shauna laughed. "Are you sure you're into

this whole retreat business? You tend to wish the time away as fast as it comes."

Sipping her coffee, Cat shrugged. "I'll get used to it. I didn't realize how much interaction we'd have with the guests. And they all think they know what's best for me after knowing me for less than a week. I get advice on my love life, my clothes, even the retreat. I can't believe how intimate the whole experience is."

"What, did someone tell you to put a ring on Seth's finger again?" The buzzer went off on the oven, and Shauna pulled out a double batch of chocolate chip muffins. One half of the muffin tins was chocolate on chocolate, the other vanilla cake with the big chocolate chips. The cocoa smell filled the kitchen. She sat the pans on the counter to cool. "All I have to do now is make up the fruit bowl and brunch is done. This group eats more than the last one did. My entire stash of cookies I put out last night are gone."

"Late-night writers." Cat glanced at the clock.

"What's going on? That's the fourth time you've checked in the last twenty minutes. Do you have a hot date?" Shauna put three muffins in a small basket and filled a travel cup with coffee.

"With my imaginary friends, yes, I do." Cat smiled and drained her cup. "Somedays I just want to do nothing and rest my brain."

Shauna set the basket and the travel mug on the table. "Maybe you should take today off. You and Seth could go skiing. Maybe spend some après-ski time in the hot tub?"

"Next week. I'm almost done with my first

draft, and I don't want to be too far away in case you need me here. So far, these retreats haven't been the calming, quiet getaways I'd thought they'd be." Cat put her cup in the sink and gathered the treats. "Today should be all free writing. I think Bella has some interviews with town folk. Can you make sure she doesn't go alone? I'll come down and go with her if you can't get away."

"You worried about people going off on their own?" Shauna paused, her hand on the fridge. "I don't think they are in any danger."

"Maybe not, but something about that mystery guy who keeps appearing has me spooked." She stretched her neck. "It's probably a reaction from him knocking me over earlier this week. My subconscious knows he's trouble."

"At least for you." Shauna took bags of fresh fruit out of the fridge. "Go write. I'll babysit the clan."

"Thanks. I'm taking a spin up to the ski lodge this afternoon. You'll be around, right?" Cat tried to say this very casually, hoping that Shauna wouldn't realize what she was planning.

Shauna cocked her head and stared at her. "Your uncle is going to flip."

"I might just be going up to buy Seth a gift. He needs a new ski parka. And if I happen to do a little snooping around for clues . . . ?" Cat shrugged. "Just don't tell Uncle Pete and everything will be fine."

"As long as you text me when you get there and when you leave. I'm not exactly sure what you're looking for, but I know it can't be good."

* * *

The guest rooms were still quiet when Cat paused on the second floor landing. No shower water running, no clicking of keyboards, and more importantly, no one in the hall to stop her from reaching her office. She hesitated a second and then wondered if she wanted to be distracted. Shaking off the doldrums, she took the final set of stairs to the third floor and set the coffee down on a hall table as she unlocked her office.

She booted her computer, then opened the document.

Ten minutes later, when she hadn't written a word, she opened her calendar and updated it with the deadlines and conferences she wanted to attend. Cat needed to develop a workshop she could pitch to the organizers on the value of retreats. Or at least writers' retreats where there wasn't a murder affecting the process. She closed the manuscript and opened a presentation program. Within an hour, the project was done. Now all she had to do was reach out to the different writing groups. Denver groups would give her the experience to pitch to the bigger venues.

Soon, she had one talk scheduled for each week next month. She made notes to start pitching the bigger events after her first dry run with the Denver Historical Writers Group in late November.

She bit into a muffin and almost groaned at the richness of the chocolate. One thing she hadn't done was mention the importance of good food for the guests. She was lucky she had Shauna to handle that part. Late-night writers snacked as much as stoners.

She froze. Maybe that's why the cookies disappeared last night. She'd be sure to ask Shauna if she had smelt any weed in the rooms when she went in to bring new towels and dump the trash. The contract said retreaters were not supposed to bring in drugs, but maybe someone thought since they were in Colorado, a joint or two wouldn't matter. Or maybe they bought the stash here. Several of the local guys made their living with a summer crop of hemp grown deep in the forest where no one could find it.

Cat didn't do the stuff mostly because of seventh-grade health class. They'd been shown films about the dangers of IV drugs and the images still stuck with her. She knew pot wasn't heroin, but still, a drug was a drug. And for her, she'd rather relax with a beer or a glass of wine at dinner. Besides, she'd never get any work done if she smoked pot.

She focused on the computer screen. Not like she was getting a lot of work done this morning. Her mind kept going back to the trip to the ski lodge she would take later that day. Uncle Pete would be mad if he found out, but she could at least look at the coats while she was there. Just to make the excuse for her visit plausible.

She reopened her manuscript, reviewing the last few pages. As she started typing, Kori and the story took over.

It was noon before she stopped writing. A totally great day.

* * *

Seth stood and took the empty coffee carafe and basket out of her hands when Cat entered the kitchen. "You're just in time. Pete's coming by for lunch, and he said he wanted to update us on the library theft, especially since it was your guests who found the missing book."

"I hope he's close by. I'm starving." Cat sank into a chair. She lowered her voice, not knowing where the guests were. "Hey, did you see anyone buying weed when we were at Little Ski Hill?"

"You think you've got a stoner in your group?" Seth shrugged. "You know it isn't illegal here, right?"

"Not illegal, but it is against the contract they signed. I might be old-fashioned, but I want this place to feel safe for all my guests." She chewed on her thumbnail. "And I want them to be successful in getting something done this week besides just chilling. It's the whole point of the retreat."

"I didn't see anyone, but I've heard rumors that you can get anything you want up at the lodge."

"Seriously? And how did you hear this?" Cat rubbed a kink out of her neck.

He stepped behind her, pushed her hands away, and started massaging the top of her shoulders. "I have my sources. Mostly it's people over at Bernie's. I've been told by a lot of people that I must do drugs to keep my girlish figure."

"Oh, really." Cat bent her head, relaxing into the rhythm. The man had great hands. And between hours of writing and the craziness of the week, she felt tighter than a snare drum.

"They don't get that my work keeps me slim. I don't sit at a desk all day playing solitaire." He rubbed his thumbs down her spine and for a minute, Cat thought she was going to cry, it felt so good. Then his words hit her brain.

"So, that's what you think I do in my office all day? Play games?" She kept her voice steady, not wanting him to stop massaging.

He laughed. "Just checking to see if you were awake."

The door to the kitchen opened and in her peripheral vision, Cat saw Shauna appear, a basket of laundry in her arms. "Whoa, I hope I'm not interrupting."

Cat tilted her head up to see her friend's face. "Not interrupting. Seth is just working some knots out of my neck."

"I don't think that's what they called it in my day." Uncle Pete stood in the doorway.

"You don't remember what anything was called back then." Cat squeezed Seth's hands as she leaned forward and stretched. "Glad you're finally here. I'm faint from lack of food."

"I don't think that's really what you're feeling, but you can humor an old man. I like to think my niece is pure as the driven snow." He pulled off his coat and sat on the bench to take off his boots.

"You remember I've been married, right?" Cat moved to the cabinet to pull out soup bowls. Shauna had clam chowder simmering on the stove.

"Details." He walked over and kissed her on the top of the head. "How's the writing going?"

"Slow." Cat looked at Shauna who had sat the laundry basket on a worktable near the door. "Is this ready to dish up?"

"You sit down. I've got it." She hurried to take the ladle out of Cat's hand.

"I can dish up soup, you know. I'm not totally helpless." Cat stared into the silverware drawer. "Just spoons?"

"Spoons, knives, napkins, and a small plate." Shauna pulled a tray out of the oven. "I made fresh rolls too. Grab some butter out of the fridge."

They worked together to get the meal served, and then after everyone had savored the first few bites, Cat looked at her uncle. "So why were you at the ski lodge yesterday?"

"You heard about that?" He kept his gaze down and grabbed another roll to butter before he continued. "Your guests just seem to be in the wrong place at the wrong time this week. Can you believe they found that book?"

Cat studied her uncle. "Way to avoid the question, but I'll play along. I know it looks suspicious, but none of them were even in town the night that the book was stolen."

"I wasn't accusing them of anything. It's just that girl was hanging around with Tommy before he died, the group of them discovers the missing book, and they were all up at the lodge last weekend."

"Yeah, skiing."

Seth shook his head. "I wouldn't call that skiing.

I'd call it drinking. I think Nelson and Jennifer were the only two who actually got on a ski lift that morning before hitting the bar."

Cat focused on her uncle. "So spill: What happened at the lodge?"

"Why do you think something happened?" He dipped his roll into his soup and then took a bite.

"Because you lumped their presence at the lodge with two other crimes?" She smiled. "I was an English professor, you know."

"Stop grilling your uncle. I'm sure there's some things he can't tell us." Shauna reached for Uncle Pete's empty bowl. "Can I refill that?"

"Please." He set his spoon down on his napkin. "What Shauna said. But what I did come by to tell you is the college wants to thank your guests for helping return the book. They have a little reception planned for Friday night, if that will work. The librarian lady is supposed to call you this afternoon."

Shauna set the filled bowl in front of Uncle Pete. "That's a lovely idea. They will be ecstatic to be recognized. You should have heard them chattering last night when they came in from dinner."

"Do you have any suspects in the book theft?" Cat asked.

"According to my sources, there's a professor's exit where the scanners have been deactivated, just in case they need to use the library during off hours." He paused as he lifted his spoon to his mouth. "The librarian thinks the book left that way. She said she's had problems with that lately."

Cat's face felt hot. "Students aren't allowed to use the exit. So she thinks it's a professor?"

"Or someone who used to be one." Uncle Pete sighed, and he grudgingly put his spoon down. "I'll be honest with you. When I was talking to Miss Applebome, your name came up in this discussion."

"Why would I steal a Hemingway?" Cat ripped a bite of her roll and buttered it. "I don't even write literary fiction."

"She didn't accuse you of stealing. She just said you had borrowed a book last month that wasn't supposed to leave the library." He waited but when Cat didn't respond, he asked, "Is this true?"

"Kind of. I took a yearbook to show Linda Cook a picture during the whole Tom Cook mess. I took it back the next day. If Miss Applebome didn't have eyes in the back of her head, she never would have known."

Uncle Pete laughed. "Well, she might have eyes in the back of her head, but she also has security cameras on all floors of the library. She saw you put the book in your bag. I guess she never gets people on that floor, so she was curious what you were researching."

"Michael showed me the exit when I first started teaching at Covington. He said most professors didn't use it, that the library was trying to discourage them from leaving without checking out books, but he didn't see the harm."

Cat shrugged. "I only borrowed one book that way. The yearbook to show Linda."

"Well, from what your librarian told me, I believe the professor exit is being locked down next week. There has to be approval from the fire department, but I don't see where they'll stop her."

Seth stood and took his bowl to the sink. "I need to get going. Hank's coming into town today with the final estimate, and he wanted to meet over at the library so we could copy off the original blue prints. Setting up a second heating and cooling system is tricky in an old house like this." He grabbed his coat and quickly left.

"That boy always disappears when your ex-husband's name is brought up. Have you noticed that?" Uncle Pete finished off his soup. "I'm heading back to the office to try and finish some of this paperwork. It's hard to write a report on having something disappear only to be returned in a freak way. The boxes on the report form don't seem to fit the situation."

Cat made circles in her soup with her spoon after her uncle had left. Shauna paused her hand. "What's got you wound up? The Michael/Seth thing or the probable cost of the new heating unit?"

Cat sat the spoon down on the table and sighed. "Can I say both?"

Shauna took her bowl to the sink. "It's your story; you can lie to yourself all you want."

The hard part was Cat *wasn't* sure what bothered her most. She needed to get this Michael thing settled so if there was a future with Seth so the ghost of her past wouldn't be living with them forever.

The heating unit addition was just money. Money came and money went. As long as they didn't find another one of Michael's secret rooms while they did the installation or worse, a body, she'd be happy when it was complete. When they'd started remodeling the attic a few months ago, Seth had found a secret room where Michael had set up a home office. Or should she say a second home office. One where he could hide the work he was doing for his second job. A job, Cat still hadn't pieced together to see if it had been the reason her ex had been killed.

Cat walked out of the kitchen and up the stairs to her room. She needed to change into jeans for her excursion. She decided she'd just have to trust Seth about getting the addition done. The way her luck was going, she better count on finding another body.

Chapter 10

Cat made her way to the elevator leading up to the lodge's hotel rooms. According to Christina, the room Tommy had rented was on the third floor. The elevator doors opened, and a couple in ski outfits stepped out. She took their place and quickly closed the doors before anyone else could get on.

The doors opened on the third floor, and she walked down the hall. A maid's cart stood abandoned about half way down. It must be break time. A few doors down, the yellow crime scene tape was flapping loose, and the door to the room stood open. She paused at the threshold and leaned inside. A large bed took up the left side of the room. The bed looked like it hadn't been slept in, the comforter still in place. On the back wall was the fireplace, and the small table still had the room-service tray on it. Glass shards sparkled on the rug. So far, Christina's story was holding up to the physical evidence. She made herself look to the right where the hot tub was sunk into the floor. She knew Tommy's body had been taken to the morgue, but in her mind's eye, she could still see him lying there. She hadn't known what to expect, but she wasn't learning anything new by visiting the room.

"I'm sorry, no one is allowed in that room." As she turned to leave, a voice came from behind her causing her to jerk. Cat turned to see the maid standing there, watching her.

"I heard there was a murder. Did you know the guy who was killed?"

The woman shrugged. "I talked to him that day. He said his girlfriend was coming up and he wanted extra towels since they would be spending some time in the hot tub. So I got him more towels."

Cat didn't want to look at the hot tub again. "Well, I guess I should get back downstairs. My boyfriend thinks I went to the bathroom."

"Men are easy to fool." The woman laughed, her cackle sounding hard. "I guess this guy didn't get the night he'd planned either."

As Cat headed out of the lodge to her car, she wondered what had really happened in that condo and who had decided that Tommy wasn't going to need to live another day.

Later that afternoon, she was back at the house waiting for the guests to appear. She expected she'd get at least a phone call from her uncle sooner or later about why she'd visited today, and since she'd forgotten to even look at a coat for Seth, she had no excuse for being at the lodge, much less on the third floor. But maybe the maid wouldn't say anything. From her response, she had to be used to people trying to sneak a peek at the death scene.

The phone rang and as she listened, Cat doodled on the notebook in front of her as she cradled the phone in between her ear and neck. She had been reviewing January's retreat guest list when Miss Applebome called. The woman was ten minutes into the conversation and had just now gotten to the point. The crew was invited to an afternoon tea at the library to thank them for finding and returning the book.

The first part of the conversation had been a not-so-subtle interrogation to make sure Cat hadn't stolen the book herself.

The bell over the door rang, and she looked up to find a delivery guy holding a large bouquet of purple flowers. She held up one finger asking him to wait.

"Sorry, Miss Applebome, I need to cut this short. I'll make sure the gang is over at the library a bit before six. They're going to be so excited about this. Thank you for thinking of them." Before the librarian could respond, Cat disconnected the call. She grinned at the guy. "Thank you for rescuing me. So, who are these for? Bella, Jennifer? Maybe Shauna?"

Shauna had been dating a guy but had kept him away from the house. Cat hoped that Shauna's reluctance to introduce him to Cat only meant that her friend wasn't quite sure yet.

The guy set the bouquet on the table. "None of the above. This is why I always confirm the delivery." He looked at his clipboard. "So you don't have a Catherine Latimer staying here?"

Cat felt her skin cool. Yes, the flowers could have been from Seth, but if he'd sent them, the name would be Cat or, if he was in a teasing mood, Kitty Cat. No one sent flowers to her under *Catherine*. At least not since she divorced Michael. Swallowing hard, she nodded. "I'm Catherine. Who are the flowers from?"

He looked back at the paper. "That's funny; it doesn't say. Someone paid a wad of cash for this bouquet, though. My designer had to order in the lilacs special. Who orders spring flowers in November?"

She handed the guy a five she'd scrounged from the desk drawer and then waited for him to leave. When she saw the Aspen Hills Floral delivery van pull away from the curb, she reached for the card.

"Lovely to meet you last week, even if the circumstances were less accommodating. I hope we can talk again. I enjoyed our banter. D." No name, just an initial. What was it with men that they thought signing with an initial was cool? She put the card in the trash and moved the antique bucking bronco statue off the oak table by the stairs. Coffee, now flowers. Why did this feel like more than just a casual meeting?

Her mind went to Seth. "I haven't done anything wrong." She muttered the words under her breath, but even as she said them, it felt like she had. She returned to the scheduling and setting up room assignments for each person, made a note for Shauna stating they only had room for one more registration, and closed out the registration software. Then, putting on her heavy winter coat and gloves, she headed outside for a walk to clear her head.

As she passed by Mrs. Rice's Thanksgiving display, she heard someone call her name. Looking up, she saw Bella making her exit off the porch. Mrs. Rice waved and then shut the door.

Bella didn't speak until she'd closed the gate behind her. "I'm so glad to see you. After talking to Mrs. Rice and your lecture last night about safety, I'd rather not walk to the library by myself. Are you going that way?"

Cat put on a smile she didn't feel and nodded. "Sure. I hope your interview was successful." She didn't know exactly what Bella was writing, but she thought she was relying way too much on research and not spending enough time actually putting words down on paper. The woman wrote fiction, for goodness' sake.

"She knows everything. Of course, she's a little hard to keep on track." Bella turned to look at Cat. "She's very interested in your relationship with Mr. Howard. She just kept pumping me for gossip, but I didn't say anything. Did you know the stories going around about the two of you? Star-crossed high-school sweethearts."

"That part is actually true. Seth and I did date in high school." No use hiding that fact; it wouldn't have even been news to Mrs. Rice, since she'd lived here as long as Cat could remember.

Bella laughed. "When she saw the florist stop at your place, I almost had to drag her back to the couch. She wanted to know who would be getting flowers. So I lied and said my husband must have sent them for our anniversary."

"I didn't know you were married."

"That's because I'm not. I just wanted to get back to what she knew about the mob kids attending Covington. And, man, did I get a list of names. I'm looking through the yearbooks to corroborate what she said, but if this is even partially true, my book is going to shoot up the best selling rankings. Of course, I've had to fictionalize the town and the college. I don't want the boys to put me in their cross hairs. But really, they probably won't even know I wrote the book."

Cat considered what she'd heard. "Are you scared they won't like the book and how it portrays them?"

They'd arrived at the library. "They should be the ones that are scared of being found out. Those guys are stone-cold killers for the most part. And they'd do anything to protect their family."

"Call the house when you're ready to come back. I'll send someone." Cat wanted to avoid getting cornered by Miss Applebome again, so she didn't follow Bella inside. Instead, she wandered through the campus and then through town before finding herself in front of Bernie's.

The bar looked empty, but Cat knew it opened at noon, so she pushed the wooden door open and stepped into the darkness. It took her eyes a moment to adjust, but then she saw Brit at the bar, a clipboard in her hand.

"Come on in, I won't bite." Brit waved her over to the bar. "What can I get you?"

Cat pulled off her gloves and rubbed her hands. "I wouldn't turn down a cup of coffee if you have some."

"I keep a pot on just for me during the day. At night, I keep one for the guys who think drinking coffee will get them sobered up before their wives notice they've been drinking." Brit poured two cups and set them in front of Cat. Then she walked around the bar and sat on the stool next to her.

Cat sipped the coffee. It was surprisingly good. "I'm sorry about Tommy."

Brit sighed. "Well, I'm not. I think I dodged a bullet on that one. How do you know if a guy is going to be a cheater?"

Choking on her coffee, Cat wiped the liquid off the bar with a nearby napkin. "I'm not sure."

Brit helped clean up the mess, then shook her head. "Sorry, I shouldn't have brought that up to you of all people." She paused, twirling her hair with one finger. "You need to know that we never dated back then. I mean when you were married. I knew him and that fall he'd come into the bar, sit on that stool, and make notes in some type of journal. One beer, maybe two, then he was out of here. He didn't pick up any of the co-eds either, if you were wondering."

"What Michael did or didn't do isn't really the point anymore, is it? He's dead." Cat cringed at how harsh her words sounded. "I was in a bad space when we divorced. Now I'm starting my life over."

"Betrayal like that kind of kicks you in the face." Brit sipped her coffee again. "You sure I can't get you a real drink? Maybe a shot of something?"

"Not today, but I'll come back in a few days and we can have that shot." Or maybe more, Cat thought. "Christina didn't know he was engaged. She's a good kid."

"Believe me, I don't blame her. Tommy just thought he was above rules. He told me he was celebrating some big score and to be ready to party on Monday. When I told him I was covering for Dad since he had to go see his doctor in Denver, he got ticked off."

"Is Bernie all right?"

Brit nodded. "A bad ticker, he'd say. Good news is he seems to be getting better now that he's taking care of himself. I even got him to stop smoking."

"That's good to hear." The clock chimed and a bird call echoed through the empty bar.

Brit stood and threw back the rest of her coffee. "I've got to get ready to open. In an hour, this place will be jam-packed with students and people from the college."

Cat left a five on the counter after Brit had disappeared to the back to grab beer. She blinked at the bright light that assaulted her eyes as she left the bar. Brit had known Michael, but more importantly, the nights she'd thought he'd been shacked up in his office with the flavor of the month girl, he'd been at the bar, ignoring everyone and everything except his journal.

As she turned the corner onto Warm Springs,

she saw a white van someone had driven up on the curb. A woman's scream came from behind the van. Cat pulled out her cell as she ran and dialed 911. When Katie answered, Cat shouted, "Something's happening on the 200 block of Warm Springs. Send help. Guy's in a white van." The van had parked so closely to another car, she couldn't see the plates. When a second scream emitted, Cat ignored the questions Katie was asking her and sprinted, hoping she wouldn't fall on the slippery sidewalk.

She barely heard the woman on the phone tell her to stay away from the incident.

"AA549." She read off the front plate into the phone as she came around the van, then stuck her phone, still connected, into her coat pocket.

A big man had someone by the waist and was trying to push the woman into the back of the van. He wasn't having much luck as the woman had flung her arms and legs out wide and was bracing herself on the edges of the opening. Even at a few feet away, Cat could see the woman's arms shaking and her grip weakening.

Looking around, she found garden gnomes someone had placed by their entry gate. She wrenched one out of the frozen ground and then ran closer, throwing it at the guy's head as she stopped, just out of arm's reach.

The man let the woman go and grabbed at his head. "Damn," he roared in pain, turning toward her. Cat could have sworn his eyes glowed red. He turned his focus back to his victim, but she'd taken advantage of being released and had grabbed a shovel out of the back of the van.

Cat heard the sound of the shovel hitting the man's head from where she stood and she grabbed the matching gnome before stepping closer. He crumpled to the ground, and she held the cement statue over his body, waiting for him to move.

"I think he's out."

Cat turned her gaze to the woman and realized it was Christina. She still had the shovel handle in her hands, as if she was on the mound and waiting for the next pitch. "Are you okay? Did he hurt you?"

"My arms are killing me, but I think I'm fine. Thanks for the help, I couldn't have held on much longer."

Neither she or Cat moved as they heard the sirens coming up the road. Katie must have sent everyone she had on patrol that day because, before Cat knew it, five black police cars surrounded the van, and soon, every vehicle had an officer crouching behind the driver's side door with guns pointed at her and Christina.

Uncle Pete climbed out of his car. "Holster your weapons and get this guy in cuffs." He took the unthrown gnome out of Cat's hands and set it back down by the gate. "You okay?"

Another officer checked for a pulse, then gently placed cuffs on him so he'd be restrained when he awoke.

"He's not dead, is he?" Christina allowed a third officer to take the shovel from her. "I didn't want to kill him, but he tried to force me into the van. Every article I've read about kidnappers says not to let them take you from the original abduction site."

"You did great." Uncle Pete kneeled next to the prone man. He exchanged a glance with the other officer. "Call for an ambulance. He's going to have a whopper of a headache when he wakes up."

Cat realized the phone was still in her pocket and connected to the police station. She pulled the cell out. "Thanks for the help, Katie. Everything's fine here." Not waiting for Katie's response, she disconnected the call and put her phone away. She stood over the guy but focused her question to Christina. "Do you know him?"

"He's the guy who offered to buy me a drink last night." Christina took the blanket that she'd been offered. "Why would he try to take me?"

Cat and Uncle Pete exchanged a glance. This had to be about Tommy Neil's death. Cat rubbed her hands over her arms, trying to stop the chill that had come over her. "He looks kind of like the guy who ran me down the other day. I can't be for sure, but he's the right size."

"We'll run his prints and see who we're dealing with." He called over to the officer who had helped Christina. "Take these two to my niece's place, 700 Warm Springs."

"Don't you want to interview us?" Christina asked as she wavered on her feet.

Cat stepped toward her. "Let's get you warmed up first."

"I'll be over as soon as I clean up this mess." Uncle Pete turned toward the sound of the ambulance. "First, I want to make sure this guy is safely in custody. Then we'll try to figure this out."

As Cat walked with Christina toward the waiting police car, she wondered if the answer was too easy. If this man had killed Tommy Neil, he'd had a reason. She went back to her conversation with Mrs. Colfax. This is just the kind of conspiracy theory the woman would love. Especially since it made Tommy some kind of target. Then the guy would have had to think Christina was a loose end. But she'd left the room before Tommy was killed, so how would he have even known about her?

At least there was one good thing that would come out of the fact that this guy was the killer. The last few days of the retreat would be free of any further crime investigation.

Cat held the car door open for the now-shaking Christina. The girl had enough problems in her life. First a stalker, then a cheater, now this. Cat wouldn't doubt if Christina wrote off men entirely after this week.

Paul Quinn drove them home, and they went into the house through the kitchen door. He looked at Cat. "Any other entrances?"

"The front door and a cellar door, but it's locked." She handed Christina off to Shauna.

Paul pulled himself up to his full height. "Keep this door locked and I'll be out front. Call 911 if you need me; don't come outside."

"They have the guy, why are you acting like we're still in danger?" Cat snapped out the words.

Paul raised his eyebrows. "We caught one guy. Who knows if he's the only person involved or if he was just working for someone."

Cat heard Christina's sharp intake of breath. She moved Paul toward the door. Lowering her voice, she said, "You're scaring her. Go watch the front if you think you need to, and I'll keep this door locked. Just leave so I can get her calmed down."

"Don't let her change or anything. Your uncle will want to interview her in what she was wearing." Paul opened the door and then waited outside until Cat threw the deadbolt.

Locking the door was probably like shutting the barn door after the horse escapes, but at least it made her feel a little better. Now she was glad Seth had replaced the lock on the cellar door last month. The house was huge, but at least it felt a little safer with the primary doors locked and watched.

Cat poured herself a cup of coffee and sat at the table, watching Christina as she sipped the hot chocolate Shauna had given her. "You said you'd recognized him from the pizza place? Had you seen him before?"

"No. But when he stopped today, he was all friendly until he got out of the truck, then he grabbed me. I should have listened yesterday when you said not to be outside alone. I just hate feeling out of control. Why can't people just be nice?" She pulled the blanket Shauna had brought from the linen closet, closer.

"Good question." Shauna glanced at me as she

rubbed Christina's back. "But you're safe now and tomorrow this will just be a bad memory."

"Will it?" Christina wiped at her eyes. "I mean, life has been kind of crappy lately. Now I get to add in a thwarted kidnapping to my list. What in the world did he want from me?"

Cat dropped her gaze. There were many things she could think of that a kidnapper would have done with a woman. Instead of answering her question, Cat tried to distract her until Uncle Pete came to bring it all up again. "Tell me what you were researching in the library. Or were you somewhere else?"

"I went for coffee at that cute little shop downtown." She sent a sideways glance at Shauna. "Not that your coffee isn't wonderful. I just wanted to play with some plot lines alone. Except this handsome man in line behind me insisted on buying my coffee, and then I asked him to sit with me."

"Not the kidnapper, though?"

Christina shook her head. "He looked rich, and he said he knew you. Although he kept calling the place 'Catherine's Retreat,' which I thought was weird if he really knew you. I mean, he'd call you *Cat*, right? Anyway, he asked about who was attending and what we'd done so far and what we were going to do." The girl paused, understanding filling her face. "And now he knows where we'll be for the next few days and when the house will be empty. You don't think he's a burglar, do you?"

No, Cat didn't think Dante was a burglar, but that didn't mean he wasn't looking for a way to get into the house alone. She was sure that's who Christina had coffee with. She wondered what he wanted. Could he be looking for something of Michael's? Was there something that she hadn't found while cleaning up Michael's study.

Now she just needed to find out what.

Chapter 11

Cat went upstairs to her office after Uncle Pete came. He'd asked if they could use Michael's study, so she had unlocked the door. She needed to just get over people being in his study. In *the* study, she corrected herself. But not until she figured out what she'd missed. As they settled into the chairs, she'd scanned the room, trying to imagine what Dante Cornelio could want in the space. She'd cleaned out all the boxes of books from the campus office, and they were all sitting in the wall to ceiling bookcase, waiting to be picked up and looked at one more time.

She made a note in her planner to sort through the books next week, once the retreat was over, and to donate anything dealing with his academic studies. She should just have the library take the whole batch. But she wanted to page through them one more time, making sure they didn't hold a secret clue. She had too many things to worry about right now. She turned on the computer. But instead of going into her manuscript and actually working, she opened an Internet browser and started searching for information on Dante Cornelio. He had mentioned knowing Michael. He knew her and where she lived. Now she was going to find out what she could about him.

By the time her uncle knocked on the door, she had two notebook pages filled with notes on the guy. His charities, his love life, and his family's reported link to the crime world. Of course, the articles that mentioned mob connections treated it like ancient history. Like the fact he'd come from such bloody beginnings was a joke. She had been staring at a picture of Dante with a tall blond woman at a charity ball when she heard Uncle Pete's knock. She clicked out of the browser as she pushed away from the desk. "Come on in."

"Sorry if you're working. I know it's probably been pretty rough getting some quiet time this week." Uncle Pete sank into the sofa and closed his eyes for a second. He let out a big sigh. "A guy could fall asleep here no problem."

"I won't tell." She sat in the rocker under the window. The backyard was still covered in untouched snow, and with the forecast for more next week, she thought they might be assured a white Christmas this year.

"You ever consider just renting this place out to a wandering circus or selling it for a school for the performing arts? Having twenty teenagers running through town might be easier on me than your monthly retreats. Aren't writers supposed to be homebodies who always have their nose in a book?"

"They aren't that bad." Cat turned her gaze from the window to her uncle, who was grinning. "Okay, so it's been a rough two months. We'll rush through December and pray January is boring."

"I have a feeling that nothing you set your mind to do will ever be boring." He opened his notebook and reviewed his notes from the first interview. "Christina said she screamed, then all of a sudden the guy went down and you were standing there. I think I already know, but I should ask. What did you hit him with? The hospital would probably like to know."

"A concrete garden gnome. That sucker was heavy. But he didn't fall; he was just stunned and let go of Christina." Cat thought about the details of the fight. "Then Christina grabbed a shovel out of the van and hit him in the head with that. That's when he went down. I grabbed the other gnome, just in case he moved and, well, that's when you arrived."

He made some notes, then looked at her. "Did you recognize him?"

Cat shrugged. "I don't know. Maybe."

"Maybe, what?"

"He looks about the same size as the guy who almost knocked me over that day. The day I met Dante." She leaned back into the chair. "It could have been him, or it could have been some random guy in town that day who was late for an appointment."

Uncle Pete closed his notebook. "I looked at

the coffee shop's videos and the guy over at the hospital had coffee with Dante Cornelio ten minutes before you did. In fact, you guys sat at the same table."

"So he knows Dante." Cat's thoughts jumbled with possibilities.

He leaned back and looked out on the backyard too. "It's really not too late to sell this and move to Florida with your folks."

"It's not all that bad here," Cat said.

Her uncle met her gaze. "If I'm right, the guy you took down with garden implements is a contract hit man for the mob. He might be a little embarrassed by his ultimate capture."

"And what? Come kill me just because I took him out with a fantasy creature?" Cat shook her head, but the pit in the bottom of her stomach was growing larger.

"Weirder things have happened." He stood and patted her on the shoulder as he walked by her and out of the office. "Don't fret. I should be able to connect him to enough murders to keep him in jail for a long, long time."

"Wait." Cat followed him out of her office. "If he's a contract killer, does that mean he's the one who whacked Tommy? And why?"

"All good questions. Maybe you should have gone into police work instead of writing." Her uncle paused at the top of the stairs. "But no, apparently from the plane tickets we found in his luggage, he came in the morning after Tommy was killed. His first stop in town was meeting with Dante. And you know how that turned out."

She followed him downstairs, where Shauna

had set out a supper of sandwiches, potato and macaroni salads, and chocolate cake for dessert. Cat and Uncle Pete paused in the dining room and watched Shauna finish unpacking the spread.

When she noticed them, she shrugged. "What? I figured you'd all be hungry."

"I've got to get down to the hospital." Uncle Pete kissed Cat on the cheek. "I'd say see you soon, but I'd rather not jinx your last few days."

"Wait," Shauna called after him. "I have a dinner for you too. I figured you wouldn't stay, so I boxed up a sandwich and salad for you."

He took the bag and glanced inside. "And a slice of that cake, I see."

"A man's got to eat. Sorry it's not homemade." Shauna patted him on the arm. "We'll do a family dinner sometime next week after we get the house cleared out."

"You spoil me." Uncle Pete waved his hand and exited out the front door.

Cat went to the window and noticed him stopping by Paul Quinn's cruiser. The men talked for a bit. Then Uncle Pete pulled away, but the other car stayed put. "Looks like we have a protector for the night. You might want to take him dinner too."

"Already delivered. And we actually have two night watchmen. Seth's coming over with his suitcase and staying in the extra room until Sunday." Shauna didn't look at her as she walked back to the dining room. "And he's picking up Bella at the library on his way."

"I'd forgotten all about her." Cat rubbed a hand over her face. "I'm a horrible retreat hostess."

"You told her to call the house when she was ready and she did. You don't have to do everything, you know. I'd say saving a guest from a kidnapping definitely outranks picking up one at the library. Besides, you're not alone here. That's what Seth and I are here for, to help. Let us do our jobs." Shauna threw a towel over her shoulder. "You can do one thing, though."

"What's that?" Cat leaned against the doorway, exhausted.

"I told the group I'd call their rooms when the food was ready." Shauna waved her toward the phone. "Go let the children know it's time for supper."

Cat laughed and went over to the desk. As she was making the calls, she thought about Shauna's reference to the guests as children. They were part of the family, at least for this week. Besides, she did have help catering to their needs. She just needed to remember that.

After dinner, the group disbanded. They'd all eaten in the dining room that meal, guests and staff alike. Shauna was in the kitchen, boxing up leftovers and cleaning up the dishes. The guests were in their rooms writing, or at least Cat hoped that's what they were doing. And Seth had gone out to his truck to get his suitcase.

He came back through the front door, stomping his feet on the entry rug. "It's starting to snow again. I bet we have three inches by morning."

"At least we'll be able to see tracks in the snow if anyone comes close to the house tonight." Cat sat at the lobby desk, doodling and looking at the flowers Dante had sent her. What was his connection to the recently deceased Tommy Neil, or was it just coincidence that he showed up into town now? She realized Seth had stopped in front of the desk. "Sorry, I was daydreaming."

He lifted his eyebrows. "About him? I'm really going to have to up my game if I hope to compete with a guy rich enough to send those flowers."

"You aren't in competition. And I'm not sure why he even sent the flowers." She yawned. "Anyway, I'm beat."

"So am I staying in your room?" There was a crinkle around his eyes when he laughed and right now, those eyes were staring at her.

"No." She dropped her gaze before she said yes with her body and contradicted her words.

"Then I need a room key."

She could hear the humor in his voice. She grabbed the key from the only empty room on the second floor and set it on the counter between them. "Have a nice night."

"I was hoping for something on the third floor. That way you could sneak into my room without anyone noticing." He twirled the key in his hand. "I'll leave the door unlocked, just in case."

"In your dreams, buddy." She stretched. "The only man I'm having in my room tonight is the sandman. And we have a date as soon as I make sure everything's locked up."

"I checked the cellar before I went out to the truck. And Shauna locked the kitchen door as soon as everyone was in the house." He pointed to the front door. "You handle that, and I'll wait for you. We can walk upstairs together."

She rubbed her face then grabbed the keys. "Might as well. I'm not doing anything productive here."

"Look, I know today took a lot out of you. You need to realize it's not normal to take down a man twice your size. You're a hero." He pulled her into a hug.

"I threw garden statuary at the guy." But she let herself relax for the first time since she'd come upon the van and Christina. All she could think about at the time was saving the girl. She'd read too many books where the situation didn't work out and the police didn't save the victim.

Seth's scent filled her senses, and now she didn't understand why in the world she'd said no to sharing her bed. She looked up at him, and he kissed her. "You're a good guy, Seth Howard."

He stepped back raising his hands as if he was warding off a blow. "Don't let that get out. Something like that would ruin my reputation as a hard-ass."

"You are the only person that thinks of you that way." She locked the door and looked out the window at the police cruiser. The snow had started to stick. "Poor Paul. It must be freezing in that car."

"Shauna set him up with a carafe of coffee along with dinner. She's a food pusher." Seth waved her toward him. "Come on, I'm beat and I know you're tired. Let's go to bed."

They walked slowly up the stairs and when

they reached the second floor landing, he kissed her again—this time quick, like he was off to work a busy day at the office. "See you in the morning. Sleep well."

"That won't be a problem." Cat climbed the rest of the stairs to her room and collapsed on her bed.

Within the hour, she'd realized her words had been a lie. Sleep wasn't coming. She'd taken a warm bath, slipped under the covers in warm pajamas and socks and, still, her mind wouldn't shut off.

Glancing at the clock, she threw her covers off and grabbed a robe. She'd go downstairs, make some hot cocoa, and then start packing up Michael's books. Maybe if she lugged around enough of those crazy-heavy volumes, she'd wear herself out.

The process was slow. She'd kept several folded boxes in a closet in the room, so now she had to tape up a box, take all the books off one shelf at a time, then replace the books she wanted to keep. So far, that had been five. And she had three boxes already to take to the library. Maybe the size of this donation would get her back on Miss Applebome's good side. Or not.

Cat didn't think the librarian forgave much, and Cat knew she didn't forget anything. She flipped through each book, looking for notations or a loose scrap of paper. So far, she'd found class notes and a receipt from the hotel where they'd spent their honeymoon. She sat that on a table, not sure what to do with something so personal after a divorce. Did she trash it? Burn it? Now that she believed Michael had staged the whole event to get her out of his life, she didn't have the anger anymore to do either. But she'd burned the love card out of her heart because of the betrayal, fake or not. Michael had still betrayed her by not trusting her to be able to deal with the whatever mess he was in. Besides, she'd never be completely certain that he didn't have at least one fling. Men don't change their patterns. They are who they are. She and Michael had taken vows for better or worse, and he hadn't trusted her to be able to deal with the worse. Still, keeping physical reminders of memories made its own problems.

Like what about Seth. How could she keep memories alive on one man when dating another. What did widows do with the remnants of another life when they began a new one? It didn't help that she was back in the very house where she and Michael began their lives together. When she came in here, she felt connected to the past. A past that no longer threw daggers into her heart. Instead she felt, if not love, contentment. Her life with Michael had been a matching of the minds. He got her, challenged her, and loved her. And then he'd driven her away, she reminded herself.

Back and forth—her heart didn't know what to feel. She knew she needed to get this last room cleaned out and figure out what Dante might be looking for in her late husband's things.

"One more box," she promised herself. She

was finally beginning to feel tired. She pulled a new stack of books off the shelf and realized they weren't on economics. These were history books. Maybe these she should save for the retreat library. She cleared the shelf, then sat down to examine each book.

Flipping through the first one, she saw it dealt with American history. Very general, but Michael had put a bookmark in the section dealing with the 1920s. Michael *never* marked up books. He said it was defacing them. He would copy whole pages onto his working notebook by hand.

Cat's thoughts went back to the journal Brit had mentioned Michael writing in. She'd assumed it was the diary that sat on the side table waiting for Cat to read her ex-husband's thoughts about their lives together. Thoughts he hadn't trusted her enough to tell her directly.

But there should be another journal. Before he'd even think about teaching a class, he studied the subject and wrote pages in a cheap spiral notebook. Cat used to tease him that he could save a whole forest of trees by working on a computer. Michael would shake his head and smile, holding up the notebooks. "Someday, these will be worth millions, once the world learns that your husband was an economic genius. These will pay for our retirement cottage by the sea."

Michael hadn't lived long enough to become an economics superstar or even get close to retirement. But if she could find the notebook where he'd worked out what was bothering him, maybe he'd left her more clues than she thought as to what really happened. As she thumbed through the stack of books waiting to be sorted, she realized one thing: Michael had been studying the history of organized crime in America. She'd found the link between Michael and Dante. But what, if anything, did it mean? She needed to find *that* notebook.

She heard a crash in the lobby and without thinking ran to the front. She flipped on the overhead light. Jeffrey lay on the floor, his legs twisted around the coatrack. He blinked into the bright light.

"What are you doing here?" He peered up at her.

Cat came over and took the rack off him, setting it back on the edge of the wall where it belonged. "I live here, remember?" She grabbed a coat and hung it back on the rack, noticing it smelled of cigarettes. She looked at the grandfather clock that showed it was already two. "What are you doing up?"

"I was just checking to see if the doors were locked tight. Christina's had a very bad day, and I wanted to make sure she was safe." Jeffrey pulled himself up to a standing position. He peered out the front window. "Is that a police cruiser out there? Why is he here?"

"He's been there all evening." Seriously, had the guy even listened when she'd mentioned Paul's presence at dinner? "Christina's fine. She's in her room sleeping." Cat didn't say the rest of the words—right where you should be.

"Fine, I get it." He spun on his heel and sprinted up the stairs. Then she went to the front door to check the locks. The police cruiser still sat in front of the house, just as Jeffrey had said, but for some reason that didn't make her feel any safer.

She went back into Michael's study and turned off the lights. She'd finish the project next week. Now that she thought she knew what she was looking for, she could relax. And besides, she realized the only stack of notebooks she had of Michael's had been boxed up a few weeks ago and put in the basement. That's where the answers lay.

Now all she had to do was ask the right question.

Chapter 12

"You look like hell." Shauna set a cup of coffee in front of Cat. "Okay, what's got you not sleeping now? Seth or Michael? Or is it all this Tommy Neil stuff?"

Cat sipped the warm liquid, letting it seep into her bones before she answered. "How about all three? You won't believe what I found last night in Michael's study. History books."

Shauna blinked her eyes, then looked at the counter. "I'm sure I have sugar somewhere. Maybe you'll feel better once you eat."

"Did you hear what I said? Michael had a ton of American history books. And do you know what subject they were focused on?" Cat rubbed her eyes. She felt sluggish. Maybe sugar wouldn't be a bad thing. "You don't have any of those chocolate chip muffins left, do you?"

Shauna put two muffins on a plate and, after warming them in the microwave, brought them and a butter dish over to the table. She broke open one of the muffins and loaded it down with the creamy butter. She paused before taking a bite. "I don't know, maybe Colorado history? He did own a pretty nice piece of Aspen Hills history right here in the house."

"Exactly. But not only did the books cover Colorado history, he had a ton that dealt with the history of organized crime in the United States." Cat buttered her own muffin. "He was researching this whole mob connection to the college."

"Ooh, I'd love to look over what you found." Bella Neighbors stood in the doorway, her Warm Springs Writers' Retreat travel cup in one hand and a carafe in another. "Sorry for interrupting, but I must have drained the last of the hot water for my tea. Can I get this refilled?"

Shauna popped up and took the carafe and the coffee cup from Bella. "Of course. Go have a seat while I heat up the kettle."

Bella sat next to Cat. "So where did you find these books? Can I look them over before the retreat ends? My plane leaves early on Sunday, and I'd really like to see if there is something I could use for my story."

Cat hesitated. Was there a connection between Dante and Bella? She shook off the idea. Now she really was seeing ghosts. But she really had wanted to look at the books first, to make sure there wasn't any hidden messages from Michael stuffed in between the pages. Cat couldn't think of a way to put Bella off without revealing things better kept hidden. "I found them in my ex-husband's study. If you promise to keep all papers that you might find in the books right where you found them, I'll let you work in the study as long as you need to review what's there. Please don't invite any of your retreat friends to join you. I'm trying to sort through his belongings and would rather keep it closed until I'm done with the sorting."

Bella took the cup Shauna offered her. "No worries. I'll be extra careful. I'm just so glad to hear there's a local who was researching Aspen Hills' unique history before me. From all the interviews I've done, most of the people here just accepted the college enrollment as a given."

"So no conflict or strife to write about?" Cat sipped her coffee. This was why she liked writing in an imaginary world. You didn't have to worry about the facts from real life. Except maybe the strife most teenagers felt while in high school.

"Exactly. Your neighbor, Mrs. Rice, can tell me who slept with who for the last century, but she has no clue about what the families of these mob kids even did. She just said the kids were special." Bella dunked her tea bag a few times in the steaming liquid. "And that local kids were warned to stay away."

"That much is true." Cat finished off her muffin, wondering again if she should call her mother for the rest of the story. "I kind of had blinders on when I was growing up."

"You mean you were, and are, naïve," Shauna translated as she brought the now full carafe to the table. "Can I get you a muffin or something?"

Bella stood and took the carafe. "I'm good. But can you show me where the study is? I'd like to get started."

Shauna looked at Cat who nodded her assent. "Sure, follow me." Shauna grabbed the key to the room from the key board and they left the room.

Cat filled her coffee cup and threw away her muffin wrapper before heading upstairs to her own office. She might not get many words down before she had to stop, but she'd at least try. The magic of being a writer was less in the talent and the muse's guidance, and more in the consistency of sitting down to write.

By the time she stumbled downstairs for something to drink besides coffee, she'd completed a chapter. Cat hoped she could grab a soda and head back to her office without anyone noticing her. After she checked in with Bella, that was.

Shauna was in the kitchen with boxes in various stages of filled all around her. Cat weaved her way to the fridge and after opening a Coke and taking a drink, looked at her friend. "Are we moving? Did I miss a memo?"

"I'm packing up the old stuff that Michael left in the kitchen. I want you to look at it before I have Seth take everything down to the second-hand shop to donate. There are some good things in here." Shauna pulled out a knife block from the box and set it on the table. "I'd keep this, but the chef knife is missing."

"One of the economics professors gave that to us for our wedding present." Cat grinned and pulled out one of the steak knives. "The card read *For use when you get tired of each other*. I guess he thought he knew how the marriage would turn out."

"And that's why I want you to go through this stuff before I donate it. We could just box it up and put it in the cellar." Shauna moved a box to the side of the room. "I don't want you to regret giving this stuff up in a year or so."

"I'll go through it, but I'm pretty sure there's not anything I want that I didn't take when I left originally. I'd collected some nice crockware at different yard sales, and that all went with me to California. I think it's in one of the basement boxes now."

"Wait. I think I saw a mini pickling crock a few minutes ago. Let me find it."

Shauna and Cat started going through the boxes, and Cat did find a few things that were either her mother's or she'd acquired during the marriage. She hadn't realized how much she'd left behind when she'd moved out. She set the things she wanted to keep on the table next to the knife block.

"Looks like a garage sale in here." Uncle Pete's voice boomed through the doorway. "Am I too late for breakfast?"

"Never." Cat grinned and waved him in. "Shauna's uncluttering. Take a look around and see if there's anything you need for your place before we donate the batch."

Uncle Pete made his way to the table and looked at the knife block. He took his handkerchief out and pulled out one of the steak knives.

"I'm keeping what's on the table." Cat shrugged. "Well, except for that. Do you need a set of good knives? Too bad the one's gone, but

I'm sure you can replace it with something that at least kind of matches."

He sank into one of the chairs. "So you have had this since you moved in here?"

"It was stuck in the back of one of the cabinets, but yeah." Shauna stacked several boxes near the wall that Cat had already gone through. "I have my own knives and, with what they cost, I don't use anything but them."

"When did you notice the missing knife?"

Something in Uncle Pete's tone made Cat stop considering the china in front of her. It too had been a wedding gift, but Cat couldn't remember if it came from her side of the family or was from one of Michael's friends. She set the plate down and looked at him. "Why are you asking?"

He met her gaze. "Because if I'm not mistaken, the missing chef knife is sitting in my evidence locker. It's the weapon that was used to kill Tommy Neil."

Shauna and Cat both stared at the unassuming kitchen display. Simple utensils that Cat had used to chop vegetables or slice meat during her short marriage had been taken and used to perform a violent act. Cat rubbed her arms, trying to ease off the chill that had just settled in the room. "Are you sure? I bet there are tons of those sets in different houses here in town."

"With a missing chef knife?" Uncle Pete shook his head. "Sorry, Cat, I don't believe your theory. I'll have the knife tested to see if it could be part of the set. I guess we couldn't tell exactly, but it's coincidental at least."

After her uncle had bagged the knife set to take back to the station, Christina wandered in the kitchen. "Whoa, looks like you guys are busy. I was just wondering if you had some of those peanut butter cookies. I'm starving, but I want to finish this chapter before I go into town for lunch."

"Miss Powers, do you have a second?" Uncle Pete motioned to the table. "I need to clarify a few things from your original statement."

"Seriously? I don't know what else I can tell you." Christina plopped into one of the kitchen chairs, her arms crossed.

"This won't take long. Tell me about leaving Tommy's room on Monday. You said the two of you fought?"

"Not really fought. I told him I was saving having relations until I was married." Christina's face burned at the memory. "And he started laughing. He told me to get out and not come back until I was an actual grown-up."

"So you were angry?" Uncle Pete kept his gaze on his notebook.

The woman sighed and leaned back into her chair looking defeated. "Not angry, embarrassed. I know my values are old-fashioned, but it's what I believe. And if Tommy had truly loved me, like he'd said, he would have understood. That's the hardest part of this; I feel like a fool even hanging out with him in the first place. I guess I was wrong about the man's character."

"So you left the room." Uncle Pete turned the conversation back to Monday night. "Did anyone see you or talk to you?"

Christina thought for a minute. "Actually, yes, Martin was in the hallway."

"Martin the bartender?" The question flew out of Cat's mouth before she could stop herself. The look on her uncle's face told her she'd made a mistake. This wasn't her investigation; it was his. She looked down at the table trying to be quiet before he kicked her out of her own kitchen.

"Yeah. He was so nice to me. He took me back to the bar area, bought me a cup of coffee, and then introduced me to the guys who drove me home. I was a complete wreck." She looked at Uncle Pete. "What? You can ask him if you want."

"Actually, I did a couple days ago. He never said anything about running into you in the hallway. And in your original statement, you failed to mention even seeing Martin." Cat knew Uncle Pete was looking for a reaction to his statement. How many times had he told her it wasn't what the people said during the interview, it was what they left out? "So who's lying, him or you?"

"Martin is. Or maybe he just forgot. Talk to him again. He'll tell you." Christina took the cup of hot cocoa Shauna had given her and wrapped her hands around the outside like she was trying to warm her fingers. "I guess I didn't think it was important before. And you asked how I got home, so I told you."

"Well, that's the problem. Martin hasn't been to work for the last few days. Or school." Uncle Pete went to close his notebook, but then paused. "One more question: Tell me how you got Tommy Neil's blood on your clothes again?"

Christina went through the whole story about

Tommy opening the champagne bottle. "He thought it was romantic. I should have known then he was reckless. You're not taking me in to be questioned again, are you?"

Reckless wasn't the only word that described Tommy. Cocky, arrogant, self-serving—those all described the man Cat had begun to get a picture of the last few days.

"I'm not going to take you to the station. When do you leave for Seattle?" As Christina recited her flight time and number from her boarding pass, Uncle Pete wrote it down in his notebook.

Christina stood, taking the plate of cookies Shauna had given her. "If that's all, I want to get some words in before we leave for the library party. Six, right?"

"We'll drive over to the campus since Miss Applebome said it was cocktail attire. We'll meet in the lobby about 5:45." Cat wondered how festive the group would be once Uncle Pete determined the knife had come from her kitchen.

"Fine." Christina disappeared out the door.

"I've got to be going." Uncle Pete put on his coat. "I'll see you all at the library thing."

Cat followed him to the door. "Do you want me to make up a list of everyone who's been in the house for the last week? I mean, if the murder weapon is the missing knife, you will need to clear all of us too, right?"

"Probably. I'm hoping I'm wrong about the knife." He put the bagged block under his arm. "Make up the list. Better to be prepared than scrambling later. Bring it with you tonight."

Shauna and Cat stayed seated at the table as he left, neither one saying anything. Finally, Shauna stood to refill their coffee cups. "So do you still have time to help me with Project Donate? Or are you locking yourself upstairs to work?"

"I'm not sure I could even form a complete sentence. Let's finish the kitchen clear-out so at least I feel somewhat useful." Cat took the coffee and pulled a box over toward her. "There's one thing you need to put on Seth's to-do list, though."

"What's that?" Shauna opened a cabinet and started stacking everything on the counter top.

"We need to lock up the kitchen knives when a retreat is in session. Next time, I don't want the murder weapon to come from this house." Cat took an old cookie cookbook from the box. "This is mine. Seth's sister gave it to me as a gag gift one Christmas." She ran her hand over the cover, remembering the laughter that had circled the Christmas tree that year.

"See, memories. I knew you needed to go through the boxes." Shauna held up a plate. "We've been using this Fiesta ware dish set for the retreats. I guess I should have asked earlier if this was sentimental. I just focused on the set that had the most settings."

"I collected that during our marriage. It's not sentimental or valuable. I just loved the colors and the weight of the pieces." She paused and looked at Shauna. "If you hadn't started this project today, Uncle Pete wouldn't have the knife block."

"If it is where the murder weapon came from, it's a miracle he even saw the knife block. I had considered just stuffing all the boxes downstairs until this summer and having a yard sale. But I heard a call out for donations from the thrift store, so I changed my mind."

As they continued to sort through the kitchen stuff, Cat kept thinking about the missing kitchen knife.

"Are sandwiches okay for lunch?" Shauna looked at Cat. "Maybe I should cook something more substantial. Who knows what they'll serve tonight or how late we'll be there."

"Sandwiches are fine." Cat paused at the kitchen door. "I'm checking on Bella then heading upstairs to my office. Can you buzz me when it's ready?"

"I'll bring a tray upstairs," Shauna said.

When she opened the study door, books were all over the floor and every flat surface. Bella knelt in front of one, reading.

"Wow. You must be finding some interesting references." Cat wondered if leaving Bella alone in the room had been a mistake.

Bella turned, beaming. "This is exciting. I've found information in almost all the books, and now I'm cataloging the books with a brief note about what each covers. There's no way I'll get all of this read before the time my plane takes off on Sunday. But if I have the reference, I can order the book from my local library."

"Sounds like a plan. Just be careful with the books, please." Cat didn't want to explain so she stopped there and changed the subject.

"We'll be meeting at quarter to six to drive over to the library. You are coming, right?"

Bella sighed and looked around the room. "You said you keep this locked? So no one will be in here messing with my system?"

Cat wasn't sure what type of system Bella thought she had, but she nodded. Writers were a crazy bunch, and she didn't even want to ask how Bella had it sorted. "Sure. And if you want to come back early, I'll have Seth bring you home."

"Thank you. This really is the best retreat. I'm going to recommend it to all my friends." Bella returned to her note taking and Cat let herself out, shutting the door behind her.

Best retreat ever, despite the murders and pending charges against the attendees. She shook her head. Thank goodness, the next few months were already booked. Otherwise, she might just have a PR nightmare on her hands if the media got wind of the bad luck following Warm Springs Retreat. She headed up the stairs as one more motto hit her. *Killer retreat—if you live through the week.*

Chapter 13

A knock sounded on Cat's office door. She closed the game of solitaire she'd been playing, then turned her chair around. "Come in. You didn't have to bring lunch to me."

The door cracked open and Nelson poked his face in the small space. He scanned the room until his gaze landed on Cat. "Sorry, were you expecting someone else?"

"No. I mean, I thought you were Shauna. Come on in. What's going on?" Cat hadn't spent much time with the too-serious nonfiction writer. "I'm really glad you stopped in. I don't feel like we've had very many conversations."

Nelson entered the room and sat on the edge of the floral sofa. He moved the magazines on the coffee table in front of him into a neat pile. "That's okay. I really came to the retreat to write. All the other stuff has been fun, but it hasn't been my focus. I'm just a few chapters away from finishing my book on Ben Franklin."

"I'm so intrigued by history. My ex-husband

and I talked about writing a history of the house when we bought it, but that project never got off the ground." Cat moved over to the same chair where she'd sat during her conversation with her uncle. "Is your book contracted?"

Nelson nodded. "Deadline's next month, and then I have another one to write before the end of next year."

"That's an aggressive schedule." Cat admired the guy's chops. A nonfiction book a year was definitely full-time writing.

"I thought I could do it, but now I'm questioning myself. How do you keep a writing schedule? I'd like to come here and work once a month, but I didn't get that big of advance." He grinned and tapped the table with his finger. One, two, three times.

"Then set up a retreat at home. You can rent a cheap hotel room for a weekend. Get one of those where breakfast is part of the deal. Then just write from check-in to check-out. I bet if you booked mid-week, you'd even save more money." Cat was getting excited about the idea. "You could buy a video on the writing process and play it in hour break sessions, just like our educational sessions here. And then order in dinner and lunch."

"You think it would work?" He narrowed his eyes. "Or are you messing with me?"

"You wrote here, right?" She waited for him to nod. "Well, I might be giving away my secrets, but the magic is in the process, not the accommodations or the distance you travel from home.

Besides, since you're not wasting two days flying; that's all the more words you'll get done."

"And what if it doesn't work?" He leaned back on the sofa, his taut body relaxing for just a moment.

"Then you're out two days and the cost of a hotel room. You took a bigger risk coming here." She held her hands out. "Besides, you try it at home with no luck, you can come back here the month before your deadline. Maybe this place is writer magic. I've sure been happy with my production since I moved back."

Of course, she thought as she watched Nelson ponder the idea, she'd gone from working a full-time job to only writing and putting on the retreat. And she had Shauna for the hard stuff she didn't want to do, like meal prep and clean up.

Finally, he nodded, more to himself than to Cat. "I'll try it. But if it doesn't work, expect to see me in March."

"I think we have a couple openings still." Cat checked her watch. They still had hours before the reception. "Was there anything else?"

"One thing. Have you ever had a paranormal-energy reading done on this place?" He scanned the room. "I'm not picking up anything in this room, but the downstairs seems to have a presence."

"You think I have a ghost?" Cat almost laughed, but stopped herself as she realized he was serious. "Why would you say that?"

"I'm sensitive to the vibrations. It's something I've had to live with my entire life. The first floor reeks of a male presence. He doesn't seem angry, just maybe confused." Nelson shook his head. He leaned forward and tapped the table three times again. "You think I'm insane. I had better go before you won't let me come back for future retreats. Just think about what I said. Even having a reading can clean up the energy at times."

Cat sat looking out the window onto the snow-filled backyard for a long time after Nelson left. No, the problem wasn't that she didn't believe the man. The problem was she wondered if it could be true. Michael would be the likely candidate if the house *was* haunted. Trying to avenge his death? Or pass on information he didn't get to share?

There was one thing that she definitely knew now. Hosting these retreats brought in a diverse writer population. That was the good thing. The bad thing was some of them weren't playing with a full deck. She returned to her computer and opened her manuscript. She needed to write.

Lunch came twenty minutes later, as Cat was just finishing a chapter. She saved her work, then stood to take the tray from Shauna. "I told you to call me."

"I needed the exercise. Those stairs are making my butt look killer." She sank into the sofa. "How's the writing going?"

"I should be done next week. And if so, Seth and I may just take a few days to go skiing." Cat waited for the response.

"Out of town?" Shauna took one of the cookies off the plate and nibbled on the edge.

Cat moved the tray away from her. "Just up to

the Little Ski Hill. I won't go if you don't want to be alone here."

"Why wouldn't I want to be alone? You think I'm frightened easily?" Shauna tucked a leg up underneath her. "Besides, your uncle will show up for at least a breakfast or two."

"When I tell you what Nelson said, you may not want to be alone in the house." Cat went on to tell Shauna about the male presence on the first floor.

She considered Cat carefully. "You don't think it's Michael's ghost do you? I've never known you to fall for the folktales and things that go bump in the night."

Cat shrugged, not meeting her friend's gaze. "If it was true, it wouldn't be the weirdest thing I've learned in the last few months. Do I believe in voices from the other side? No, I don't. However, someone was trying to mess with my head last month by sending me his journal. And I know someone was in the attic."

"Someone. That doesn't narrow the suspect pool very much. You might as well believe in the darn ghost. By the way, who sent you the lovely flowers? I noticed there wasn't a note."

"I threw the note away. I should have dumped the flowers too." Cat closed her eyes. Seth hadn't been happy when she told him who had sent the bouquet. "Dante sent them. I'm getting the feeling he wants something that Michael left in the house."

"Like what? Most of his stuff is gone—well, except for the kitchen and his study." Shauna leaned forward. "You think Michael was working for Dante? Is that what he'd found out?"

"Maybe." Cat didn't know what she thought about Dante and Michael, and she didn't want Shauna to get involved in case it was dangerous.

"This retreat is getting more interesting as the time goes by. What's next?" Shauna put her hand up to stop Cat's answer. "You need to eat and then get into the shower to start getting ready for the reception. I'm wearing green, so you can have any other color. We don't want to look all matchy-matchy."

"Will Kevin be there?" Cat let the question hang.

Shauna stood and walked to the door. "He's one of the college's biggest supporters, so I'm sure he got an invite."

"Playing hard to get, are we?"

"Just because I don't call a man to see if he's going to be at the same party as I'm attending doesn't mean I'm playing hard to get. Besides, the phone lines work both ways; if he really wanted to know, he could have called me."

Cat laughed as Shauna flounced out of the room, her red hair bouncing off her shoulders. Cat knew her friend had more than just a crush on Kevin. She just hoped the guy wasn't playing with Shauna's heart.

Bella was the last to arrive in the lobby where they gathered to go to the library. Her dark hair, instead of being pulled back into the bun she'd worn every day that week, flowed around her shoulders, and she wore a tailored black pants suit with a matching pair of heels. As they started to leave the house, Cat stayed behind and fell into step with Bella. "You look great. I thought I was going to have to drag you out of Michael's study for this."

"Believe me, I wanted to stay here and work. I'm through about half of the books and citations, but this is really interesting stuff. Your ex-husband was a meticulous researcher. Was he working on his own book about Aspen Hills history?"

Cat locked the door behind them, pulling her coat closed with one hand. "Not that I knew about. But maybe he started something after we were divorced. I've been gone from the area for a few years." She climbed into the front passenger seat and turned to look at the group. Five retreat guests sat in the back, but no Shauna. She turned to Seth. "Where's Shauna?"

"Some guy came and picked her up in a Land Rover," Nelson said from the back. "The vehicle was sweet. I bet it ran him at least 50K."

"He brought her flowers too," Jennifer added. "She put them in the kitchen, but they are lovely. Some sort of orchid."

"Surprised the plant didn't freeze before he got in the door," Jeffrey muttered. "How cold is it anyway? Maybe going out in this isn't a smart idea?"

Cat saw Seth look up into the rearview mirror. "The reason we're taking the car is so you won't be cold. The temp is supposed to be in single digits tonight, but right now it's only twenty-two."

"What Mr. Howard is saying is don't try to walk home from the library event tonight. If you need to leave before it's over, just let us know and we'll ferry you home." She put her hand on Seth's leg. "You'll be happy to make several trips, right?"

He glanced over at her. "Ecstatic."

"This is so much fun," said Christina. "I mean how often do you get rewarded in life for doing the right thing?" The little that Cat could see of Christina's cocktail dress shimmered even in the low light of the vehicle's interior. When she took off the wool coat, she was going to be blinding. "I really need something like this. It's been a bad week."

No one said anything. Who could disagree?

"I don't mean because of the retreat," Christina added. "Heck, the retreat and writing is the only thing that's kept me sane the last few days." She leaned forward and patted Cat's shoulder. "I love your house, and it's been enlightening finding out so much about libraries. I might just have a librarian in my next book. Of course, he'll be the uptight new guy, and she'll be the complete opposite. Maybe even own a day care where the kids come in for storytime."

"Sounds like a fun idea," Jennifer said.

"I know, right? I love talking books with people. Maybe I do have the basics for my next book. *The Reluctant Librarian*?" Christina pulled out her phone and began tapping on the keys. "I'm sending myself an email about this before I forget everything."

"A good idea will stay with you." Bella sat in

the third seat in the far back. "It might evolve over time, but it will circle around in your head until you can't help but write it."

Before they could get into a discussion on writing down ideas versus letting your mind sift through the good and bad, Seth stopped the car in front of the closest library entrance to the parking lot. "I'll let you out here and then park. That way you guys don't have to walk through the snow in your pretty shoes."

Nelson jumped out and held the door open. He leaned into the cab when Cat opened her own door. "Just to be clear here, I don't wear pretty shoes."

Seth laughed. "Dude, they're polished. My boots have seen more use than those wingtips."

Nelson offered his arm to Cat. "May I escort you inside? That is, if you're not ashamed of walking with the pretty-shoe guy."

She grabbed her purse out of the SUV. Looking up at Seth, she smiled. "We'll see you inside."

Nelson closed the door, and they gingerly made their way to the entrance. The sidewalk had been shoveled and de-iced, but even so, there could be black-ice spots. Cat didn't want to end up in the emergency room tonight with a broken ankle and, worse, bruised pride.

As they walked upstairs to the main reading room, Cat gasped at the view. The room's ceiling had been covered with small white lights. The room looked more like it was out of some fantasy book than in the college library she'd thought she knew by heart. The college string quartet played baroque music in one corner, and a large table of food had been set up in another. Small, round cocktail tables covered with blinding white linens and a pillar candle filled the room. The burning candles gave a festive, yet other worldly, vibe to the room. Nelson walked her to what looked like the only empty table left, then turned. "May I get you a drink?"

"White wine, if they have it. Otherwise, I'll take a beer." She scanned the crowded room after Nelson left. She waved to a few people she knew, but there was no Shauna and Kevin. Maybe they had to make a stop before they arrived. Or maybe they were making out like teenagers in the parking lot.

Nelson dropped off her wine and then went to look for the rest of the group. Cat took a sip and relaxed, people watching. Someone touched her arm, and she turned, expecting to see Seth. Instead, Dante Cornelio stood in front of her in a tuxedo that screamed expensive. The fabric shimmered tastefully in the dim light. "I hear your group is the reason for the celebration. How proud of them you must be for finding the lost book."

"I'm not sure the book was just lost." She saw Jennifer walk by and when she got behind Dante, the girl made a silent *wow* in Cat's direction. She smiled and turned her attention back to Dante. "You really should mingle. Looking like that, you could have your choice of the women here."

"Maybe I like the choice I already made."

Cat's mouth went dry as she considered his comment. She wasn't sure if her sudden uncomfortableness was from his blatant attention or the fact her uncle had made it clear Dante was probably one bad decision from being on the board for America's Most Wanted. She wasn't a choice because she was dating Seth. The guy had to know that if he'd been in town more than a day and had any plug into the gossip chain.

He laughed. "I can see I flummoxed you. Believe me, I am not hitting on you. If I was, the man coming up behind you may just have to defend your honor, and I'm not into duels."

Cat looked over her shoulder and saw Seth approaching with two beers.

"I don't think Seth would fight for me over a conversation." Cat turned back and realized Dante was already gone. She scanned the room and finally found him across the room talking with Miss Applebome. "The man moves quickly."

Seth handed her a beer. "Not quickly enough because I saw him chatting you up. Is that the guy who bought you coffee this week?"

"The one with mob ties? Why yes, yes it is." Cat took a long pull of her drink. The beer tasted so much better than the wine had. She had to admit it to herself, she was a redneck—at least in her choice of alcohol. She looked pointedly at his bottle. "Hey wait, aren't you the designated driver?"

He turned the label around. "It's Colorado Basin Root Beer. The non-alcoholic kind. Don't worry, I've got you covered. Especially since I hear we're a go for next week's ski trip."

"Shauna really needs to keep her mouth shut." Cat scanned the room again. "Where is she? They should have already been here."

Seth shifted from one foot to the other.

Narrowing her eyes, she focused on him. "What do you know that you're not saying?"

"Fine. I saw the Land Rover in the parking lot. It looks like they're talking." Seth grinned. "Although, that's not what I'd do if I had you in a dark parking lot."

Cat took another drink. "I hope Shauna's not negotiating her signing bonus. I guess the guy is really pushing her to be his chef at the lodge."

"They didn't look like they were talking business." Seth shrugged when Cat stared at him. "What? A man knows when someone's getting told a line. And Shauna's getting a load full of crap from this guy. I hope she's just smart enough to ride it out and not hook up with this loser."

"A loser that owns half of the county," Cat reminded Seth.

He crooked his head in the direction of Dante. "Money's not everything."

"Are you asking if I'm interested?" Cat looked over his shoulder toward the food table. "If we're going to get into a fight, can we at least eat first? I'm starving."

He took her bottle and set it on the table next to his and the half-drunk glass of wine. "We're not getting into a fight. But food's a great idea."

They loaded up the small plates with all kinds of finger foods and then returned to the table. Shauna strolled over alone from the bar, a beer in her hand. Cat watched her friend sway just a bit. "Hey, where's Kevin?"

"He has to be at the Denver airport to catch a plane tonight. No wonder he brought flowers.

He knew he was going to be in trouble as soon as he told me." Shauna took a bacon-wrapped shrimp off Cat's plate. "Good, but this could use some barbeque sauce."

Seth handed over his plate. "Here, take this and I'll go get more. Anything specific?"

Shauna held up a mini crab cake. "More of these. And the shrimp. And pigs in a blanket. Heck, just get two of everything."

Cat waited for Seth to be out of earshot and then asked, "Are you sure you're okay? You know you're going to regret eating all that in about two hours."

"I won't. It will be tomorrow morning." Shauna sipped on her beer, then ate a jalapeño popper. "Sorry. Just when I think Kevin and I are in a good place, he pulls something like this."

"You said you didn't care if he even came to the reception." Cat grabbed the last shrimp on her plate when she saw Shauna eyeing it. "Remember?"

"I don't care if he comes. But then he shows up, makes a big production of us actually going out on a date, and then leaves me at the venue. I even have to find my own way home. What did he think? I could actually walk in these heels?" She put down the third crab cake. "I guess I just thought tonight might be different. Like he would sweep me off my feet. Women can still want the whole princess treatment, right?"

"I think we can want anything. It's what happens that we have to deal with." She put her hand over Shauna's. "Maybe Kevin's just too busy to date. Have you asked him if he even wants a relationship? If you're not on the same page, it could be better to cut it off now, before you get your heart broke."

"That's the come-to-Jesus meeting we're having when he gets back." Shauna tossed her hair back. "I'm going to lay down the law."

Seth appeared with a plate full of snacks. "Too soon for me to come back? I can go get a round of drinks."

"It's fine. I'm just crying in my beer over here." Shauna smiled at him. "You're a great guy, Seth Howard. Salt of the earth. I tell Cat that all the time."

"And you're full of clichés tonight." Cat pushed the plate over to her friend. "Are you sure that's your first beer?"

"My first *beer*, yes. Kevin had a bottle of Jack in the car. I might have had a couple of shots."

"And he's driving to Denver tonight?" Cat looked over at her uncle. Maybe she should report him.

"Of course not. Paul's driving. Kevin's assistant? He followed us in his car." Shauna rolled her eyes. "Paul is always there. I suspect he's even around on our dates. Of course, he drives his own car, but if something happens to the businesses, heaven forbid Kevin be more than a few steps away. Seriously, I need some time to think about this whole thing."

"So it's a good thing that he's out of town for a few days." The lights dimmed, and Miss Applebome stepped on a raised platform that suddenly had a spotlight shining on it. Cat turned Shauna toward the front. "Looks like we're getting ready to start. Did anyone bring a camera?"

Seth held out his phone. "My cell takes great pictures. I'll get several shots for you."

The group was called up, one by one, as Miss Applebome explained their role in getting back the priceless book. Seth snapped pictures as each person got a certificate and a hearty handshake from Acting English Department Dean, Professor Turner. At the end, as they stood behind him, Professor Turner started telling everyone about Hemingway and the treasure he was to the American literary field.

A woman walked up to Miss Applebome and whispered something in her ear. Even at this distance, Cat could tell something was wrong. She watched as the librarian closed her eyes, looking pained, whispered something to the woman, and then broke in front of Professor Turner. "Thank you for that interesting history lesson, but I'm afraid our time is up and the library is kicking us all out. Good night everyone, and thanks again to the brave souls who returned our missing book."

Chapter 14

"Well, that was interesting." Seth sat in the driver's seat with the car still running and looked at Cat. They'd brought everyone home and now it was just the two of them in the car.

She looked over at the doorway where Shauna was having trouble with the key. "Maybe I should go help."

Just then a cheer rose from the group, and they watched as the door opened and everyone disappeared inside.

"Looks like they have it covered." He took her hand in his. "Why don't we go have a couple beers at Bernie's and talk about this guy who's stalking you."

"Dante's not stalking me." She looked at the house one more time, then grinned. "It would be a shame to waste this dress. The reception kind of got cut short."

"Kind of? The printed invitations they gave out said there would be dancing and an open bar until ten. What do you think happened that

Miss Applebome cut it off at seven thirty?" Seth
put the SUV in drive and eased the car out onto
the street.

"Who knows. Maybe she found someone neck-
ing in the bathroom." Cat leaned her head back.
"Poor Shauna. She's really into this guy."

"The guy who always has something else to do
than spend time with her? He doesn't sound like
a good match for our girl. She deserves better,
whether or not the guy has money." Seth navi-
gated the empty streets carefully.

Cat wondered if his driving was due to the
fact he was in her car, or if he had always been
this way. In high school, Seth had always been the
one to drive and their friends had piled into his
Camaro on their trips around and out of town.
Memories flooded through her mind as they drove
through the night. When they reached Bernie's,
he shut off the engine and turned toward her.

"Are you sure you want to go in? I could just
take you home if you're tired." He lifted her
head with his finger. "You look tired."

"I am tired, but I don't want to go back, not
just yet. Running a retreat is exhausting. Everyone wants your opinion on things. And, truly,
that's all I'm giving them, one writer's opinion.
Yet they treat my advice like it's gold. A magic
entrance into the world of a published author.
Maybe this whole thing was a mistake," she said
as she reached for the door handle.

Seth stopped her and pulled her toward him.
"You don't believe that. The retreat does these
guys good. I'm sure, from where they are, the
advice you give them *is* gold. They take what

they need and leave the rest. I saw it in the last group, and I'm sure we'll see it tomorrow night in this one. You just have to trust the process. It's a great concept."

"You saw it in part of the group last time. Tom Cook died because of the retreat, and Sara dropped out of graduate school." Cat's eyes burned from holding back the tears.

"Larry Vargas did both of those things, not you or the retreat. And you know better." He kissed her gently on the lips. "Stop thinking about all the control you don't have over the real world and let's play some pool. I'll even let you win a game." Seth jumped out of the SUV and ran around the front to open her door. "My lady."

"Such a gentleman tonight. Maybe you are jealous of Dante." She took his arm as they walked into the dimly lit dive bar.

"I can't say I like him sniffing around you. I'm not convinced he doesn't have another motivation beside just being into you. I just can't figure out what it would be." He looked down at her shocked face. "Don't get me wrong, you are a prize worth fighting for, this just feels like there's something else."

They stood at the bar waiting as Cat processed Seth's comment.

"Uh-oh, I've seen that look on my wife's face too many times. What did you say to get yourself in the dog house today, Howard?" Bernie O'Malley threw a bar towel over his shoulder. "Darling, if you want I can kick him out right here and now."

"I didn't . . ." Seth paused. "What are you even

doing working tonight, old man? I thought Brit handled the night shifts."

"The girl has gone and lost her mind. She called me a few hours ago, told me to get my arse down here because she had something she needed to do tonight." He poured a shot of whisky and downed it. "Not like I didn't have plans for the evening. My college team is playing tonight. Now I have the television recording thing going. But you know someone will blab the final scores before I can get to watch it. What can I get the two of you to drink, if the lady is sure I don't have to kick you out?"

Seth ordered their drinks, and Cat turned and looked at the other patrons. For a Friday night, it was almost deserted. Four or five couples were crowded around small tables, a few single men sat at the bar in what looked to be their work clothes, and both the pool tables and dartboard area were completely empty. They might just get to hog Seth's favorite table for a few hours at least.

Cat aimed toward the pool table. "I'll go claim our table. Don't forget quarters. I think I have a few in this purse, but not more than one game."

"If you don't watch out, Howard, you two are going to be acting like an old married couple in no time." Bernie slapped the bottles on the bar.

As Cat walked away, she heard Seth's answer and smiled.

"All right by me."

Halfway through the third game, Seth didn't stand for his turn when she returned to the table. Cat finished off her beer. He still didn't move. "You know it's your turn, right?"

He rolled the cue stick in his hands. "I do. I'm just thinking about this Dante guy. You said he acted like he knew you?"

"Yeah. For one, he called me Catherine and, two, he mentioned Michael. Why would he use the same name Michael used for me? Michael never called me Cat, not even when we were dating. It became our little joke." She thought about tonight's encounter. Nothing really was said, except he insinuated he was interested in a relationship with her. But could it be something else? "What are you thinking?"

"I don't know. Could he have been mixed up with this thing that got Michael killed?" Seth finished off the soda he'd been nursing.

"Just because Uncle Pete thinks Michael's death was suspicious doesn't mean someone killed him. Suspicious doesn't mean murder." Cat pulled her coat closer, trying to convince herself that what she was saying was true. The bar had gotten colder, and she had goosebumps all up and down her arms. "We don't know anything really."

"Yet. We don't know anything yet." Seth stood and sat his cue down. "I'm going for another Coke. You ready?"

"Sure." Cat thought about what Seth had said. It kind of made sense. Maybe the extra job Michael took on was for one of the shell companies where the families laundered money. He would have been able to see quickly that the numbers didn't jive. The problem was a dead man's journal and a bunch of history books weren't proof Michael was murdered. It didn't even give her a lead to explore.

"Now you're thinking you're some sort of detective like Uncle Pete," she said as she watched Seth make his way back to the table. The smile fell off her face when the door opened and Dante Cornelio walked into the bar. He looked as out of place as a supermodel at a weight-loss meeting. She watched as he scanned the bar, then went directly to Bernie.

"Here's your beer." Seth handed her the bottle. "What's wrong?"

"Look who just came in to talk to Bernie. I guess your theory that Bernie is connected to the family was spot on the money." Cat watched the bar. Seth didn't look that way until he was seated and he turned his chair.

"Well, I'll be. Maybe I should go have a chat with the guy and let him know it's not polite to hit on my girl." Seth leaned back, studying the situation. "Except, it looks like Bernie's not very happy to see your new beau. Maybe we should let this play out."

"It's your turn to shoot. I'll watch while you play. We don't want either of them to get spooked." Cat rubbed Seth's dress shirt. "Have I told you lately that you clean up good?"

He chuckled then leaned down to kiss her. "First item of business: public display of affection— check. If he hadn't gotten the hint that you were off the market before, he will by the time he leaves here tonight."

"You're silly." Cat turned her chair so it looked

like she was observing the pool table but, in fact, she could see the bar where Bernie's face was getting redder by the minute. She heard the crack of the ball as it hit its target, then the thump into a pocket.

"Crap. You're solids, right?" Seth walked over and sank into his chair. "Seriously, I'm so not in the right mindset to be playing pool. Maybe I can't play sober."

The door opened again, and this time Brit walked in. Both men turned to watch her walk toward them. When she reached the bar, she pulled a packet out of her tote and shoved it in Dante's hands. From where Cat sat, it looked like he asked her a question, then he tucked the packet under his arm and left.

"So that was weird." Seth twirled his bottle between his hands. "What do you think Brit gave him?"

Cat shrugged. "Beats me—maybe something from Tommy? It wouldn't surprise me to find out Tommy worked with those guys even though his mother thought he was a saint." When they'd finished the game, she sank into her chair. "I'm beat. And I'm tired of trying to guess what everyone else is doing. I like it better when I'm clueless about the things going on around me."

"Come on, I'll take you home. When we reach the house, I'll need to come in for a while to let my truck warm up enough to scrape the windshield." He waited for her to button the coat and then put his arm around her to walk to the door. He waved a hand and called out, "Bye, Brit."

Cat saw the woman's face go white as soon as

194   *Lynn Cahoon*

she looked up and saw the two of them. No, it was her that was making Brit's alarms go off. She wondered what she had done.

She didn't speak until they got into the vehicle. Seth was warming it up, the defrosters going on max to try to remove the thin layer of ice that had accumulated while they were in the bar. "Did you see how she looked at me?"

"Like someone caught with their hand in the cookie jar? Yeah, I caught that." He grabbed the ice scraper off the floor. "What was that all about?"

"No clue."

The ride home was quiet, but as soon as they got into the kitchen with their coats off, her cell phone rang. She didn't get the *hello* out before she heard her uncle asking, "Where are you?"

"We just got home. Seth and I went to Bernie's, and you wouldn't believe who showed up." Cat shrugged out of her coat and hung it on the rack. Seth put her keys in the basket by the door and then went back outside to start his truck.

She went over to the stove and pulled out a pan for hot chocolate.

"Listen, I need to talk to you and your guests. Can you have everyone up by the time I get there?"

Cat looked at the small pan and switched it out for the larger one. "Sure, well, probably not Shauna. If I had to guess, the girl is going to

need to sleep off the bender she had tonight.
I'm not too happy with her Kevin right now."

The phone crackled and then Uncle Pete
came back. "Just get everyone in the living room.
I'll be there in ten."

When Seth came back in, she shook her head.
"Go shut it off."

A smile creeped on his lips. "Why, am I staying
over?"

"That depends on one thing." She stirred the
hot chocolate, mixing in chips to the milk she
was stirring.

"Do I have to beg?" He put his arms around
her.

"Won't help. The one thing? It's Uncle Pete.
He wants to question us all for some reason."
She tapped the spoon on the pan. "So go turn
off your engine, and when you come back in stir
the chocolate so it doesn't burn."

"Where are you going?" Seth headed to the
door. "And can I say, this is getting old. Doesn't
your uncle think anyone in town but us might
have some information about a crime? He's
always here."

"For the last couple months, trouble's been
camped out on my doorstep." Cat paused at
the other kitchen door. "I've got to round up
the troops. I should start charging extra for the
ultimate insider law enforcement packet. They
all can write a police procedural after the con-
tact they've had with my uncle this week."

Jennifer, Christina, and Jeffrey were still in the
living room talking about the night's adventures.
She asked them to stay put and then headed to

Michael's study. Bella was on the floor, reading a text.

"Can you move over to the living room? My uncle needs a word with each of us." Cat picked up a pile of books on the floor and set them on the coffee table.

Bella slowly moved to a hands-and-knees position, then just as slow, stood from there. "I need to walk around a bit anyway. I'm stiff as a board."

She left Bella in the lobby and went up to Nelson's room. When she knocked, there was no answer. She knocked again: still no answer. She grabbed her passkey and hoped he was in his room and dressed. She didn't need to see the guy in his birthday suit. "I'm coming in."

When she opened the door, she saw the room was empty, but Nelson's laptop sat on the bed. It looked like he'd just vanished. Then she heard a noise to her left.

Nelson poked his head out of the bathroom door. "Jeez, what are you doing in here?"

"I need to ask you to come downstairs. My uncle has some questions." She kept her gaze down just in case he was naked behind that door. "He should be arriving in five minutes. Can you please come downstairs?"

He walked out of the bathroom fully dressed. "Sure. Let me get my shoes on and I'll be down."

As she shut the door, she heard him mutter, "The one thing I don't get on this retreat is any privacy. Seriously, how am I expected to work?"

Smiling, she headed up to the third floor. She

knocked on Shauna's door and was surprised when her friend opened it. "Hey, how are you?"

Shauna shrugged and walked back over to her bed. She had a pair of sweats and a cami on and she was towel-drying her hair. "Embarrassed mostly. Sorry you and Seth had to be witness to my pity party. You sure you want to talk now?"

"I don't; Uncle Pete does." Cat leaned on the doorway. "He should be here any time now."

Shauna's hand flew to her mouth and she dropped her towel. "Tell me Kevin's okay!"

Cat held up her hands. "Hold on a minute, he didn't say anyone was hurt. Besides, he wants to see the retreat guests as well, so I'm thinking it's something about Tommy or the book they found for the library."

Shauna grabbed a hoodie and zipped it up over her cami. "Whatever it is, I'm not getting dressed up for this late night interrogation. I have to be up at five to start baking tomorrow. You know the last day is always special."

"Maybe he won't keep us long." Cat looked at her watch. "Besides, it's not really late."

Shauna stepped past her and headed to the stairs. "Says the woman who gets to sleep in tomorrow."

As they went down the stairs, Shauna looked back at her. "Maybe I should make some hot chocolate and set out cookies."

"The cookies are a good idea, but we're already on the hot chocolate. Seth should be stirring the pot right now."

Shauna's pace quickened. "If he lets it burn in

my new pots, I'm going to ban him from dinner for a month."

Instead of going into the living room, Shauna sped into the kitchen. Cat hung out in the doorway, waiting to see which door her uncle would use. Seth joined her and handed her a cup of the cocoa. "I've been banned from kitchen duty."

"If you'd messed up, she would have banned you from dinner. Which would you rather have?" Cat took the cup and sipped the warm chocolate mixed with whipped cream. "This is good. You didn't let it burn."

He stepped closer. "I do have skills."

Cat felt her body reacting to his heat, but then a rap came at the front door. Uncle Pete had arrived. She hurried to let him inside. "What in the world's going on?"

He took off his snow-covered boots and his coat and left them in the hallway. "Is everyone together?"

"I told them to go into the living room. I haven't counted yet. And Shauna's getting us treats in the kitchen." Cat followed him as he walked to the living room.

"Go get her. We don't need treats for this discussion." He turned right into the living room. As Cat pushed the door open to the kitchen, she heard him address the group. "Sorry to disturb all of you so late, but I needed to ask you a few questions about what you may have seen at the library tonight."

Cat found Shauna finishing the treat tray. "He's in a mood and says it's not a treat kind of discussion."

"Too late, I'm done." Shauna picked up the tray and headed toward the living room. "Did he say what it was about?"

"He said he had to talk to them about what happened tonight at the library." Cat snagged a cookie off the tray and followed her. "So the question is, what *did* happen tonight at the library?"

Chapter 15

Uncle Pete waited at the door to the living room. He shook his head as Shauna offered him a cookie. After Cat and Shauna found a place to sit, he looked around the room. "Sorry to bother you all this late at night, but there's been an incident at the library."

"Please tell me no one's hurt," Christina blurted out. "You all may be used to people dying around you, but I've had just about enough of the underbelly of human actions. I want to talk about snow angels and hot chocolate." She filled a cup from the carafe on the table.

"No one's hurt," Uncle Pete said.

Bella broke in. "That's a relief. I mean, one dead guy, one attempted kidnapping, one lost book . . ."

"Two. Two lost books." Uncle Pete interrupted. "The one you all found at dinner and a new one—this was a signed copy of a first-edition Hemingway. Much rarer. And it disappeared from the exhibit tonight during the reception."

Cat sank back into the couch. This was getting seriously out of hand. "We were all at the reception, so why are you here?"

"That's a good question." Uncle Pete looked around the room. "I have video of most of you arriving together promptly at six. Did anyone leave the conference room alone after you arrived?"

Jeffrey nodded. "I went to the restroom, but I didn't leave the floor."

The others shook their heads. All except Christina. Uncle Pete focused on her. "Miss Powers?"

"This is going to look bad. But I swear it's the truth." Christina looked around at the group. "I went to the restroom too, but there was a long line for the woman's facility and I knew that each floor had a restroom at the same place by the stairs, so I went down a flight."

"The floor where the collection is stored," Bella whispered. "Girl, you know how to put yourself in the wrong place at the wrong time."

Christina glared at her. "I didn't do anything. I peed, washed my hands, then went back up to the party."

"Were there lights on?" Now Uncle Pete was writing in his notebook again. "What time was this?"

"Just before the presentation. I could see they were getting ready, so that's another reason why I didn't want to wait in line." Christina paused, seeming to imagine the scene in her head. "The bathroom lights were off, but when I opened the door, the sensor saw me. But the stairwell and the rest of the area was fully lit. I didn't think anything of it except for they had the bathrooms on a different sensor. But that's not true, is it? You think that's when it was taken? Oh my God. Oh my God." Christina repeated the phrase, over and over. "I could have been killed or taken again."

Cat rushed to Christina's side when the girl started hyperventilating. "Just breathe."

"You weren't taken the first time," Jeffrey reminded her.

"All I want is a quiet life with a picket fence and a happy-ever-after. Why am I constantly being thrown into these things?" Christina started crying and Shauna found a box of tissues.

"Look, the rest of you can go unless you saw something that looked unusual or out of place tonight." Uncle Pete studied each person for a reaction. When he was satisfied with the lack of any nonverbal clues, he blew out a breath. "Miss Powers, let's go over what happened one more time. Do you think you can do that for me?"

As the group left the room, Uncle Pete moved to sit by Christina and Shauna. Cat and Seth huddled in the corner, where they could see the guests taking the staircase to their rooms. Seth took a cookie off the table. "Well, it's never boring around here."

"I would like some boring. Or at least to get through one retreat without a dead body or a stolen treasure. That doesn't seem to be that big of a wish, is it?" Cat looked at her friends. All she wanted to do was sink into Seth's arms and cry. She shook away the feeling. She knew she was tired. The problem was being tired always made things seem worse than they truly were. Sure, things were bad, but she'd gotten through worse.

Christina stood and bolted to the staircase, her hair flying behind her.

Cat, Seth and Shauna joined Uncle Pete on the couch. Cat noticed her uncle looked as tired as she felt. "So another book was taken? You don't think it's a prank like last time?"

"I'm not sure last time was a prank." He put his notebook away. "I don't think Miss Powers had anything to do with the theft, but she's darn lucky she didn't get hurt when she wandered into the crime scene. Whoever took it had to be holding their breath while she used the restroom and returned to the party."

"What about the library surveillance video? That has to show who was there." Seth leaned forward with his forearms on his thighs. "I worked on that project a few years ago. The main contractor was out of Denver, so he needed someone local to do the grunt work."

Uncle Pete considered Seth. "I knew about the surveillance system, but apparently so did the thief: All the cameras on the floor and any exits were turned off."

"I was with your niece the entire time." Seth turned his gaze on Cat. "You are going to tell him this, right?"

"Once you parked the car, you were with me for the rest of the time." Cat thought about the people milling around the room. "What about Dante? Did he leave the room?"

Uncle Pete shook his head. "The party feed shows him talking to you, then leaving when

Seth showed up. I don't know what kind of game the three of you are playing, but he didn't leave the room until Miss Applebome closed out the evening."

"I came in late, but I was with Kevin the entire time in the parking lot." Shauna arranged the plate on the cookie tray.

"We have your actions taped. Even when you and that man of yours were doing shots in the parking lot. By the way, that's against school policy to drink in the parking lot. You should have come into the party; the library had an open bar."

"I think Kevin had other plans." Shauna stood. "So, if we're done here, I'll take this to the kitchen. Then I'm going to my room. I'm beat."

"I'm heading home too." Uncle Pete covered a yawn. "Miss Applebome will be calling first thing tomorrow for an update on the missing book. That woman is relentless and not afraid to tell me how to do my job."

"I'll start up the truck, then hang out in the kitchen until it defrosts." Seth kissed Cat on the cheek. "You go on upstairs. I'll use my key on the deadbolt."

Cat followed her uncle to the front door. "You really didn't think any of the guests were part of this heist at the library, did you?"

"I didn't, but Miss Applebome did. She wanted to make sure I talked to them before they start disappearing on Sunday." He put his boots on and then ran both hands over his head. "What about you? Do you think any of your guests might be involved? You tend to have a good gut sense about these things."

"I know Christina didn't have a thing to do with this. That girl is running on her last nerve. I'm afraid it will only get worse when she gets home and returns to Stalker Land." Cat tried to hide a yawn behind her hand. "The others? Who knows. None of them look like practiced thieves."

"Well, I'll let you get some sleep. I'd hoped this book nonsense had been put to bed. You don't think someone's just getting a kick out of reading something a famous guy had signed, do you?"

Cat pondered the question. "I'm thinking it's going to be a collector. But I don't know any one who would give back a book once they stole it for their bookshelf. That part doesn't make any sense at all."

"Unless he already had the book he returned in his collection. Why do people do anything?" Uncle Pete kissed her on the top of her head. "No use thinking about it tonight. Time to grab some z's. I'm sure this will make more sense in the morning."

Cat doubted that, but she locked up after her uncle then checked the kitchen. It was already dark. Shauna upstairs and Seth in his truck. Cat went over to the doorway and checked the lock, just in case.

When she started to head upstairs, a light shown down the hallway from Michael's office. Bella must have left it on when she came to the living room to talk to Uncle Pete. Cat opened the door and stepped back when she saw someone at

Michael's desk. When her heart stopped racing and her vision cleared, she realized Bella was furiously scribbling into a notebook, a text open in front of her.

Just like Michael used to do.

Bella looked up, confusion at the interruption filling her face. When she saw it was Cat, she smiled. "Sorry, burning some midnight oil here. This stuff is a gold mine. I already checked your December retreat to see if I could just come back next month. But it's full. You are popular."

"If I had another room ready, I'd be glad to open up another spot. Maybe January?" Cat leaned against the doorway, not wanting to enter the room. The feel of Michael still had such power in this room. Maybe it was because she was tired, or maybe she was reacting to Bella working in the study. If she was going to open it to guests, she probably would have to redecorate.

"I hope to be editing by then." Bella rolled her shoulders. "I should have most of what I need before I leave on Sunday. I feel like I won the lottery on the subject, though."

Cat wished her a good night and, as she left the floor, wondered if she would find the woman asleep on the desk in the morning. Michael had claimed that chair was as comfortable as the bed. Cat couldn't see it. Memories of her marriage were coming faster these days. She wondered if it was because she was opening his part of the house up for use, or maybe because she herself was opening up her heart again.

She started the last flight of stairs, a layer of

fatigue settling in on her. No matter what, she wouldn't worry tonight. She was beat.

Waking the next morning, Cat thought, *one more day*. Not the most charitable thought and she hated wishing away time, but it had been a long week. She only had to play hostess for one more day. Then the group would start to disappear to the airport, and by dinnertime, she and Shauna would be alone in the house again. They hadn't even started to talk about plans for Thanksgiving, but Cat assumed they would host a dinner at the end of the month for Uncle Pete, Seth, and maybe Kevin. If he was even in town. Or out of the doghouse by then. She'd mention it to Shauna on Sunday once the retreat guests had left.

Thinking about the holidays got her planning how she wanted to decorate the living room, with its large mantel. The lobby would host the tree. And she'd put a flameless candle in all of the guest room windows. Feeling more cheerful than she had in days, she dressed and headed downstairs to the kitchen for coffee. Time for writing, but first, she had to fuel her caffeine habit.

Before going into the kitchen, she checked Michael's study. No Bella. She crossed over to the desk and looked at the notebook with what appeared to be a genealogy chart. Dante's name was highlighted with a few generations filled in, but she saw the question marks on the next generation's names. Apparently, Bella was digging deep into the family connection to the college. Even though it was interesting, Cat thought Bella was going down the research rabbit hole. Sometimes, fiction needs less reality.

Cat shut the door but left it unlocked so Bella could continue her work once she awoke. She would pop in when she heard the woman come downstairs and impart her unsolicited wisdom.

As Cat stepped into the kitchen, Shauna called out a cheery good morning. If Cat had drunk half of what her friend had the night before, she'd be in bed all day. "Just here for coffee. How are you doing?"

"If you mean, am I hung over? No. I don't seem to get sick from drinking. My metabolism burns off all the alcohol. I was 90 percent sober by the time your uncle left." Shauna was mixing together something in a large bowl.

"I'll let you get back to the baking, then." Cat filled her cup and a carafe. "I'm upstairs working until the dinner tonight. If someone needs to talk to me, send them up."

"Will do." Shauna turned up the volume on the radio and started swaying to the beat. "I love this song."

When Cat reached the second floor, she heard a scuffling sound. Peering down the hall, she saw Jeffrey lean down and stuff something under one of the room doors. She took another step and he scurried back to his room, not even looking to see who had watched him. Counting off the doors, she realized he'd been at Christina's door. Had the poet taken a chance to reveal his feelings for the woman before the retreat was over? Or was something else going on?

Christina needed some good in her life, but was Jeffrey what she needed? The guy was intense.

As she thought about the idea, a scene for the book filled her mind and her fingers itched to get into her office and writing. Maybe having retreats wasn't going to kill her writing energy as much as she'd thought. Being around other people could make her own writing more realistic and emotional.

A knock on the door pulled her out of Kori's world. She glanced at the clock—almost eleven. "Come in," she called as she saved her work for the day.

Bella peeked in around the door. "Sorry to bother you, but—Wow, this is a great office. Look at your view." She walked inside and paused at the window looking out over Warm Springs.

"I've always loved this office. I can't say it makes the words fly faster, but it certainly doesn't suck." Cat leaned back in her chair and watched her guest. "I was planning on coming to talk to you anyway. Are you just stretching your legs? I was glad to see you at least got a few hours' sleep last night."

"Well, technically, it was this morning." Bella turned back and watched Cat. "I do have one question I need to ask about your ex-husband."

"Shoot." Cat wondered if it would be the

standard question about Michael: How did you let this smart, funny, organized guy go?

"He writes about putting copies of articles in 'the blue folder.' Do you have any idea where that could be?" Bella had dark circles under her eyes, and Cat figured she must have gotten only a few hours' sleep. She could sleep on the plane, Cat guessed, but she hated seeing anyone dragging this badly.

"Really, I don't. I have several boxes they brought over from the college, but he didn't keep much in his home office." Cat thought about the hidden office and boxes of files she'd taken from the attic last month. Had any of those been blue?

"Well, it was worth a shot. I thought maybe he might have a list of some additional resources he used." She stretched her arms over her head. "A couple more hours, then I'm taking a nap before we go out tonight. My plane leaves early so, if it's okay, I'll spend most of tonight after the dinner in the study."

"Whatever you want. I can set a wake-up call for you tomorrow. Ask Shauna for some snacks to get you through the session. Sugar tends to keep me running long after my normal bedtime. Are you starting to write?" Cat asked, hoping she wouldn't have to do the lecture.

"The book's written. All I have to do is go back and make sure my family theory is valid. I thought I told you that." Bella smiled as she said, "You must have thought I'd be falling into the research twilight zone."

Cat watched as Bella made her way out of the office. At the door, Bella paused and turned to face Cat.

"You told me to leave the note papers in the books?"

Cat nodded. Next week, either before or after her couple days at the ski lodge, she was planning on going through the rest of the books in his office. It was time to put that part of her life away. "Please."

Cat mimicked Bella's shoulder roll and stood to follow her. When she reached Michael's office, Bella wasn't there. She stood at the desk, wondering what she had found. When she turned around, Shauna was watching her. "Do you know where Bella is?"

"She just left for the coffee shop. She said she wanted to buy a bag of beans to take home with her." Shauna leaned against the doorway. "Why?"

Cat laughed, but the sound was tinny, even to her. "She said she found some notes I wanted to look at. I'll just talk to her later." She left the room and headed back upstairs to her office and to her computer. She might be able to finish this chapter if she forgot about her real-life craziness and just focused on Kori and the gang.

The fictional world without a missing blue folder.

Chapter 16

Thirty minutes later, Cat gave up on the writing. Instead of writing, she'd been staring out toward the street. For some reason, the idea of a walk nagged at her. She hadn't been to the Written Word, Aspen Hills' one-and-only bookstore, since she'd moved home. She'd meant to stop in several times. But then the retreat had started, and she'd fallen into the trap of being too busy to do the work that wasn't in front of her face. She grabbed a copy of her latest release and a business card and headed downstairs. At least by spending some time marketing her series, she could pretend this visit was more than just the much-needed break from writing and the retreat guests.

She met Shauna on the stairs. "I was just coming up to get you. Do you want me to make you some lunch?"

Cat shook her head. "I'll grab something when I get back. I'm going for a walk into town."

"What for? You going to the library? I think

that's where everyone but Bella is right now. She's back to being holed up in Michael's study. Having her work in there isn't bothering you, is it?" Shauna followed Cat down the last few stairs.

"Visiting the bookstore to talk to the owner and leaving one of my books. I hope that, since I'm a local author, she'll stock the series. I guess I could sell copies here, but that feels a little commercial. Besides, I like shipping her some of our retreat business." Cat didn't want to talk to Shauna about her feelings right now. And she didn't want to find out what Bella had found. Instead, she grabbed her coat and the hat her mother had crocheted and sent last Christmas, even though then Cat had still been in California and had no need for the warm topping.

"See if they have that new Emeril cookbook. I'm thinking we might just need to spice up some of our breakfast menus for the winter."

Cat nodded, not really listening. She needed to get out of the house and clear her mind of all the thoughts that were circling. Bella, Michael's books, Christina, the list was long.

The chill of the winter's day bit her cheeks and made her wrap her scarf a little tighter. She loved the Colorado weather. Cold, snowy, and bright, the air even smelled cleaner in the winter than it did during the summer. She was briskly strolling toward town and turning left out of the front walkway when she saw Mrs. Rice standing by her front gate talking to the postal carrier. One obstacle avoided. How many more would she encounter before arriving at her destination? She felt like she was in a damn video game.

By the time she'd made it to the bookstore, she was cold and grumpy. Walking had not been a good escape from writing. She hoped the store would be slow so she would get a chance to actually talk to the owner. Tammy Jones was standing at the counter, looking at a book, as the bell rang over the door.

"I can't believe you are really here. I love your books. When Seth told me you were opening that retreat, I'd hoped to meet you." Tammy came around the counter and took Cat's hand in a vigorous shake. "Of course, if I'd thought about it, I should have come and visited you. But you know how crazy running a business can be. That is so not an excuse."

"No, I'm the one who should be apologizing. And I understand how crazy it can be." The woman's over-the-top energy made Cat smile and put her at ease. She pulled out the book she'd brought. "I take it you're already aware of what I write."

Tammy squealed and picked up the book. "I'd love it if you signed the copies we have in stock. And if you ever want to do a signing here, please let me know. I'd love to have you." The door's bell rang as a new customer entered. Tammy held up a hand toward the front of the store, but then turned to the back office. "Hold on a second, I'll be right back."

Cat looked at the display of Colorado-themed bookmarks and picked out several to give to the retreat guests. Her mood was improving by the second. She always felt better just by wandering through a bookstore. The shelves of books calmed her. Like everything in the world could be put on hold until she'd finished reading the story.

"Those are lovely." Dante stood behind her, looking at the bookmarks Cat had laid out.

She spun toward him, her hand on her chest. "Mr. Cornelio, you scared me. I hope you're not following me. I'd hate to have to let my uncle, the police chief, know I'm feeling less than safe."

"You don't seem like the type who would hide behind a relative." He held up his hands. "I'm not here to see you. Actually, Miss Jones called me earlier and told me a book I'd been asking about had come in. I'm afraid I have a horrible collection habit. I can't seem to pass a bookstore without buying something."

"I'm the same way." Cat let her guard drop just a bit. She needed to know why Dante was involved in her past, but this meeting might be just a coincidence. She decided to push the envelope. "So did Michael work for you? I know he was doing some analysis for a company before the divorce."

"Work for me? Why would you ask me a question like that?" Dante turned and scanned the closest rack of books. "Anyway, I did want to talk to you. So this meeting is kind of serendipitous. I hear you've been having some issues at the house. Possible break-ins?"

"Where did you hear that?" Cat didn't say anything more. Let him tell her what he knew rather than her blurting out everything. Who could he have been talking to? The only people who knew were people she trusted, like Uncle Pete, Shauna, and Seth.

"I hate to admit it, but I'm afraid my nephew had been playing pranks on you before I arrived. He knew your husband . . ."

"Ex-husband," Cat interrupted.

"Sorry, ex-husband." One of Dante's eyebrows raised just a tad. "Anyway, like I said, the boy played a few pranks."

"Like?"

"The old phone game of call and hang up. I hope he didn't scare you." Dante leaned on the counter, watching her reaction. "I gave him a suitable punishment as soon as I found out about the problem."

Did this explain the noises she'd heard in the attic, the phone calls, and the white carnation? The fact she'd been scared out of her wits as soon as she moved back to town wasn't just a prank. Or was Dante's nephew actually looking for something in the house? Something Michael had hidden that she hadn't found or had found, but didn't understand the significance of the item? Before she could ask what else the boy had done, Tammy Jones returned with a stack of Cat's books.

"Go ahead and sign all of these. I'm not returning any of them. In fact, we'll have a local-author mini shelf right here by the cash register." Tammy set the books on the table and then looked up, startling when she saw Dante. "I didn't know you were here. Sorry, I should have greeted you. Hold on, I have your book right here in the back."

She disappeared as Cat took one of the books and signed the title page.

"You're famous." Dante's lips curved into a smile.

"Just a little local celebrity." She held up the book. "I'm an author. I thought I told you that."

He shrugged. "Possibly. But seeing Miss Jones so excited to meet you, that must be pretty exciting."

"You're teasing me." Cat kept her head down and kept signing. She just needed to get this done, pay for her bookmarks, then she'd be away from Dante. When was the guy leaving town, anyway?

"I do like seeing the blush in your cheek." He straightened a pile of paper bookmarks on the counter. "I hope your uncle isn't looking at any of your guests for the latest library incident. I can't imagine that would be good for your business."

"I didn't realize many people knew about the second book being taken." Cat narrowed her eyes and watched him.

"Have you forgotten I was at the library last night?" He put a hand over his heart. "I'm wounded. And I thought I'd made such a good impression on you."

Logically, she knew he was trouble but her body tended to ignore that part every time she saw him. Cat realized she had seen him somewhere else last night too. "Wait, you were also at Bernie's last night talking to Brit. What was that about?"

"Let's just say Brit did a favor for me. The girl is devoted to her father." He stood straight as

Tammy came back with a bag. "Put that on my account, please. And thank you for your diligence in finding this book."

As he walked out, Tammy sighed. "I know it's crazy, but I can't help but think he'd be a perfect hero in a romance novel. Maybe a duke." She looked up at Cat. "He's a hottie, right? It's not just me."

"It's not just you." Cat thought about the barista's comments about Dante. The man made all the girls swoon. She put the pen down on the counter and moved the bookmarks toward her. "Here are the books. And I'd like to buy these. They'll make perfect going away gifts to the retreat guests."

As Tammy rang up her purchase, Cat thought about Dante's nephew. She was glad they'd changed the locks on the house but if anything else weird happened, she'd go right to Uncle Pete. She was done with the so called pranks.

When she left the shop, all ideas of doing anything but head straight home left her head. The wind had picked up, and it looked like a new storm was coming into town. She should get home before the snow started, but wouldn't if she detoured and went to see her uncle. She dialed his cell. Busy. She left a message and headed back to the house to get ready for the dinner. Thank God they'd asked Seth to drive the guests to the dinner. She would hate to have to navigate the icy roads tonight.

When she came in through the kitchen door, Shauna hurried over to her. "You look frozen. I can't believe you went out in this."

Cat shook off her coat and put on the jacket she kept in the kitchen. "It was sunny when I left."

"Sit down and eat some soup." Shauna moved to the stove. "Then we both need to get ready for tonight."

Cat hurried to the table. As Shauna set the bowl in front of her, Cat grabbed her arm. "Sit down with me. I've got to tell you something." She went through the conversation with Dante and included seeing him at both the library event and the bar afterward. Finally, after she'd laid out the incidents, Cat asked Shauna the one question that had been nagging at her since leaving the bookstore. "You don't think Dante took the book, do you?"

Shauna tapped a finger on her lips. "Eat while I think this through. You think because Dante was at the bar, the library, and the bookstore, that's evidence that he stole the second book? Was he even in town for the first theft? And why would he steal a book?"

Cat pointed her spoon for emphasis. "Because he's a collector, that's why."

"Then why would he give the book back? Wouldn't a collection with two Hemingway's be more valuable than a collection with just one?" Shauna grabbed her notebook off the side of the table. "Who did you say his nephew was?"

"He didn't tell me," Cat admitted. With a bowl of soup in her stomach to warm her body, the idea sounded more and more farfetched.

"But he basically admitted the kid was responsible for the weird hang-up calls you got last month." Shauna wrote a note on the paper.

"Maybe your uncle can check out any kid with the same last name or with Dante listed as a next of kin. If he's here visiting, the college should know who he said he was seeing."

"I'd feel stupid telling Uncle Pete this. One, he didn't believe me when I told him the first time someone was in the house and making prank calls. I think he even said I was lost in my fantasy worlds." Cat took the bowl to the sink and rinsed it. "So why would he believe me now?"

"You and I both know he was trying to hide how Michael died back then." Shauna stared at the page. "Bugger. What if this nephew was the one who actually killed Michael?"

"Or he could have been the contract hit man who tried to kidnap Christina. Or anyone within a ten-mile radius." She paused at the sink. "I'm going upstairs to shower. I promise I'll talk to Uncle Pete tomorrow after we get everyone out of the house."

Seth came through the front door with another man before she got up one stair.

"Hey, Cat, this is Hank, the heating and cooling guy from Denver? He's here to do an estimate for us finally." Seth turned toward Cat. "Hank, this is Catherine Latimer. She owns the place and likes being called *Cat* for some strange reason I could never decipher."

Hank held out his hand for a handshake. "Sorry it's taken me so long to get back. Apparently, your house is under consideration for historic preservation. Believe me, you don't want that headache label placed on you. It took me a month just to get permission to give you a quote." He smiled. "Although I'm pretty sure they didn't have systems anywhere as nice in the old days as the one I'm going to sell you. And you already have a security monitor."

"Pleased to meet you." She looked upstairs. "I'm invested in getting that attic section livable— and not just on soft spring mornings or Indian summer days."

"Seth said you wanted to set up a library. I think that's a great idea. Too many homes I work on installing windows don't have even one book in the house. Unless you count the cookbook on display in the kitchen that—from the way it looks—I don't think anyone used for years, if not ever." He looked at Seth. "My man here tells me you're an author? I'm going to go buy your books for my daughter. You think a twelve-year-old would like them?"

"I think she'd love them. Thank you." She smiled at the guy. "I'm afraid we make up for a lot of homes without books. We have books all over."

Her gaze automatically drifted to the hallway to Michael's study. Turning her head back, she saw Seth watching her.

"We better get upstairs if we're going to get this done before six." Seth slapped Hank on the back. "I'm also the chauffeur around here when retreats are in session."

"Sweet gig." Hank tipped his baseball hat toward Cat. "Nice to finally meet you. This guy talks about you all the time."

The men headed toward the cellar door to

inspect the current heating unit. Cat heard Shauna from the kitchen doorway. "He seems nice."

"You could have come out from behind the doorway and actually met him," Cat pointed out.

"I wasn't eavesdropping. I just came to see who was out here. I heard Seth's voice, but didn't know who the other guy was." Shauna smiled.

"That's a bad habit you know." Cat started up the stairs. "You may not like everything you hear."

"That's what my grandmother said when she caught me the first time. But ever since I was five, I've never regretted knowing what I heard." Shauna paused at the bottom of the stairs looking up toward Cat. "Besides, you won't tell me what's going on between you and Seth, so I have to figure it out by other means."

"Maybe it's none of your business."

Cat heard Shauna's laughter all the way up to the third-floor landing. When she opened the door to her room, all she wanted was to take a long shower and wash all her doubts and worries down the drain.

Her plan worked for a little while after she'd gotten out of the shower she'd felt lighter. Then her phone rang. Glancing at the display, she turned down the television she'd been kind of watching for the last hour. "Hey, what's going on?"

"Hey, yourself," said Uncle Pete. "I saw you called earlier. Is this a good time to talk?" Her uncle sounded worn out on the phone.

Cat swung her legs over the side of the bed. "Of course." She glanced at the clock. She still had two hours before she even had to think about getting ready. Three if she threw on a favorite dress, boots, and makeup.

"I just wanted to let you know that I may not make dinner tomorrow night. I know you wanted to have a relaxing meal, but with this new book disappearing, I'm up to my waist in alligators."

"Not in Colorado, you're not. Maybe black bears." She looked at herself in the mirror. She looked as drained as Uncle Pete sounded. And her hair was sticking up on one side. So much for showering early for the event. Now she looked like she'd been sleeping the day away.

"Whatever fierce predator you'd like to use. I keep forgetting my niece was an English professor." He chuckled into the phone. "At least my missing lodge bartender showed back up this morning. Apparently, he'd been visiting family and forgot to tell his boss. Of course, he also forgot to tell his boss about his little drug dealing arrest back in Boston. I swear, sometimes I think working in a big town would be so much easier."

"Wait, is that Martin? We met him last Sunday. The kid seemed on top of everything. He was a great salesman." Cat thought about the little extras like how he proposed adding alcohol to Seth's coffee or the condo suggestion.

"I really can't say, but the lodge only has two bartenders, and one is the sixty-year-old sister of the manager of the place." He paused. "So you do the math."

"So it is Martin." Cat thought about her meeting with Dante this morning. "Stupid question, but is his last name Cornelio?"

"You mean like Dante?" Her uncle paused. "No, but he still might be related. Why are you asking?"

"I ran into Dante again this morning." Cat paused as she heard Uncle Pete's long, drawn-out sigh. Before he could say anything, she went on. "Just let me talk, then you can lecture me about staying away from the bad guys, even though this was so not my fault." She told him what Dante had said about his nephew trying to scare her a few months ago and that he'd had a long talk with the kid and it wouldn't happen again. When she finished, her uncle didn't respond. "Are you still there?"

"I'm just trying to figure out what motive Dante's nephew would have to play these pranks on you, unless that's all it was. Maybe the kid was in Michael's classes and thought it would be funny to scare the widow?" Cat could hear Uncle Pete's pencil tapping on his desk.

"That's pretty creepy."

Uncle Pete cleared his throat before responding. "Yes, it is, but it may not be the worst thing a member of the Cornelio family has done recently."

Chapter 17

Uncle Pete's comment whirled in her head. Of course, he'd hung up after dropping that bombshell; some emergency at the college made him cut the conversation short. He promised to try to come for coffee tomorrow evening even if he couldn't make dinner. Cat took out a notebook and, from what she could remember, made a timeline of the prank calls that occurred during the last retreat. She'd thought maybe it had been one of the guests since it seemed to stop as soon as the retreat ended. Now she wondered if it had only stopped so it would look that way.

She pictured the smiling bartender and wondered why the kid would want to scare her. He'd said his major was in accounting, but had he taken any classes from Michael?

Cat heard the distant chimes of her grandfather clock downstairs. She had an hour before she would be hosting dinner. Looking in the mirror, she tried to push down the cowlick that had formed while she lay on her bed watching the home-decorating channel. The brothers in the show had been putting in crown molding, and Cat had been fascinated at how it made a room look more historical. None of the guest rooms had the treatment, and she had wondered what it would cost to install.

Now she realized she'd been trying to focus on anything else besides her talk with Dante. And she'd forgotten to mention when she talked to Uncle Pete that she'd seen Dante at the bar with Brit. She felt like she was whacking moles. If she got one to stay down, two others popped up to distract her.

She gave up and jumped into the shower to wash her hair a second time. Dressed and ready, she glanced at the notebook. This Michael stuff just kept coming up. The more she tried to sweep it under the rug, the more it kept showing up. At least now, with the help of Dante, Martin should be leaving her alone. If she could trust Dante. The man was like a bad penny, he kept just showing up at the oddest times. Who knew what kind of control he had over his nephew. The one thing that bothered her was how did he know Michael used to give her carnations? Or had it been a lucky guess?

She headed downstairs and practiced putting on a smile until it felt comfortable. Time to play retreat hostess.

Shauna pulled her aside. "Hey, I'm glad you're down early. I have something to show you."

Cat followed her over to the lobby desk. "What's going on?"

"I found it." Shauna held up a manila folder.

Cat took the folder from her grasp. "You found what?" She opened the folder and found a paper with Covington College printed at the top.

"The contract we were looking for. Along with agreeing to provide a professor for an hour each month, it also outlines the library privileges for our guests in exchange for including the college on our website and advertisements." She held her arms up in triumph. "Ta-da! The magic of paper files. I bet this got filed under the wrong year over at the school, which is why Professor Turner didn't find it. And I hear that the university filing department has been using interns to run the file room and has to evaluate the last two years because the system is such a mess."

Cat read through the contract. Not only did they have a one-year agreement, but the contract allowed for a five-year extension if the advertisements were published in venues with a national distribution. "Make sure you send the marketing department a copy of our *Writer's Magazine* ads. That reach isn't just national, it's international."

"I'll send it next Monday with a cc to Professor Turner asking who he's going to schedule for our December retreat." Shauna grinned. "At least one thing turned out good today."

"After this dinner, it will be two." Cat hugged her friend. "Thanks for handling this, I'd almost forgotten about Dean Turner's request."

"Again, it's what you pay me for, remember? We're in this together, no matter what." Shauna took the file and put it in the top drawer. Then she turned her head toward the stairs. "Well, I'll be . . ."

Cat turned to see what she was looking at and saw Nelson. He was in a black suit with a tie and looked like he could rival Dante in formal-dress competition. He smiled as he crossed the lobby. "Ladies. I hope I didn't keep you waiting."

"You're actually the first one here." Cat gave him a head-to-toe once over. "I have to say, you clean up good."

"Now you're just making me blush." Nelson fiddled with his pocket handkerchief. "I didn't want to embarrass you all at the retreat dinner."

"Well, you make me look like the help." Seth came through the kitchen door. He wore good dress slacks and a dress shirt but no jacket. He held his hand up for a high five with Nelson. "You are going to be on fire with the ladies tonight."

Cat didn't think it was possible, but Nelson's cheeks burned a bit redder after Seth's pronouncement.

Nelson dropped his head. "All I want is to look normal. Maybe I should go change?"

"Are you kidding? You look amazing." Cat took his arm and led him away from the stairs. She glanced at the clock. "Five more minutes and we'll start calling rooms. We have a reservation, people."

A flurry of sound echoed on the stairs. "We're here, we're here . . ." Bella called.

Bella, Jennifer, Christina, and Jeffrey pounded down the stairs. The women were in conservative cocktail dresses and Jeffrey wore a suit, like Nelson.

Seth moved closer to Cat. "Now I am officially underdressed. Do you want me to go change before we leave?"

"You're fine." She patted his blue dress shirt. "But maybe we can keep a jacket here in the coat closet just in case you feel uncomfortable next month."

"Sounds like a plan." He kissed her full on the mouth.

"Okay, love birds, we need to go. I'm starving." Bella chuckled and started to lead everyone out to the SUV.

Seth grabbed the door before Bella could reach for the handle. "Let me. Welcome to the closing ceremonies for the Warm Springs Writers' Retreat."

As the group filed out into the cold, Seth waited for Cat to lock up the house. "Maybe you can tell them the story of how you were a radio DJ?"

She rolled her eyes. "Maybe you should just shut up?"

He chuckled and held her arm as they went down the stairs to the walkway. "You're such a feisty one."

"And that's a surprise to you now? What, don't you remember high school at all? We were always fighting over something." Cat held his arm tightly.

"Discussed. We never fought; we always discussed." He helped her get in the passenger seat and closed the door.

The guests kept the chatter up during the ride, discussing the advantages of first- or third-person point of view. She looked at Seth who stared ahead at the road. "You're bored, aren't you?"

"I've heard people fight over the weirdest things. This isn't weird." He smiled at her in the dark. "Besides, you're probably digging this."

"Get a bunch of writers together and you'll never know what will come up to talk about. That's why I love hosting these events, even with the crappy two sessions we've had so far."

He reached out and took her hand in his and kissed the top of it. "Then I can deal with any conversation. Besides, maybe I'll learn something."

Their dinner reservations were at the local Mexican restaurant down the highway toward Denver. Blanco Montanas had opened up a few years ago with a young and hungry chef and rave reviews. Cat enjoyed the more casual dining atmosphere with the gourmet menu. As they pulled into the parking lot, she announced, "I am so getting a margarita."

Seth laughed as he parked the SUV near the door. The parking lot appeared clear of ice and snow, and they had scored a rock-star slot. "I kind of expected that."

"Don't tell me I'm drinking too much." Cat glanced behind her as the retreat guests piled out of the vehicle. "I'm not, am I?"

"After what you've gone through this week? I'm surprised you're still standing." He climbed out of the car and came around to open her door. "I was teasing you."

"I just worry. I don't want to ruin the guests' last night with the retreat." She put on a smile. "There, now do I look like a successful author?"

"You look like a very pleasant, and hot, author." He took her arm and remote locked the car. "Stop stressing. It's just dinner. Everything will be fine."

As soon as she walked in the candle lit dining room, Cat knew that Seth's prediction had been off. Way off. Near the back of the room, Dante Cornelio sat with three other men. He saw their group enter and held up a wine glass in greeting.

"Seriously, that guy's getting on my nerves. It's like he has a spy in the house telling him exactly where you're going to be and when." Seth growled in her ear as he held her chair out for her.

"Relax, remember? We're just having dinner." She looked around the table as their waiter came for drink orders. "I'm having a margarita. Who's with me? Shall we do a pitcher for the table?"

Jennifer and Nelson joined her. The others ordered beer and wine; Seth ordered a large iced tea with lemon. He grinned at her over the menu after the waiter had left. "Sometimes it sucks to be the designated driver."

"Maybe I should take turns with you." She leaned back as the waiter brought her glass and poured her first drink. Sipping the strawberry mix, she shook her head. "And maybe not. This is perfect."

"You're evil, you know that right?" Seth squeezed her thigh under the table, raising his eyebrows in response to her squeak of surprise.

Cat quickly ordered her meal along with a few different appetizers. After the waiter left, she scanned the table. "So this is the place where we talk about what worked, what didn't work, and what you would do differently if you came to a second retreat."

Bella set down her wine glass. "I've gotten so much done, mostly because of the local-history resources you and the library have tied me into so I'm happy with the retreat, although it could be a few days longer."

Nelson nodded. "I can't believe how much writing I've gotten done in the last week. I mean, even with the mandatory library trips at the beginning, I've written more this week than I did in the last six months. And it's good stuff."

"I can't say that." Jennifer took a sip of her beer. "I've been editing since I got here and realized how much work I still have to do on the book. Of course, it's better to clean it up before sending it off, especially since this work is also going to be my thesis project. I'm going to have to bust my butt to get everything done by end of semester in a few months."

Cat noticed neither Christina or Jeffrey joined into the conversation. She understood Christina's hesitance to rank her week, so she looked toward Jeffrey. "So how has the retreat been for a poet? I'm interested if the structure works for a writer in a different medium. What made you choose Warm Springs Retreat?"

Jeffrey looked like she'd stuck him with a knife rather than a simple question. "I don't know. I guess someone said something about how much work they got done here, and I wanted to see if it would work for me."

"And did it?" Cat pressed the question. Something didn't ring true about his answer, probably because she'd only had two sessions total. Who did Jeffrey know from the first session?

"Did it what?" Jeffrey's face looked hard. He issued the question more as a challenge and Cat got the message loud and clear. *Don't mess with me.*

"I was asking if the retreat worked for you." Cat didn't let her gaze leave Jeffrey's face. She'd dealt with bullies before, but she hadn't expected this type of behavior from the normally shy and reserved man.

Jeffrey glanced quickly over to Christina, then blushed when he realized Cat had seen the movement. He leaned back in his chair as the appetizers arrived. Finally, he picked up a small plate and started dishing up salsa and chips. He didn't look at Cat when he answered her question. "I've gotten a lot accomplished this week."

As the chatter about the food took over, Seth leaned closer to Cat as he put a wedge of chicken quesadilla on her plate. "That sounded ominous. Or is that just a poet thing?"

Cat's hand shook as she picked up her fork. The man had spooked her. "It's definitely not a poet thing. Maybe I should ask Uncle Pete to check on our guest a little closer."

"I thought you started doing background

checks on the guests when they signed up." Seth took a bite of the cheesy tortilla.

"Not really; a full background would cost a fortune. However, Uncle Pete hooked me up with a private investigation firm that runs everyone's name through the crime databases. So we don't have any serial killers at our table."

"At least not any that have been caught." Cat almost choked at Seth's whispered response. She looked up from her plate and saw Jeffrey staring at Christina again. Yes, she was definitely having Uncle Pete check on his background. The girl attracted loser men like a moth to a flame.

When the main courses were served, Cat noticed Dante and his group leaving the restaurant. Cat held her breath as they walked by their table. *Don't stop, don't stop, don't stop.* She turned away from that side of the room and started chatting to Seth about the attic heating and cooling. As soon as they had passed by, he took her hand.

"I guess you really didn't want to know what Hank said?" His smile made her relax.

She shook her head. "Not really. But thanks for the distraction."

"Cat." Christina hissed from the other side of the table. "Cat, look."

Cat looked at the woman, then followed her pointing finger to see Dante's group. In the middle, slipping on a wool coat, was their bartender from the lodge, Martin.

"Cat." Christina called again. "That's the

guy who was outside Tommy's room when I left Monday night."

Seth turned his head and nodded. "He's the bartender. But how is he involved with Dante?"

As they left the restaurant, Dante's hand on the younger man's back, Cat thought she knew already. Martin was Dante's nephew and the guy who had terrorized her last month because he thought it was funny.

The group was subdued during the drive back to the house—partially due to the fact that everyone, including Cat, was stuffed to the gills with their dinner; partially due to the fact that the group had consumed their share of alcoholic drinks. And, at least for her, partially due to the fact that she was trying to figure out what role Dante and his nephew had in the murder of Tommy Neil.

"A penny for your thoughts?" Seth made the turn on to the road leading to Aspen Hills.

Cat snorted. "I think you'd be overpaying." She rubbed the outside of her coat, brushing off the light snowflakes that had stuck during their walk from the building. "Let's talk when we're alone."

They were both quiet until he parked the car in front of the house. Shauna helped the guests out, then paused at the back door when neither Cat or Seth moved. "Are you coming in?"

"Give us a few minutes."

"You love birds are going to freeze out here. Don't stay too long." Shauna slammed the car door shut.

Cat watched as the group moved onto the porch and into the house. "Actually, I've been trying to figure out if the guy who attempted to kidnap Christina could have been trying to cover up his killing Tommy."

"I thought your uncle said he tracked his flight into Denver and the guy arrived the next morning." Seth turned up the defrost vents as snow started to stick to the windshield.

"That's right. The obvious contract killer didn't kill Tommy." She chuckled, but the noise sounded humorless even to her. "Of course, why would the killer walking around town be the one who actually killed someone?"

"I think you have something there. Keep talking." Seth turned the lights off and Cat looked down the empty streets. She shivered.

"Wait: So why was a contract killer here in the first place?" She was missing something. Something important. The alcohol she'd consumed was already giving her a headache. One more reason she didn't like drinking hard liquor. Tequila hid in that sweet strawberry mix and then attacked once it was in your body. She rubbed her temples.

"Exactly—why was the guy here in the first place?"

Cat thought about standing outside the coffee shop after paying her respects to Tommy's mother. The guy flying out of the coffee shop had been mad. And he'd met with Dante just a few minutes prior. Had Dante just cancelled the contract the killer had come to perform? Because by the time he got here, Tommy Neil was already dead. She turned to Seth. "He was brought here to kill Tommy. And Dante is at least a middleman in the whole exchange if not . . ." She sucked in a breath, thinking how close the man had been to her so many times.

"If not the person who ordered the hit," Seth finished.

"I've opened a writers' retreat in the middle of a mob town." Now all Cat could see were the deepening shadows in the picture perfect neighborhood.

"Don't say that. Aspen Hills isn't a mob town. We just have families wandering in and out at times." He rubbed the back of her neck. "Besides, even if Dante did hire a hit man to kill Tommy, that's not what happened. Tommy was already dead."

"Somehow I don't find that more comforting, since it means someone who lives in Aspen Hills is a murderer." She closed her eyes, not wanting to say the next idea. "Do you really think Brit could have been mad enough about Christina to kill the guy? I understand betrayal. It's a hard emotion to deal with, but murder?"

"No." Seth's answer was so quick and forceful, Cat opened her eyes to watch him in the dark. He shook his head hard. "Look, I don't think Tommy was as good a catch as everyone else did for Brit, but I know the kid couldn't have killed someone. Especially not someone she thought she loved."

"Sounds like you know her pretty well."

A sigh came from the driver's side of the car. "Did I date Brit while you were gone? Yep. We had some fun. But I didn't marry her."

"Not like me and Michael." Cat added the part of the sentence Seth had left off. "Look, I've got a headache and I can see this conversation might go downhill fast. Let's talk tomorrow."

He didn't stop her as she climbed out of the car, but he did meet her at the other side. Seth handed her the keys after hitting the button to remote-lock the vehicle. "Sorry."

She watched from the window next to the front door as he made his way to his truck and after a few minutes pulled away from the front of the house.

"Uh, oh. Trouble in paradise?" Jeffrey Blank had come up behind her and was now looking over her shoulder at the taillights of Seth's truck.

"Not in the least. I'm just worried about him driving in this weather." Cat shook off the feeling of unease the man caused in her and then secured the locks on the front door. "See you in the morning."

She started up the stairwell as the clock struck eleven. The retreat was almost over and in less than a day, she'd have her house back. And hopefully, she'd know how to react to Seth's revelation about dating Brit. Hell, she knew he hadn't been a monk, but for some reason the sting was still there. Maybe because she suspected Michael had been involved with the girl too. Although Brit claimed they were just friends, Cat didn't feel like she could trust the woman's statement.

Two out of the three guys Brittany O'Malley had dated that Cat knew about were now dead. Was that a total coincidence or would Seth be number three?

Chapter 18

Cat paused as a knock came at her door. Her jeans were half way on and the dress she'd wore earlier lay on the bed next to a dark sweat shirt.

"Cat? Are you all right?" Shauna called through the locked door.

"I'm fine. Just tired, and I have a whopper of a headache." All these things were true, but not why she didn't want Shauna to see her dressing to sneak out of the house. She felt like she was back in high school and avoiding being grounded for taking off to Denver for a concert. But if Shauna knew what she was going to do, she'd either talk her out of going or, worse, demand to go along. If she was going to get answers, she had to be alone. And for some reason, it felt like it had to be tonight. Tomorrow morning with the bright sun shining through the windows, this mission might seem foolhardy.

Sometimes doing was better than asking permission. This was one of those times.

"Do you want me to make you some coffee? Sometimes the caffeine can drive your headaches away." Shauna was still at the door.

Cat felt like a real heel. Sucking in a deep breath, she called back. "I've got a Coke. I'll take a warm bath, then head to bed. I'll see you in the morning."

She glanced at the clock. Eleven thirty. The bar didn't close until one. She had plenty of time. But only if Shauna believed her lie.

"Okay then." Shauna hesitated, then added, "Sleep well."

Cat waited to hear Shauna's door close, then watched the clock tick by ten more minutes. She finished dressing, pulling on an old pair of boots to wear under her jeans, put a cami under her sweater for extra layers, and then sat, waiting. She'd go out the back door, where her heavy parka hung along with her gloves and hat. By midnight at the latest she'd have walked to Bernie's and could talk to Brit.

Cat had already decided not to bring up Michael or Seth in the conversation. No, she wanted to know what Brit and Dante had talked about last night. Bernie's didn't seem like the type of bar the well-dressed player would hang out at, even on a business trip. Dante was more likely to have a bottle of expensive Scotch in the fully stocked condo he had probably bought when Martin had started going to Covington.

Okay, so this was all conjecture, but that was her job. As a fiction writer, she filled in holes, and this story had more holes than a pasta strainer.

Dante was the key to this whole thing. Her uncle wasn't able to ask the hard questions since there wasn't a speck of evidence pointing to the man—but she wasn't law enforcement, now, was she?

She could hear her uncle saying that same thing when he found out what she'd done. "You're not law enforcement, Cat, I am."

Maybe he wouldn't find out.

She passed by Mrs. Rice's house. A single light burned in the second level, and Cat couldn't be sure, but she thought she saw the woman standing in the window. Great. Now by morning, everyone would know that Cat left the house alone the night before. Probably most of the gossip would be about her sneaking out to sleep with Seth.

She pushed through the what-ifs, and by the time she'd reached the bar, her head was clear. She opened the outside door to find the bar dark and almost empty. She checked the clock on the wall; it had just turned midnight. Brit stood at the bar, watching her.

"Where is everyone? It's Saturday night, right?" Cat pulled off her gloves and her hat and stuffed them in her pocket.

"The storm has everyone hunkered down. You know it's supposed to snow five to eight inches tonight, right?" She waved to the last couple who were at the exit now. "See you guys next time."

"I won't be long," said Cat.

Brit grabbed her pack of cigarettes and took one out. She held out the pack to Cat. "Want one?"

Cat shook her head. "I don't smoke; besides, it's illegal, isn't it?"

"What, are you going to tell your uncle? No one's here but you, me, and George." She nodded to the man sleeping at the bar as she lit the cigarette, drawing in a long, deep breath. "You're like that song: You don't smoke, you don't drink, what do you do, Cat?"

"I drink." She glanced at the pool table. "I've had a few in here since I got back."

"Fine, you have some vices. How long do we have to do the polite chitchat before you ask me what you want to know?" She leaned against the other side of the bar, watching Cat. "I'm betting it's about Seth. I think you've been over Michael for a while."

"Surprise: It's not about either." Cat noticed the coffee pot on the side of the bar and inclined her head toward it. "Can I have coffee?"

Brit poured her a cup and set it in front of her. "Well, then, what has you walking to my bar in this snowstorm? Can't sleep? Need a friend so you can cry on their shoulder?"

Cat sipped the hot liquid. "I want to know how you know Dante Cornelio." The shock on Brit's face reinforced Cat's feeling her intuition was spot on.

"Why do you want to know?" Brit looked around the bar, but except for a man sleeping at the end of the bar after, apparently, one too many, they were alone.

"I think he has something to do with Tommy's death." Cat laid her cards on the table. For some reason, right now, she trusted Brit. At least she didn't think she'd have Cat killed for asking. Not like Dante.

"What's between me and Dante has nothing to do with Tommy." Brit crushed the half-smoked cigarette into an ashtray. She didn't look at Cat.

"I don't believe you. I guess I'll just have to ask Dante why he was here last night." Cat stood.

Brit waved her down. "I don't think you want to do that. Dante's complicated."

"You mean connected." Cat sat back down on the stool.

Brit laughed as she poured a cup of coffee for herself. "So you aren't as naïve as you look. Yes, Dante's connected. I had to pick up a package for him yesterday, so he came to collect it from me. No big deal."

"What was in the package?" When Brit didn't answer, Cat watched her face to see if she'd give anything away. "It was a book, wasn't it?"

"Isn't there a law saying I don't have to incriminate myself?" Brit shrugged then set down her cup. "Look, my dad had agreed to get something for Dante because he owed him money."

"Gambling?"

Brit's laugh was short and hard. "If you call running a business gambling. No, Dante lent my dad some money when the bar was having a downturn. So when he couldn't pay back the loan, he offered a barter of sorts."

"And it wasn't Tommy's death?" Cat couldn't even imagine why Dante would want to have the ski bum bumped off.

"No. Tommy messed up the original barter and, yeah, Dante was steamed, but I guess someone else was just as mad and Dante's hired guy came too late." Brit considered her. "If you're wired, I don't think I've said anything that would hold up in court."

"I'm not wired. My uncle doesn't even know I'm here." Cat's gut twisted. If she'd guessed wrong about Brit, she'd just told her that no one would stop her if she decided Cat knew too much.

"Michael tried to keep you safe, and now you just walk straight into the fire. Can't you just be satisfied that I didn't have anything to do with Tommy's death?"

This time, Cat was the one not to answer the question.

"I'll tell you one more thing, then I'm closing up the bar. I'll drive you home if you want."

"I can walk." Cat took her gloves out of her pocket. "So what are you going to tell me?"

A horn sounded outside. Brit turned off the bar lights and walked over to rouse the sleeping man. "Your cab's here, George."

After he was gone, she stood at the door, motioning Cat to leave as well. "Michael taught me how to get a book out of the library without a valid card."

Cat thought about Brit's last statement all the way home. Did it mean what she thought it did? Brit had stolen the book? Both books? But why steal a book, just to return it? Her mind was reeling, and she had more questions now than she had before she'd left to visit with Brit.

As Cat opened the kitchen door, she saw a movement at the table. Stifling a scream, she flipped on the overhead lights. Shauna sat at the table, a bottle of whisky, and a shot glass sitting in front of her.

"You aren't as sneaky as you think you are." She held up the bottle. "Want a shot while you tell me why you snuck out of the house tonight? I'm pretty sure it's not to see Seth since he called here a few minutes ago and wanted to know if you were awake."

Cat closed the door behind her, got her own shot glass, and sat next to her friend. "You're right. I didn't go to see Seth. I went to Bernie's."

Shauna poured her drink. "We had alcohol here."

"I went to find out why Dante was there last night." Cat took the glass and quickly threw the liquor down her throat. She shivered as the liquid burned all the way down to her stomach.

"Did you?"

Cat nodded. "I think so."

"Do you want to share?" Shauna's eyes twinkled in the dim light.

"Brit took the Hemingway book. At least the second one. I can't prove it, and she knows that, but she took the book and gave it to Dante to pay back her father's debt to him." Cat shook her head. "And Tommy probably stole the first one, but he got the wrong book. So Dante killed him."

"I don't think Dante's the type to do his own dirty work." Shauna swirled the amber liquid in her small glass.

The wind started up and Cat listened as the shutters outside the kitchen window threatened to blow off their hinges. Finally, she nodded. "You're probably right about that. And since we know he was talking to the hit man the day after Tommy's death, we know he knows people."

"John. The guy who tried to kidnap Christina is named John." Shauna smiled when Cat stared at her. "Your uncle let it slip yesterday. He will chatter about anything when he's eating a slice of my pumpkin pie."

"You're sneaky." Cat rolled her shoulders. "I guess I better get to bed for real this time."

"No more sneaking out, at least not tonight." Shauna took both glasses and rinsed them at the sink.

"Yes, Mother." Cat paused at the door. "I didn't mean to worry you."

Shauna put the bottle away in the cabinet and turned off the lights. "You might not realize this yet, but you're not alone any more. You have me, and Seth, and even your Uncle Pete. We all care about you."

"It was pretty stupid to sneak out." Cat flushed. She didn't like admitting she was wrong, but at least this failure of logic had gained her some new information. Just not about Tommy's death. "This investigating thing is harder than I thought it would be."

"Things will look clearer in the morning, Nancy Drew." Shauna followed as Cat went upstairs. "They always do."

* * *

Cat rose before five on Sunday. She looked at the red-eyed woman in the mirror and patted down the cowlick that always appeared on the right side of her head in the morning. She turned on the water for the shower and mumbled, "Last day of the retreat."

By the time she'd gotten dressed and headed downstairs, her mood had improved and she had a plan. One that didn't involve trying to figure out why a book would go missing or who would kill a local ski bum. Today all she was going to focus on was saying good-bye to the guests. But first on the schedule, after grabbing a mug, a carafe of coffee—and maybe a muffin— would be writing time.

"Good morning," she called out to Shauna when she entered the warm kitchen.

Her uncle turned around and looked at her. "Glad you're up. We have some things to talk about."

Cat tried not to groan as she went to the coffee pot and poured a normal-size cup. She side-eyed Shauna who stood at the counter putting warm pumpkin muffins in a basket for the retreat guests. In turn, Shauna shrugged a nonverbal answer to her unspoken question: She hadn't called her uncle. This impromptu visit was all on him.

"Don't think I don't see you two communicating over there." Uncle Pete chuckled. "I swear, you are turning into an old married couple who can talk without even opening their mouths."

Shauna held out a muffin, and Cat took it and

the coffee to the table. "I don't know what you're talking about."

"Shauna didn't call me to come over, but now I'm wondering what I don't know." He peered at her. "You haven't been out investigating again, have you? Or is Dante just showing up here at the house, feeding you information?"

"Is Dante a person of interest?" Cat peeled off the paper wrapper on the muffin and took a bite. A cream-cheese filling topped off the pumpkin muffin and almost made her sigh in pleasure.

"Wherever Dante Cornelio goes, he's a person of interest. So stay away from the guy. I hear he's been putting the moves on you." He studied her over his coffee cup. "Besides, I thought you were dating Seth. I'm in the pro-normal-guy camp."

Cat set the muffin down on a napkin. "So Dante isn't a normal guy? Huh. And I thought all he had going for him was his immense wealth and crazy good looks. Billionaires are popular in the romance genre right now; maybe I'm doing research for a new book."

"Cut the crap. I wasn't born yesterday. You know Dante's connected." Her uncle set his cup down a little too hard. "I'm worried about you."

"The rumor mill is going way too crazy on this one. I'm not interested in the rich mob guy, okay?" She shook her head. "I can't believe you came over this early just to ask me about my love life."

"Actually, I didn't. I got a call from Miss Applebome at four this morning asking me to come over to the library. Apparently she wants to amend her statement on what was stolen."

Shauna brought over the coffee pot and re-filled their cups. "They're missing more books?"

"No. She wants to rescind the entire report. Apparently, she says there was just a misunderstanding about the book. It's on a special loan program." He leaned back into his chair. "Honestly, I think she's been coerced into changing her statement. So now I have to figure out if she really means to drop the case, or if I need to look into someone strong-arming her. It's never easy around here."

"At least she doesn't think it's me anymore. That woman can hold a grudge forever." Now, with this revelation, maybe she didn't even need to mention what Brit told her last night. She wanted to get the subject off her and the non-relationship with Dante. "What about the murder? Do you have any suspects yet?"

"I've confirmed our hit man wasn't in the area when Tommy died, so he's going down for the attempted kidnapping and a few other murders. Seems like he's a trophy killer and likes keeping his memories close. He had a briefcase full of items that we've matched back to at least five murders all over the country. It's above my pay-grade, that's for sure. The feds are coming to take him into custody on Monday." He sipped his coffee. "I hate to say it, but I doubt the kid-napping charge will even go to trial. We've got a few people ahead of us that want the guy for worse activities."

"Doesn't seem quite fair, but I get it. Was he your only suspect?"

He shook his head. "You're not getting much more out of me. At least not this morning. Let's just say I'm looking at a few additional people of interest, and no"—he held up a hand—"before you ask, it's not one of your guests."

"Christina's a good kid. There's no way she could have done this." Cat relaxed back into her chair. "I feel bad about what's been going on in her life lately. She doesn't have it easy."

"I've talked to the police chief in Seattle. They're going over the evidence in the stalker case now, just to make sure they didn't miss something. It's a good time since she's out of harm's way." He looked at the clock. "They told me they'd give me a call if anything hit, but I think that was more a professional courtesy. I've got to get over to the library and see if I can change Miss Applebome's mind about withdrawing the complaint."

Cat sat at the table long after her uncle had left. Shauna refilled her cup another time. "Something you want to talk about?"

"Just thinking about Christina. The girl can't catch a break, you know?" Cat laughed and took another muffin. "She's all into the bad boys, which gets her in trouble. And I'm not sure the next one doesn't fall into that category."

"You mean Jeffrey Blank?"

Cat rubbed the back of her neck. "Why can't she attract the solid, down to earth types? You know, like Nelson."

"Nelson is a little old for her. Besides, Jeffrey's

quite taken with our Christina. It would be kind
of lovely, a poet and a romance writer, don't you
think? At least it would be if he didn't give off
the creep-a-zoid vibe. He doesn't live near her,
does he? Maybe this is just a vacation infatua-
tion."

"I don't remember. I'll look it up. Are they on
the same plane out of here today?"

Shauna pulled out her day planner. "Actually, I
am taking them both to the airport late tonight."

Cat stood and grabbed the filled office coffee
carafe. "I hope it's just a connecting-flight situation. Christina doesn't need another problem
relationship."

Chapter 19

A knock came on Cat's door about nine. She'd had a great morning writing, so she welcomed the interruption. Besides, it was probably Shauna stopping in to tell her she was leaving with the first airport shuttle. "Come in."

Bella came into the room. "You sound cheerful. The writing must be going well."

"I'm that transparent, am I?" Cat waved her into the room, pointing at the couch. "You want to talk?"

"You're such a normal writer. I get antsy when my roommate comes into the office, especially on days where each sentence comes hard. Then there's other days when my fingers can't fly fast enough. Someone needs to bottle the muse on those days. They'd make a fortune selling the magic," Bella said as she sat on the edge of the couch.

After Cat moved to the side chair, she watched the woman take in the office. It wasn't like this was the first time Bella had been in here, but it felt like she was videotaping the images in her mind for playback later. "So, what's up?"

"I just wanted to thank you for opening up your husband's office for me. I talked to Shauna yesterday, and she told me how hard the breakup between the two of you was." Bella didn't meet Cat's gaze. "When I'm researching, I can be a little one-tracked and insensitive. So I wanted to apologize for being pushy on the subject."

"No worries. If I hadn't wanted you to have access, I would have said no." Cat thought about the room and having others use it. She needed to open up her life and that part of her history. She tended to react first then think later, but she had been okay with Bella using the room. "Besides, it was good for me to let a little light into that study. I've been going over the same information and still not coming up with a good answer."

"Your husband, I mean ex-husband, was an interesting man. It's not often that business types get so involved in history research." She patted a notebook she had in her hands. "But I'm glad he did. I do have a favor, though."

"Anything." Cat templed her fingers together, wondering what exactly Bella would ask. She should have said, *Ask and I'll think about it.* She really needed to get better at this people thing.

"If I have a question on what I scribbled, can I call you and ask you to fax me a few pages? Or if I can't find the resource in my library? I'm very detailed in my notes, so it wouldn't be a lot, and I'd be able to guide you directly to the information I needed." Bella spoke fast. Cat wondered if Bella had expected her to say no.

"That wouldn't be a problem at all." Cat saw the relief on Bella's face.

"Thank you. I better get downstairs. Shauna's waiting for me." Bella turned to leave the office.

"Hey, wait a second. Can I ask you a question?" Cat stood to follow her. "It's about the books you reviewed."

"Of course." Bella paused.

"Do you think there's a value in keeping them for the retreat? Are they specific enough to the location that other guests might enjoy looking at them?" Cat shrugged. "Or are they more academic research books, and I should give them to the library?"

"I sorted the books into two piles. Books about Aspen Hills and Colorado and then the more general, American history books. If I were you, I'd keep at least the first pile here at the house. They are quite remarkable and hard to find. But look through the second pile before you just give them away." Bella laughed. "I guess if it were me, I'd keep all of them. You have such a lovely work area in that study, and from what I hear, you'll have a great library upstairs. Why not keep the books he curated for the retreat?"

"Thanks, I didn't want to just be acting on emotion here." She gave Bella a quick hug. "Keep in touch and come back soon."

Bella walked toward the stairs. "One more thing. I found an envelope addressed to Catherine and left it on the top of the pile."

"Thank you." Cat's stomach tightened. The last letter she'd found from Michael had led her to the hidden office in the attic. Who knew what this letter would reveal?

Cat watched out the window as Shauna backed the SUV out of the driveway. Bella sat in the passenger seat. She saw Cat in the window and waved. Waving back, she smiled as she thought of the portly writer. The great thing about running the retreat were the friendships she made during the week.

She went right to Michael's office to find the envelope. Time to let the white rabbit back into her life. Opening the door, she saw someone sitting in Michael's chair. The chair slowly spun around, her heart beating faster and her breath quicker.

A smiling Dante Cornelio sat in the chair. Stifling a scream, she managed to control her emotions and ask, "What are you doing here?"

"Miss Latimer. Catherine. I'm sorry to intrude on your Sunday, but I'm on my way out of town." He smiled toward the window that overlooked the backyard. "I believe, in the spring, your view from this spot will be quite beautiful. I do so love Colorado due to this amazing scenery. Everywhere you look, it's a different calendar picture. You can see the tops of the mountain crest from here."

"Thanks, but I'm well aware of the view from my own house. How did you get inside?" She leaned against the doorway, hoping it would look nonchalant and not like she needed the support to keep standing. When she'd opened the door, she'd almost thought . . . she brushed away the idea. Michael was dead. At least that part of the puzzle was certain. Now she just had to determine why Dante sat in his chair and what he wanted. "I'd ask you again how you got in, but I'm not sure I want to know. So I'll go with the obvious: What do you want?"

He chuckled. "I suspect my reputation has preceded me. Maybe your uncle has been warning you off, perhaps. Anyway, I wanted to give you this."

He held out a blue notebook.

"Is that one of Michael's?" She took a small step toward the desk, then paused. Time to put at least one of these mysteries to bed. This could be the blue folder Bella said Michael had mentioned.

"I'm afraid my nephew helped himself to this during one of his nocturnal visits. I have told him that he is not to come within blocks of the house. Or you." Dante set the notebook on the desk next to the pile of books. Cat could see the envelope sticking out of the book. She hoped he wouldn't notice it.

"I don't understand. Why would he steal one of Michael's work books?" Now she did step closer, opening the cover of the book. The handwriting on the first page confirmed this was Michael's. Was it the blue folder that Bella had asked about? Could she have been confused? "And when was he in my house?"

"We've gone over this, Catherine. I told you my nephew had been bad. But you don't have to worry about him breaking in anymore. I've also told him to stop with the phone calls. If you even feel uncomfortable in the house, just call me and I'll take care of it." He held up his business card. "I'll leave this with you."

"I should call my uncle and tell him what you said." Cat closed the notebook. She knew what she was proposing was a bluff, since she'd already told Uncle Pete about Martin. "Maybe then Martin would do some time for his actions."

"You could, but rest assured he will have air-tight alibis for the days in question. I made sure we were covered before coming to talk to you. In case you were, well, unreasonable." He shrugged. "I thought we were becoming friends."

"Friends don't break into each other's houses." Cat pointed out the obvious.

A smile curved Dante's lips. "Touché. Although I did feel that returning your property was a good reason. I guess I'll have to try harder to show you the value of my friendship." He stood from the desk. "It's been lovely to meet you, Catherine. However, I'm needed back in Boston. I'm sure our paths will cross again very soon."

"I don't get to Boston much, so I'm sure our paths won't cross." Cat straightened the pile of books on the desk, moving the envelope deeper into the book and out of sight.

"That's a shame. But I do visit Aspen Hills quite regularly. In fact, I just set up a library endowment that will be requiring me to come into town a lot." He walked around the desk, pausing next to her. He looked down into her face, his gaze smoky and demanding. "Maybe we'll be able to have dinner next time."

"I'm seeing someone." She wanted to take a step backward, but didn't want him to know his closeness made her uncomfortable.

He pushed a strand of hair out of her eyes. "That's unfortunate. I guess my timing is bad."

"I guess so." Was it rude to tell someone that there was not a chance she'd go out on a date with him? Probably. Besides, he was on his way out of the house, which is what she needed. Him out of her house.

"One more thing." He paused before exiting through the doorway. "You are under my protection. However, I might not be able to keep you safe if you keep digging into Michael's untimely death. You need to leave this alone."

"What do you know about Michael?" The question hung in the air as he gazed at her.

"I will see you soon, Catherine." He ignored the question and disappeared into the hallway.

She didn't respond, wondering if the parting statement had been a threat or a promise. She shivered, not liking the implication from either one. Cat didn't know what was going on in Dante's head—or worse, how he was related to Michael's death—but she did know one new thing since because of his visit.

Dante Cornelio knew who killed Michael and why. Now she just needed to figure out what he wasn't telling her. Of course, she didn't have any evidence strong enough except her suspicions to take to Uncle Pete. But she would sit down with him and share this new information as soon as the retreat was over. She was done with not knowing.

She heard the front door close and then walked around the desk, sinking into Michael's chair. No, she corrected herself, the desk chair. Nothing in this house or this room was her ex-husband's property any more. Even as she thought it, she wondered if she was fooling herself. Would she ever be able to walk into this room that was so Michael and not think of it as his study?

She slipped Dante's business card into the desk's top drawer. While she was there, she thumbed through the contents, wondering if it held any answers to the ton of questions running through her mind. Was anything missing? How long had Dante been in the office? She went through the drawers, trying to figure out what wasn't there. She took out several nice pens and set them on the desktop. No use letting them dry up. Finally, she pushed the drawer closed. She was stalling.

She took the top book off the pile and opened it to the page that held the envelope. She slipped Michael's letter opener into the edge of the envelope and sliced it open.

A single sheet of paper fell out. This time, there was no key to a hidden office. This time, Michael had only written an address: 846 Willow Lane. Then he'd signed the paper.

Another clue that didn't tell her anything. If Michael wasn't dead, she'd kill him for being so cryptic. She stared at the address for a long while.

"Cat? Are you here?" Seth's voice broke through her confusion. She picked up the notebook, shoved the envelope and the note inside, then grabbed the pens. She'd take them into the kitchen for Shauna to use. Or to the lobby desk. And the notebook would go upstairs for her to read once the retreat guests had left. Maybe then she could figure out what exactly was at the address and what it had to do with Michael.

She locked the study door behind her, then set the notebook and pens on a table in the hallway. She didn't want Seth asking what she had. "I'm coming."

He met her at the door to the kitchen, almost knocking her down. He caught her, his arms surrounding her waist. "Hey, I guess you don't have your phone on you."

Cat instinctively reached for her pockets. Empty. She'd left the phone on her desk when she'd come down with Bella, expecting to return to her office sooner than later. "I left it upstairs. Why, is something wrong?"

They walked into the kitchen, and he took a soda out of the fridge. He offered her one, and she nodded, her mouth feeling like a desert, and waited for him to answer her question. "Kind of. Bella's flight is late, and Shauna didn't want to just leave her, so she asked me to drive Nelson to the airport. Have you seen him yet?"

"No. I've been . . ." She paused, not wanting to tell Seth about Dante's visit, but not knowing for certain why she wanted it to be kept secret.

"Writing. I should have known." He smiled.

"Anyway, I told her I'd do this shuttle run. Do you mind? Or do you want to go? You can borrow my truck."

"Driving to Denver isn't on my top-ten list of things to do today. You are more than welcome to take him." She frowned at the clock. "Although you might be pushing the time, especially if he's not packed yet."

As if on cue, the heavyset writer swung open the kitchen door. "Oh, there you are. I just wanted to say good-bye and ask who will be taking me to the airport."

Seth held up his hand. "That will be me. Are your bags in the lobby?"

"Right by the door." Nelson walked closer to the table as Seth left the room to retrieve the bags. "Thank you for your hospitality and for opening this retreat. I will be taking your advice to set up my own version as soon as I get home. I've got tons of projects that are screaming to be written."

"I'm so glad you found your time productive." Cat stood and gave Nelson a quick hug. "Come back anytime."

"I might just take you up on that." He waved good-bye, then followed Seth to the lobby and his waiting truck.

"Two down, three to go," Cat said to the empty room. She went over to the stove where Shauna had left a pot of beef stew simmering on the stove. She ladled a bowl for herself and sat at the table, thinking about the events of the morning.

Not wanting to wait, she grabbed Shauna's laptop and keyed in the address from the note.

There were several hits, but only one was in Denver. She kept blowing up the map until she found the business that occupied the building. It was a dry cleaner. Had she gotten a note about where he'd left his suits? Michael had always been particular on where he took his overpriced wardrobe.

No. There had to be something more about the building or the address. She just needed to dig deeper into the clue he'd left for her. Why had he been so brief? Maybe the address wasn't an address. She keyed it into Google to see if any other "non-street" hits came up. Nothing. Not a book or a movie. Puzzled, she wrote the address onto the first blank page of the notebook she'd retrieved from the hallway after Seth had left.

A knock sounded on the kitchen door. When she looked up, Martin—the lodge bartender and, she knew now, Dante's nephew—stood at the door. He must have seen the fear in her eyes as he held up his hands, like he was surrendering.

She stayed frozen to the chair, but the more she sat there, the madder she got. Then the land line rang. She walked over to the kitchen extension and picked up the receiver, even though she thought she knew who was calling. "Hello?"

"Let the boy in; he has something he needs to tell you," Dante said. Then he hung up.

"This is stupid. Like I'm supposed to take your word for it?" she muttered as she hung up the receiver even though Dante couldn't hear her. She walked to the door. "I wouldn't let my Kori act like this in a book, why am I?"

She didn't unlock the door, but looked out the window at the young man. He held open his coat, apparently showing her he wasn't armed. That didn't mean he couldn't overpower her. She still had three guests here to protect. Along with herself, of course. But Dante must be close by if he knew Martin was at the door.

"What do you want?" She raised her voice so he could hear her through the door.

"I wanted to apologize. Can I come in? It's freezing out here." Martin blew warm air into his cupped hands.

"Your uncle told me you were going to leave me alone," she called back.

He shrugged. "Seriously, I feel like a jerk. I'll be in and out. Then I'll leave you alone."

Cat paused with her hand on the lock. "Stupid, stupid." But she unlocked the deadbolt and let him in. He took off his coat and laid it on the bench.

"You can frisk me for weapons if it will make you feel better." He raised his hands over his head and waited.

"Don't be stupid." Cat's gaze drifted up and down the well-built man. You could tell he skied. A lot. As tight as he wore his shirts and pants, a weapon would have been obvious. "Spin around for me."

He did as she instructed, a big grin on his face. "Satisfied I'm not packing?"

Cat watched him. He reminded her of a big

kid. She wondered what all he'd tell her if he thought she was relaxed. She walked toward the stove and the pot of stew. "Do you want some stew?"

He laughed. "I can't believe you. I know Uncle Dante told you what I did, and you still want to break bread with me? What are you, a religious nut?"

"Actually, you interrupted my dinnertime and I'm hungry. And I don't like eating alone." She shrugged. "I don't care if you eat or not. Why are you here?"

"I was wrong to break into the house and try to scare you. I thought if I found out what Michael knew, the family would let me leave school and I could go to work with them. I hate hanging out here, waiting for them to say I'm grown enough to be part of the business." He stopped by the stove. "This does smell good. You really don't mind if I eat?"

"If you're not here to kill me, I'll feed you." Cat smiled at Martin's reaction. He looked like she'd hit him with some invisible whip.

"Honestly, I'm not much of a killer." He poured stew into a bowl, picked up a spoon, and then joined her at the table. "Not like that guy Uncle Dante brought in. Man, he was scary. Too bad Tommy had already left the building by the time he got here."

"I heard the contract killer got stiffed." Cat wondered why he was telling her all this. Had his uncle told him she was trustworthy? Boy, Dante had gotten that wrong.

"Yeah." Martin laughed. "The guy was POed.
Then when he tried to kidnap that girl to see if
she was the one who took his mark, Uncle Dante
wanted to shoot him just for the fun of it. Sometimes people are too single-minded for their
own good."

"Christina said you helped her find a ride back
Monday night. I appreciate it." Cat finished her
stew and watched the kid eat like he hadn't had
a home-cooked meal for years. "So I take it you
didn't kill Tommy either?"

"Believe me, I wanted to. I was going to the
suite to get rid of him. Heck, I set him up with
the free room, just for that purpose. But then he
goes into town to get the girl, and she didn't need
to see that. So I thought I'd come back later, after
I got her off the mountain." He dropped his gaze.
"Don't tell Uncle Dante any of this, okay? He's
already afraid I'm too soft for the business. If
he hears I played white knight in this deal, he'd
tell me to become an accountant for real."

"Why did your uncle want Tommy dead?"

He scraped the bottom of the bowl and held it
up. "Do you mind if I get more? This is so much
like Mom's stew."

"Go ahead." Cat watched as he jumped up, refilled the bowl, and returned to his seat before
she could change her mind.

He took another bite. "The why?" He shrugged.
"I probably shouldn't tell you this, but Tommy
was an idiot. He was on probation with the
family anyway, and then he messes up a simple

assignment. Can you believe he stole the wrong book? What a joke."

"And your uncle was mad enough to put a hit on him for that?" Cat pushed her bowl away. The conversation had soiled her appetite. "That seems excessive."

"Uncle Dante has a temper. But anyway, Tommy was dead before anyone on our side could do the job." He drained the last of the stew. "Look, I wanted to say I was sorry, and I hope you and your friend take the lodge up on our weekday specials sometimes. I'll keep you in alcohol all night. Free of charge."

"We're thinking about it." Seth was going to be sad he missed this. It was like watching a television show where it was opposite day. "Thank you for apologizing. That means a lot to me."

After he left, Cat relocked the door and watched as the young man sprinted out to a waiting stretch Hummer. She leaned against the wall, trying to get her heart beat to slow. "Oh, Michael, what did you get yourself into?"

She remembered the last journal entry she'd read. Had Martin been tormenting Michael too? She needed to stay out of this. To take all the notebooks out to the middle of the yard and have a bonfire. Definitely, that's what she should do. Her last doubt about what happened to Michael disappeared as his words haunted her.

I've been officially warned. The dead rat on my desk at the house wasn't just sent to me, I know they meant Catherine to see it. Thankfully, I got it out of the house before she saw the creature. I can tell she thinks something's going on, but she won't ask. In order to get her to leave, I'm going to have to up the stakes. I hate to do this to her, to us, but maybe once this is over, we can be together. Or am I just spinning this pipe dream for my own well-being? I hope she can forgive me for what I'm about to do. ~~ Michael

Chapter 20

"I thought I heard you talking to someone?" Jennifer Simon looked around the empty kitchen. Spying the stew, she squealed and ran to the stove. "Is that for us? Can I have a bowl before I head back to the dorm?"

Cat rinsed her bowl and turned toward the stove to make a cup of tea. "Go ahead. Shauna hates to have anyone leave the retreat hungry."

"This is totally the best. All the guys in my graduate classes were way jealous when I was chosen for this week. You know, everyone has their name on the list to be chosen. It's a real coup." She filled a bowl and headed to the table. "Of course, that first chick, Sara, she almost ruined it for all of us. Can you believe she was sleeping with that old goat?"

Cat pressed her lips together to keep from agreeing with Jennifer's assessment of the last English department dean's age. "It was apparent that Larry Vargas had some mental issues. I don't blame Sara for being taken in. Sometimes women can be naïve, especially when they think they are in love."

"I hope I'm never that way. I mean, look at poor Christina. All she's done this week is run after one guy and then another. And now *they're* fighting." Jennifer sipped her stew. "Women should get their degree and start a career before they even think about adding a love interest to their lives. I mean, look at you—you were a professor before you were married, right?"

"It happened about the same time. But I dated one person all through high school and college." Cat thought about her last fight with Seth. He'd wanted her to give up graduate school and move to Washington with him.

Okay, well, that wasn't quite fair. He'd suggested she transfer to a Washington program. She'd been the one to go off about losing all the contacts she'd built over the last four years. She'd been planning on teaching at Covington probably since she could walk. She still felt loyal to the school, even with all the dirty little secrets that had come to light in the last year.

"Well, I still feel women should wait. Men don't give up everything to have a baby or get married. They keep working, keep developing their career. My thesis deals with this gender inequality in fictionalized form." Jennifer looked at her watch. "I'm meeting my study group at two. I guess I better get going. Thank you again for a lovely retreat. It felt like I was on a luxury vacation rather than just a few blocks from the college."

Then Jennifer's words sank in. "Wait, who's fighting?"

But Jennifer had already taken off at a trot, and Cat's question fell on an empty hallway.

Cat took her bowl to the sink then walked toward the kitchen door. Restless, she grabbed the accounting she'd promised to review for Shauna. Actually, she'd asked her to put a standing appointment each month on her calendar, but with the book deadline and now the retreat, Cat had been wanting to do anything but numbers in her free time. This seemed like as good a time as any.

Fifteen minutes into the review, a tap sounded on the kitchen door. She looked up to see her uncle standing on the back porch. Opening the door, she waved him in. "Sorry the door's locked. I'm alone this afternoon. Well, alone with two guests left. I'm just being cautious."

"Not a bad thing, especially with your track record." He went to the stove. "This place smells like home. What is Shauna cooking today?"

"Beef stew. Go ahead and have some. I think we're going to have to cancel dinner tonight. Shauna and Seth are still at the airport. I'm hoping at least one of them gets here to drive the last shuttle to the airport or I'm going to have to squeeze the remaining guests and their luggage into Shauna's little compact." She grabbed two sodas out of the fridge and returned to the table. Closing out the accounting program, she made a mental promise to finish the review first thing in the morning. "So how did your library visit turn out?"

"The woman is stark raving mad. First she's yelling at me that I let the thief take the second book; then she's all, 'What second book?'" Uncle Pete sat across from her and dug his spoon into the stew. "Maybe she's got that old-person disease. The one that makes you forget stuff?"

Or maybe someone paid her off well enough to look the other way. Cat wanted to tell her uncle about the latest Dante visit with her new best friend, Martin. But honestly, what could she add to his knowledge of the situation? Uncle Pete had already told her that the hired killer hadn't been in time to do his job. And he suspected Dante was the guy who set the hit in motion. All of this over a little book. She sighed.

"You look like you need to confess something. Like when you and Seth took off for Denver for the SATs and forgot to tell your mom you were staying for a concert that night." Uncle Pete was watching her.

"I just don't know that what I know is important." She stood and returned the laptop to the desk. "Can we talk about Tommy's death and the other weirdness this week in hypotheticals? That way, you don't get in trouble for leaking information on an open investigation, and if I do have more info than you, I don't feel guilty."

"Cat, I've told you to stay out of this." Uncle Pete stood to refill his bowl. "But since the murder investigation is at a stall right now, I guess reviewing the facts wouldn't be a bad idea."

"I'll start then." Cat went on to tell her uncle

about how she'd learned Tommy had taken on the job of stealing the Hemingway book. And, according to Brit, Tommy had taken the wrong one.

"I've known Bernie O'Malley was on the fringes of the family, but getting a loan from them is like signing a deal in blood with the devil. I didn't think he was that stupid or desperate." Uncle Pete finished his stew and pushed the bowl away. "No wonder Tommy was acting so reckless with Christina. He knew he had nothing to lose since, sooner or later, he'd be paying for his mistake."

"Exactly. But then hit man didn't kill him." Cat sighed. "And if I'm right, Martin didn't either."

"You've figured that out?" Uncle Pete's mouth turned up into a grin. "You're kind of good at this investigation thing."

"What, that Martin's Dante's nephew? He kind of outed himself to me a few minutes ago. In fact, you just missed him."

Uncle Pete choked on the sip of soda he'd just taken. "What do you mean? He was here?"

"He came to apologize for terrorizing me when I first moved back. I guess he was behind all the noise and the creepy phone calls." She paused. "Although he didn't admit to sending the carnation or the journal."

"I'm amazed he even admitted that. Maybe I should have a talk with him about boundaries and what a locked door means."

Cat waved her hand. "No need. I told you he apologized, and I have a feeling his uncle is keeping him on a pretty tight leash from now on. It's hard to be a hard-ass when your family just wants you to get a degree."

"Katie wanted me to tell you she didn't find anything on the Jeffrey Blank out of Phoenix. She said it may be he's clean, or it may be he's not really from Phoenix." Uncle Pete looked at her. "You want to tell me why you're running background checks on your guests through the department?"

"Not through the department. Katie's husband owns that private investigator company that you told me to use." Cat shrugged. "Jeffrey was giving me the creeps, so I wanted to make sure there wasn't something outstanding."

"Just because nothing came up under that name and address doesn't mean he's not in trouble. You've heard of fake IDs, right?"

"For a writer's retreat? I don't think one week of hiding out in Aspen Hills is going to make a difference if someone is wanted by the authorities." She refilled his soup bowl. "Besides, they shouldn't hide here; you're too good of a police chief for them to stay undercover long."

"I'd rather not be challenged so often. You know this place was pretty quiet before you moved home." Uncle Pete's phone chirped and he glanced down to look at the text. After he read it, he frowned. "Which two of your guests are still here?"

"Christina and Jeffrey. They are on the same plane out of Denver." She glanced at the clock. "Shauna or Seth should be back here in thirty minutes to shuttle them out. Why?"

"That was the police chief from Christina's

hometown. Apparently, they have a lead on the stalker, but according to his roommate, he's gone on a ski vacation. They are trying to track down the airline, but so far no luck."

"That poor girl. I wonder if he'll ever leave her alone." Cat looked up toward the ceiling.

"Well, you just keep the doors locked. If there's a choice between Shauna and Seth driving her to the airport, let Seth do it. It's probably a coincidence and who knows where he really went, but I don't like it." His phone beeped again. "I have a three o'clock with the mayor to update him on my lack of progress."

Cat followed him to the door. "I'm going to be glad when this retreat is over this time."

"You and me both, kiddo. At least you keep things interesting around here." He kissed her on the top of the head. "Call me if you need someone to transport your guests. I don't want you going alone. And . . ."

"Keep the doors locked. I get it." She helped him into his heavy coat. "Now get out of here before the mayor comes looking for you."

After he left, Cat's phone rang. The display said it was Seth. "Hey you."

"Hey yourself. Look, flights are getting sent out early so I'm coming to get the rest of your guests. If they don't get on this flight, they might not leave tonight. They're talking about closing the airport due to the storm."

"I didn't think it looked that bad." Cat stared out the window at the gently drifting snow.

"In Aspen Hills maybe not, but Denver's a mad house." He uttered a string of swear words.

"Look, I'm almost there. Twenty minutes out. Can you have them packed and waiting downstairs when I get there?"

"No problem. Just drive safe."

She heard the chuckle on the phone. "I will, but we're leaving my truck in long-term parking when Shauna and I come back. We'll have to make plans to go get it once the storm clears. I don't want the California girl to go careening down the mountain side."

"Sounds like a plan." She hung up the phone and went out to the lobby. Checking the living room and finding it empty, she took the stairs up to the second floor. At Christina's door, she lifted her hand to knock. A loud voice stopped her. Was Christina watching TV? She knocked loudly on the door. "Christina? I hate to rush you, but your ride to the airport is on its way. The roadways are getting dicey, and we don't want you all to be stuck here."

The door opened slowly and Christina peeked around the edge of the door. "I'm almost packed."

"Seth will be here in"—Cat looked at her watch—"fifteen minutes. Is there anything I can do to help?"

"No." The answer came out rushed. "I'll be down in a few minutes. Thanks for letting me know."

Christina shut the door and Cat heard the lock engage. Cat lowered her voice as she walked away. "Okay, then, sorry to disturb you."

She went down to Jeffrey's room and, when she knocked, the door swung open. His suitcase was packed and sitting on his already-made bed.

The guy was neat, that's all she had to say, which wasn't a bad habit for a hotel guest. She called into the room. "Jeffrey, are you in there?"

When she didn't hear an answer, she called out again. "It's Cat, I'm coming in."

She stepped into the empty bedroom and crossed the floor to the bathroom. Again, when she knocked, the door swung open. Something was definitely off about this. "Jeffrey? Are you okay?"

She snuck a peek around the corner of the door, but the bathroom was empty. A used towel hung neatly on the towel rack. All of Jeffrey's belongings had already been packed. At least once she found him, all she'd have to do was get him downstairs. Maybe he was in the attic creating his poetry.

Cat left the room and headed back to the stairwell. She took a cursory glance around the third floor, but both her and Shauna's rooms were empty. And her office was still locked.

Making her way to the attic, she took a deep breath before opening the door. The remodeling had slowed, mostly because Seth didn't want to put up walls that would then need to be torn down when the heating ducts were installed. He'd been busy driving the group around for the last few days. In truth, Seth had become a strong member of the retreat team. She counted on him more than she realized she would. The room was filled with uncut boards, sawhorses, and a thick layer of sawdust. No Jeffrey.

Had she missed him downstairs? She hadn't looked in the dining room. Maybe he had been getting a soda or a cup of coffee. She headed back downstairs. As she cleared the last step, she knew one thing. This house was way too big to be playing hide-and-seek in. She slowly went through all the rooms on the main level. No Jeffrey. She checked the doorknob on Michael's study, still locked. Then she looked up the stairwell. She'd go up one more time. She couldn't believe he might have taken off for town, not in this weather.

Jeffrey. Something was off about the guy. It wasn't just that she couldn't find him now. Or the fact that Harry couldn't find him at the address Jeffrey gave on his application. She thought about the reaction he'd had to Christina this week. Like he'd known her. Like he'd cared about her. Cat stopped at the stairwell as the thought hit her. Christina's stalker was Jeffrey. She'd lay money on it. She needed to get downstairs and call Uncle Pete. Then he could figure out where Jeffrey had gone.

As she reached the second floor, Cat heaved a sigh of relief when she spotted Christina with her bags coming out of her room. The girl turned pale when she saw Cat and with a jerky movement waved her back toward the steps.

"What?" Cat whispered.

Then a male voice boomed through the open door to her room. "I just have one question, Christina. How many men are you going to make me kill?"

Chapter 21

Jeffrey Blank walked into the hallway, staring at a clearly shocked Cat. "You may want to close your mouth, darling. It's not attractive."

"What do you mean, kill for her?" Cat froze in her tracks, unable to run or scream. All she could do was look at the eager-to-please poet.

"Women aren't very smart, are they?" He grabbed Christina's arm and squeezed until she choked out a sob. Apparently, she wasn't going to talk to anyone. "Christina knows what she did wrong. And now that we're together, nothing will stop our love."

"You just met her." Cat didn't want to let on that she knew that Jeffrey wasn't really Jeffrey. She moved away from the stairwell, but not toward the now-sobbing Christina and the clearly insane man. "Love doesn't work that way."

"Now, see, that's where you're wrong. Christina gets it. You should read her books. She understands love." He leaned his head onto the shoulder of the shaking woman. Christina let

out a short scream, and his face contorted and
he closed his eyes for a second, apparently trying
to get control.

Cat had used the seconds to position herself
in front of a wall. Seth would be here in ten minutes, but he'd be walking in blind, not knowing
that one of the retreat guests had gone insane
since he left earlier. "She's obviously upset. Let's
go downstairs and get a cup of tea while we talk
this out."

Jeffrey shook his head and held up a jagged
hunter's knife. "I don't think so. Knife trumps
queen." He grinned as he drew the tip of the
weapon down Christina's cheek. A tiny line of
blood followed the blade's path. "Get it, like in
chess? Knight trumps queen?"

Cat didn't like where this was going. If he
heard Seth come in, he might react and kill
the woman he now held so tightly. What would
Uncle Pete do? Besides draw his gun and shoot
the psycho? Since she didn't have that option,
she searched her brain for another way.

Keep him talking. The voice in her head sounded
above all the flight-or-fight responses she was
considering. *Just keep him talking until you figure
out the rest.* Well, it wasn't a full plan, but it had
merits.

"So, you fell in love with Christina this week?"
Cat's hands were shaking, and she pressed them
against the sides of her legs, hoping Jeffrey
wouldn't see the fear. Right now, he wasn't even
focused on her. She could, she should, run. But
something kept her from moving.

"What?" He turned his head toward Cat. She

realized he'd been whispering in Christina's ear. Terms of endearment? Plans for the future? Or just ways he was going to torture her before he killed the girl. Cat couldn't tell from Christina's facial expression: All she saw was fear.

"Tell me when you fell in love? I'm crazy about meet-cute stories. Apparently you must have fallen for her at first glance." Maybe this was just a temporary wiring issue in Jeffrey's head. Poets could be intense. If she brought him back to reality, maybe he'd drop the knife on his own.

Jeffrey did lower the knife, but then he laughed. "Seriously? You want a good story for the retreat marketing? Star-crossed lovers meet and fall in love in a restored Victorian, in a small Colorado town? Maybe you are the one who should be writing romance instead of those teenage books."

"I don't have Christina's skill in that genre. So tell me, when did you know you loved her?" Cat was beginning to think the voice in her head was wrong, that all she was doing was postponing the inevitable. Jeffrey would kill Christina, then her, and then Seth when he came back to the house. He'd steal the car and drive off, getting away with at least four murders, maybe more?

"Fine, I'll play. She was in the grocery store picking out apples. I've never seen someone so beautiful. And funny. Christina read all the different signs the grocery store had posted about the apples. Which ones were tart, which ones were good for eating. Then she got a bag of both kinds. When I followed her home, I watched through the kitchen window as she baked a pie.

What kind of woman today actually bakes?" He got a dreamy look in his eyes as he remembered the day.

The better question was, What kind of man follows a woman home from a grocery store? This had been his end game. To romance her at the resort, then they'd go home and start their life together.

Instead, at the romantic ski lodge, she'd fallen for Tommy's good looks and charming ways.

Christina must have come to the same conclusion as she turned toward Jeffrey. "I haven't made an apple pie since last fall. You're the one who's been following me?"

He shook his head. "This week hasn't turned out the way I'd planned. When I saw you had signed up, I hurried to get the last slot. You're so easy to track on your computer, you must know that. This was supposed to be our"—he turned toward Cat—"what did you call it, a meet cute?"

"You're insane." Christina's eyes got dark. "Do you know how scared I was?"

"Sure, but I had a plan. We'd meet at random, then we'd go for coffee and, well, I never could engineer it at home. So when I saw you signed up, I thought this plan would be perfect." His eyes narrowed. "Then you had to ruin it, going off with that playboy. Everyone in the bar was laughing at you. The silly girl who was to be Tommy's last fling before he married that slut bartender."

"Tommy cared for me," Christina blurted, which Cat saw was the exact wrong thing to say.

The knife in Jeffrey's hand twitched. Christina saw it too, and backtracked. "I was silly. I thought he cared for me. That's why I left Monday night. I knew then that he wasn't the one. Why didn't you leave him alone?"

"He shouldn't have played with you like that." Jeffrey's shoulders relaxed, and Cat took a deep breath. "I made him pay for hurting you."

"Wait, how did you get up to the ski lodge?" Cat studied the man's reaction to her question.

"When I saw Christina climb into his truck, I knew where they were going. Of course, the tracker I bought online and put in her purse did its job too. Those things are amazing. I got back to my room, checked the coordinates on my phone, then hitched a ride up to the ski lodge." He shook his head. "Ski bums—what can I say? You all are way too trusting out here in the boonies. I got rides up and back, right to your door."

Cat wondered about the luck of the criminal mind. How many times had he been within reach of Christina, and she'd never known? Now that she could put a face to the man who'd stalked her for years, now, he'd walk away again because of a snowstorm and a late ride to the airport.

He laughed, not looking at Cat, but down at Christina. "You should have seen the guy beg for his life. He told me he didn't even want you. That he had some hot bartender lined up to marry in the spring. You were just a trifle to him." He leaned over and kissed her on the top of her head. "You'll never be just another piece to me.

We'll be those old folks in a retirement home, and when one of us dies, the other will follow within days."

"That's creepy." Cat slapped her hand over her mouth. She hadn't meant to say it aloud.

She saw the anger flash in his eyes, then heard the front door open.

"Where is everyone? We need to get going if we're going to make your flight." Seth called up the stairwell. When they heard his footfalls, all hell broke loose.

She turned and yelled down the stairs, "Get out of here. Go get Uncle Pete." She felt the cold steel blade on her throat. And shortly after, a grunt from the man hovering over her. Then he went down, holding his privates as the knife he'd held clattered to the floor. Christina kicked the knife away from his hand.

Then Seth was holding her and watching Christina tie Jeffrey with a curtain tie she'd grabbed from her room. She looked up at the two of them. "Call the police. He's not going to stay down long."

Seth pulled out his cell from his pants and dialed 911. Christina now had Jeffrey's ankles tied together. She sat back and looked at her handiwork. "We need a gun. Anyone have a gun?"

"I think we're good." Seth handed the phone to Cat. "Talk to Katie until your uncle gets here. I'm going to retrieve that knife, just in case he thinks about moving."

"Man, she kicked me in the balls. You should have *her* tied up. She's a menace." Jeffrey groaned.

"Why can't you just take my love and devotion? Why do you have to be such a bitch?"

"You think this is love? Holding me at knife-point? Killing men I date one time? That's just being a psycho. That's not love. Not in any book or real life." Christina sank into a chair near the stairwell. "Well, at least we got one mystery solved. Wait, no, two: I finally know who is stalking me."

"And he'll be the guest of the state of Colorado for a while, once he's convicted of murdering Tommy." Cat leaned into Seth. "I was worried you'd either find our bodies or he'd kill you too. All I could think was to keep him talking."

"At least those two years of self-defense classes didn't go to waste." Christina tipped her head, listening. "I think your uncle is here. And I'm going to have to spend another night here explaining what happened."

"You can be our guest. The guy was going to kill me. I saw it in his eyes." Cat shivered a little as Seth hugged her closer.

"I was not," Jeffrey said from his place on the floor. "All I wanted was for you to stop yelling for your boy toy there. We would have left and been long gone before your uncle even knew it was me."

"In your dreams." Cat was never so happy to hear her uncle barge through the door. "And here comes your ride to the police station."

"Cat? Seth? Where are you?" Uncle Pete yelled up the stairwell.

"Second-floor hallway. Come up and get the

trash. Christina's already got it all bagged up for you." Seth grinned at the romance writer.

"Well, you know what they say: If it doesn't kill you, and you're an author, you use it in a book." Christina shivered. "Although I'm not sure I could even try to write about this week."

Chapter 22

Monday night, Shauna served dinner in the dining room. She'd baked a ham, au gratin potatoes, green salad, fresh rolls, and a pumpkin pie for dessert. There was so much food on the table, Cat had to wonder how many guests Shauna had invited.

Tomorrow, Christina would head home after being held up one day for Uncle Pete's interviews and another day for the storm, which finally cleared. For the first time in a long time, she wasn't going to have to worry about her safety. Uncle Pete had charged Jeffrey—aka Adam Stevenson of Seattle—with Tommy's murder along with a couple of incidents of assault for Sunday's events. Even if he didn't get life for the murder, having the other charges could keep him locked away for years. But just to be on the safe side, Uncle Pete had pulled some strings to get Christina into a witness protection program. She'd be set up with a new name, and a new life, as soon as the trial was over.

As Cat sat down, Seth took the chair next to her. Uncle Pete and Christina were already sitting across from them, talking in hushed tones. Shauna kept looking at the door.

"Come sit down and eat. Or are we expecting someone else?" The table had two empty place settings. One for Shauna and one for—Cat paused. "Kevin? You invited Kevin? Seriously? We get to meet the boyfriend?"

"Don't get so excited. He's just back in town, or should be by now. I thought it was time for all of us to hang out together." Shauna looked at her watch. "He said he'd be here ten minutes ago."

"Roads are still a mess out there." Uncle Pete reached for a roll. When he saw everyone looking at him, he set it down on his plate. "What? It's going to get cold if we don't eat soon."

Shauna sank into her chair. "He's right. Go ahead and eat. I guess Kevin had better things to do."

"Now, darling, there's nothing better than having dinner with you." Kevin walked through the dining room doorway with a dozen red roses and a bottle of wine. "I had to stop at the store before I arrived. My mama taught me to never come empty-handed to a dinner invitation."

Shauna stood and went to his side. She took the flowers and set them on the sideboard along with the wine. She kissed him on the cheek and straightened his tie. "Everyone, this is Kevin."

"Hi Kevin," came a greeting in unison from the people at the table. As Kevin and Shauna got seated, Uncle Pete looked around the room.

"Well, I know it's not Thanksgiving yet, and I'm not the head of this house, but I'd like to propose a toast." He held up his wine glass. "To my niece Cat and her friend Shauna, and one more fairly successful writing retreats."

"At least none of the guests died this week." Seth held up his glass. When Cat slugged him in the arm, he shrugged. "What? It's true. You may have had one arrested for murder, but I see that as a good thing."

"To Cat and Shauna," Christina said. "Thank you for saving me from being kidnapped."

"And thanks for the amazing food this session." Cat smiled at her friend. "We made it through another retreat."

They all took a drink. Then, after setting his glass down, Kevin looked around the table at the group. "Apparently I've missed out on a few things since I've been gone."

Seth grabbed the potatoes and scooped a big spoonful onto his plate. "We'll catch you up later. Let's eat before the food gets cold."

"Sounds like a plan." Uncle Pete started carving the ham. "Who wants the first piece?"

Shauna held her plate out. "Did anyone see the big story about the library's new benefactor? Apparently they got a substantial donation."

Later, as Kevin and Shauna hung out in the kitchen doing dishes and talking, Cat sat in the living room with Christina. "So, are you going to be okay going home tomorrow?"

Christina curled up on the couch, her legs

tucked underneath her. "I'm looking forward to it. I'll get all packed up and ready to start my new life. No job is worth what I've been going through lately. I guess I'll have to start writing something else than sweet romances, though."

"What are you thinking?" Cat smiled. "Certainly not about poetry."

Christina shuddered. "Heavens no. I'm not sure yet. Right now, all I want to do is find a job where I can start rebuilding my life."

"I'm glad you're okay. Those were some amazing ninja moves you pulled on Jeffrey." Cat closed her eyes, a memory of the anger in his face making her frown. "He can say all he wants now, but I knew he wanted to slash my throat."

"He didn't like to be questioned. And you were too strong." Christina sighed. "I know one thing: I'm going to stay away from men for a long time. Maybe forever."

"Is that why you don't want to write romance anymore?"

Christina nodded, gazing off in the distance. Cat didn't know what she was seeing, but she knew it wasn't really there. "I can't seem to relate to a happy-ever-after right now."

After everyone had left, and Christina and Shauna had retired upstairs, Cat went to the kitchen and got the key to Michael's study. She turned on the light and went directly to the desk. Opening the desk drawer, she took out the blue notebook that Dante had returned. It was filled with notes from his classes, comments about students, and questions to follow up on for the next class. She had piles of these notebooks in the cellar.

But she knew there was a specific one she needed to find. At least one that didn't deal with the economic solutions he was developing in his classes. A notebook that talked about his side project, the theories he had about the college and the company he had been working for on the side.

She went through Michael's desk to see if she could find the blue notebook Bella had told her to read. Or the blue file? What had she said? Dante's blue notebook had been one of Michael's class explorations. All about economic theory.

There wasn't anything like that in the desk. It had to have been in the boxes they took downstairs. The boxes she hadn't wanted to open yet.

Dante's warning echoed in her head: *Stay out of this.* He'd promised to protect her if she just kept her nose out of the Michael puzzle. But she couldn't do that. Right now she was in limbo. She couldn't go back to hating the man she'd been married to. And she couldn't go forward and build a relationship with Seth until she knew what had happened to her husband. She probably was risking everything she'd built in the last few months, but it was time.

It was time. Time for her to figure out what had happened to Michael once and for all. She reread the last entry in his journal.

With Catherine away on her first academic conference, I've been able to construct the new office in the attic. I hired a contractor out of Denver who charged

*me a premium price for the travel time as well as his
silence so she'd never hear about my renovation project
from any of her old schoolmates. I hate keeping things
from her, but I know it's for the best. Now I can work
in private while she sleeps and not worry about leaving her alone and unprotected.*

*Oh, the ease with which one lie turns into the next.
How will I ever be able to stop? I'm afraid I'm not only
lying to her, I'm beginning to lie to myself. ~ Michael*

Tuesday, after Shauna left to take Christina to
the airport, Cat went down to the cellar. She lo-
cated the boxes she and Shauna had carried
from the attic and deposited not in Michael's
study, but instead in the damp darkness underground. Had she hoped his secrets would stay
buried with him?

She carried the first box upstairs and set it on
Michael's desk. She turned it over, letting the
jumble of notebooks and loose pages cover the
desk. Then, she set the box next to her and
slowly started reading through what appeared to
be a madman's ramblings.

When Seth found her, she'd gone through
four boxes. And as he stood by the doorway,
watching her, she burst into tears.

"You know you don't have to do this to yourself. He's dead. What he did, or didn't do, doesn't
matter now. Why can't you just leave it alone?"
Seth's voice echoed Dante's last words in the
study. And less than half way through the jumble,
Cat wasn't any closer to understanding what her

husband had been working on than when she started.

"I feel like I'm stuck in quicksand. Every time I try to move forward, either with us or with my life, Michael comes back. Maybe moving back here was a mistake. Maybe I should have sold the house and stayed in California." Cat pushed the rest of the unread notebooks off the desk and into the waiting box.

"No. You should be here. We'll work through this." He walked over and, taking her hands, lifted her out of the chair. "Look at me, being all understanding and crap. Anyway, come with me. Shauna called me and we have an assignment."

"I don't think I can do anything today. All I want to do is crawl back into bed and cover my head with my comforter." She leaned on him as they walked out of the study. As she reached to close the door, he stilled her hand.

"Leave it open. We need to get some light into this room and the secrets it's been holding on to for too long." He kissed her gently. "Now go get your parka on. We're leaving."

She walked toward the front door, not wanting to go on an adventure, not today.

"What are we doing? Where are we going?" She pulled on her snow boots and her blue parka. Seth put her hat on her head.

He smiled. "We're buying a Christmas tree. Shauna wants to host a decorating party tonight. She's going to stop at the store on the way home and buy ornaments and lights. She figured you'd want new rather than using any from your past."

"A Christmas tree? Why on earth does she

want us to get a Christmas tree?" Cat squinted up at him.

"You are a scrooge. You know Thanksgiving is Thursday, right? And what holiday comes after Thanksgiving?"

"I know what comes after Thanksgiving, but . . ." She'd been about to say Christmas was months away. But she was wrong. She had less than a month, when you took out the week for the December retreat. She looked around the lobby and pointed. "There."

"There what?" Seth looked confused.

Cat smiled, feeling the warm emotion seeping into her veins and throwing out the darkness that had surrounded her for too long. "We'll put the tree there."

As they walked out into the bright sunshine of the day, she felt even more of the darkness fall away. Keeping secrets didn't keep away the darkness. Keeping secrets let the darkness fester and grow. She'd figure this out. Looking back at the house, she thought she saw Michael standing in one of the upstairs windows. He waved a hand at her, then disappeared.

"What are you looking at?" Seth put his arms around her and brought her next to him in a bear hug.

She looked up at him and kissed his neck. As they walked hand in hand to his truck, she realized how light she felt. She leaned toward him and said, "Nothing. Absolutely, nothing."

Be sure to read

A Story to Kill

Available now from Kensington Books
To see how it all began.

And check out
The Tourist Trap Mysteries

Available now from
Lyrical Underground.

Connect with U s

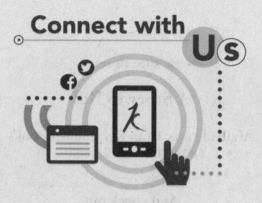

Visit us online at
KensingtonBooks.com
to read more from your favorite authors, see books
by series, view reading group guides, and more.

for sneak peeks, chances to win books and prize packs,
and to share your thoughts with other readers.

facebook.com/kensingtonpublishing
twitter.com/kensingtonbooks

Tell us what you think!

To share your thoughts, submit a review,
or sign up for our eNewsletters, please visit:
KensingtonBooks.com/TellUs.